DAD BOD
—HAMMERED—

D1028749

Jasinda Wilder

HAMMERED

ONE

"**D**AMN YOU, NICHOLAS IRVING," I SNARL, HEAVING at the stuck window. "You lazy, good for nothing, cheating bastard."

After one last futile heave, I let go of the window and climb down from the kitchen counter where I'd been perched in my effort to get better leverage. The window over my sink was stuck, and I wanted the damn thing open. It's ninety-five degrees outside, with almost a hundred percent humidity, and there's no central A/C in the house. Not even a window unit. The summers are so hot here that I'd wanted to at least get a window unit for our bedroom, but Nicholas had refused, insisting he'd spring for central A/C this summer. I'd begged him all winter and spring, to no avail. Well…now it's August, one of the hottest summers on record, and there's no central A/C, and no window unit, and the house is like a blast furnace.

To top it off, having survived three brutal months

of divorce proceedings, I'm now the *ex* Mrs. Nicholas Irving. The divorce was finalized about a month ago. And the bastard—the *bastard*—had spent the six months preceding the divorce helping himself to the money in our joint savings account. Yeah, our joint account, the one I've been dumping every penny of my salary into for *years*, to afford the remodel of this cheap-ass, broken-down, money pit of a fixer-upper *he'd* wanted to buy. Now, the bank account is all but empty. Zero. He'd spent it all. *Our* money. *My* money—my forty to sixty hours a week at Dr. Bishara's practice, six to seven days a week, no vacations, not even a weekend into the city—gone.

Turns out I'm too trusting, and maybe too naive, and perhaps a little bit stupid. My paychecks were on auto-deposit, and I never bothered to check the account, trusting that my little nest egg was growing each month. I intentionally *didn't* look at it so I wouldn't be tempted to spend it on things like wine, or new scrubs, or new shoes. Or A/C. Or a working dishwasher. Or repairs for my broke-ass, piece-of-shit car.

No, I trusted my husband. "We're saving for the remodel," he said. "We'll start this summer," he said.

Nope.

I was saving—he was helping himself. While I was working my ass off to pay for the remodel, he was tapping the ass of the local science teacher, and then he moved on to his secretary—and spending our money on presents and dinners and wine.

Now I'm flat broke, stuck with a mortgage I can barely afford on a house with no A/C, a stuck window, no dishwasher, and at least a hundred thousand dollars worth of other repairs I can't afford and can't do myself.

I stare hard at the window, cursing it silently, willing it to budge. Even an inch! One inch, just enough to get the tiniest bit of air circulation in here, that's it. I've got all the other windows open—all of them that *will* open, at least—and six box fans running, but this house has zero airflow because it's ninety years old. Open-plan design was not a design concept in the early 1900s.

All I want, right now, is to open this damn kitchen window so I can feel a little bit of air stirring in the kitchen while I wash this sink full of dishes. That's it really. One open window. Not so much to ask, is it?

Apparently it is. I've pounded on it, I've checked the lock, I've even gone around outside with a stepladder to see if it's nailed shut, but I can't see any reason it won't open. It's just stuck, and I'm going crazy.

To top it off, today was a day from hell.

On the way to work, three songs into my favorite playlist, my car audio died. Just…dead. No AM, no

FM, obviously no XM, not even my aux cord would work.

Then, about ten minutes after clocking into work, with a waiting room overflowing with patients, the computer system crashed. The whole system—throughout the whole office. Computers, iPads, phones, everything—kaput. Dead. All our appointments, patient notes and records, prescriptions, everything, gone. Yeah, we had the paper records obviously, but that adds about ten to fifteen minutes per patient. And we were slammed with appointments from open to close, plus all our walk-in slots were triple-booked. The waiting room was a zoo from the moment we unlocked the doors and it never slowed down. And, oh yeah, Jackie called in sick; leaving me to pull double duty on the busiest day I can remember.

And then, when work was finally over, I dropped my phone on the way to my car, shattering the screen.

Did I mention that my car is twenty years old—the same car I bought thirdhand for five grand the summer before my freshman year of college? It was a piece of shit then, and that was fifteen years ago. The A/C is broken, and has been for years. The windshield wipers spazz out randomly, switching from low to high gear by themselves, whether or not it is raining. The transmission sounds like a garbage truck, the muffler has a hole in it and there's a spiderweb crack in the windshield which is gradually getting larger.

And now the radio is broken.

And my phone is on life\ support.

And there's no A/C at home either, and it's hotter now at six o'clock in the evening than it was at noon.

AND THE FUCKING KITCHEN WINDOW WON'T OPEN.

I fight the urge to cry as I fail yet again to get the damn thing to even budge.

Screw it. Just screw it. Now I'm mad. I'll get that thing open if I have to pry it open.

I hop down from the sink, lose my balance, and fall flat on my ass on the warped laminate floor. Good thing I've got plenty of padding back there, huh? I stand up, brush the dirt off the butt of my scrubs, and march out the back door. The backyard is one of my favorite places, and one of the reasons I agreed to buy the house—there's a giant spreading oak tree that shades most of the yard, with a white-painted porch swing attached by two huge ropes to the lowest, thickest branch. Flowerbeds run around the perimeter of the fence line, planted with colorful, easy to maintain perennials, filled in with rocks instead of mulch, which keeps the maintenance even easier. There's a cute little shed in the back corner of the yard, painted red with white stripes in an X on the door so it looks like a miniature barn.

I head over to the shed to get some tools. In it are an ancient push mower, a weed whacker, some pruning shears, a few trowels and buckets and spades, and a fifty-year-old Craftsman toolbox handed down from Nicholas's grandfather, full of equally old tools. I open the toolbox and find a screwdriver and a huge, heavy hammer.

I march back across the grass, which desperately needs cutting, but guess what? The mower doesn't work.

I slam through the back door, climb up onto the kitchen counter yet again, and wedge the screwdriver between the window and the frame. I give the back end of the screwdriver a solid whack with the hammer, and it bites back hard into my hand. I do the same thing on the other side of the window and then set the tools down and try to open the window.

Nothing.

DAMN IT.

I try again on both sides, higher, near the top of the window. Still nothing.

Getting more frustrated than ever, I decide to use a bit more force; this window WILL open, dammit.

Wedging the edge of the screwdriver between frame and window, I take a deep breath, line the hammer up with the screwdriver, and smash it as hard as I can.

The frame splinters apart, and the glass cracks. I curse floridly, and then set the tools down and try to open the window. I heave, and tug, and yank, and then, with a creaking, cracking noise, the window slides upward...sort of. It tilts in the frame, the right side moving slightly while the left side moves marginally. One more mighty heave and the window slides up all the way...

And the glass, already cracked, breaks entirely, chunks and shards of glass shattering on the counter and hitting the ground outside.

It's open! Broken, but open.

I clear the broken shards away, inside and out, and, of course, I cut myself on a piece of glass. Sucking at the blood and cursing nonstop now, I deposit the bag of glass into the garbage can outside my garage, and go back inside. I wash my cut finger, squeeze a paper towel around it until it stops bleeding, and then wrap a Band-Aid on it, all the while staring at the mess of my kitchen window. The frame is splintered in several places and cracked from top to bottom, and the glass is shattered.

And it's supposed to rain tonight and tomorrow.

I consider, for about six seconds, doing the dishes like I'd intended.

Nope. Not gonna happen tonight.

Screw it.

I have a couple bottles of red wine—one of my few splurges—so I open one, pour a nice big glass, and dump half a bag of Skinny Pop into a big bowl, grab my iPad, and curl up in the corner of my couch.

I need moral support. I have precisely one number in my favorites list: Audra Donovan, my best friend. I touch the number, put the phone on speaker, and then set it on my knee.

She answers on the fourth ring. "Hey, babe. Sorry, I can't talk. I'm with a client."

I hear music thudding in the background, and a deep male grunt of exertion.

"Ugh, fine," I grumble. "Be that way. Your best friend needs you, but it's fine. Whatever."

She says something, but it's muffled and meant for her client, and then I can hear her properly. "Oh quit being passive-aggressive, Imogen. You know I hate it when you're passive-aggressive."

"I had the worst day ever, Audra," I whine. "I need a drinking buddy."

Audra sighs. "You know I would, but I have clients until nine tonight and then again early in the morning. But we're having tacos and margs on Friday, right?"

"Yeah, but that's *days* away still."

She just laughs. "Wow, you really had a shitty day, huh? You're never this whiny."

I can't help laughing with her. "You have no idea how shitty."

"I'm sorry, babe. Look, I've gotta go, but I'll see you soon, okay?"

"Fine," I moan, perhaps somewhat melodramatically. "Go be more important than me."

She just laughs again. "God, you're being ridiculous. Drink some wine and go to bed. You'll feel better in the morning."

"Kay-bye," I say, turning it into one word.

"Bye!" she calls in a singsong.

I haven't had dinner, and I'm going to end up drinking this whole bottle of wine and eating the entire bag of popcorn but hell, after the day I've had, I don't even care. It's Skinny Pop, so it's not THAT bad, right? And they say red wine is good for you…

Honestly, at this point, I don't even need an excuse.

As I try to relax by catching up on Facebook, my mind begins to wander, and I think back on the past couple of years. Nicholas stopped looking at me as an object of attraction roughly fourteen months ago. Actually, fourteen months, three weeks, and two days ago. And…four hours.

How do I know, down to the hour, when my

husband—*ex*-husband—stopped desiring me?

Because it was fourteen months, three weeks, two days, and four hours ago that I had my last miscarriage after our third and final attempt at IVF. Close to $60,000 in fertility treatments and medications— debt which I bear almost entirely. We tried for years to get pregnant. Countless doctor appointments. Funny positions, lying with my legs in the air for half an hour after lackluster sex with my distracted husband, shots, pills, transvaginal ultrasounds which I attended alone…

After that last miscarriage, Nicholas just checked out. He stopped looking at me. Stopped seeing me at all, much less seeing me as a woman, as his wife, as his friend, even less as a woman with sexual appeal.

He reserved all that attention for Tanya, his secretary. Clichéd, but true. He's an associate principal at the local high school, and he has his own secretary. Tanya is a twenty-two-year-old, size-three, fake D-cup, community college drop-out, who apparently has a thing for forty-four-year-old balding, overweight, associate principals with a low sex drive, lower sperm count, and a twenty-four-hour refractory period.

With those thoughts running through my head, I notice I've already finished my first glass of wine, and think about what I'm going to watch on Netflix. I take my iPad with me to the kitchen and pour another glass of wine. I can't decide between season four of The Tudors, and the latest Ali Wong special, so I scroll through my Instagram feed for a minute.

My cousin Sheila and her husband are having a baby—woohoo for them.

My favorite reality star is in Tahiti, drinking rum and looking fit and fabulous—I mean, she has a six pack and guns, and she's older than me. No fair.

Nicholas's sister is posting a series of selfie-stories, mostly loops of her posing at the gym—she's a personal trainer, and I followed her on the idea that it would motivate me to get in shape, but instead it just makes me feel even more lacking and unmotivated.

Bloody Hell. Why do I do this? Why do I go on here when all it does is make me feel like shit?

I'm about to close out the app when an ad catches my attention.

Instead of a fitness model, it's a photo of burly, tattooed, sexy male arm holding a wrench, about to tighten a pipe under a sink.

There's a caption with it:

Dad Bod Contracting—for ALL your domestic contracting needs. Have a leaky faucet or clogged disposal? Need a new patio with intricate paving designs? Want your garage transformed into a yoga studio? Dad Bod Contracting has you COVERED. Our clean, well-mannered, and friendly professionals pride themselves on attention to detail.

Every job comes with a 100% customer SATISFACTION guarantee. No job is too small. Hand us your "honey-do" list and we'll get it done, and we'll look good doing it! A good job well done is one phone call away, so call Dad Bod Contracting today!

There's a phone number with a local area code, and an email address.

I have zero dollars, I remind myself.

Not true—I have just enough in the bank to pay the mortgage, utilities, and buy exactly $126 worth of groceries.

The kitchen window will cost more than $126 to fix, guaranteed.

I have just under two grand available on my credit card, though. That is meant for emergencies, and I've been trying to pay that *down* rather than put more on it.

But it's going to rain, and I have to at least get a board or a tarp on that window until it can be properly fixed.

I really don't have the money for this.

But screw it.

I use Siri to dial the number, since my phone is near death. The phone rings for a few moments— three rings, four, and then five, and I resign myself to going to leaving a voicemail message and dealing with a wet kitchen in the morning.

Then, a miracle happens.

"This is James." His voice is deep, rough, curt, but not unfriendly.

"Hi, um, I saw an ad on Instagram… is this Dad Bod Contracting?"

"Yep. I'm James Bod, I own the company."

"Is that your arm in the photo?" I hear myself asking. Why did I ask that?

A pause, and a hint of amusement in his voice when he answers. "Ah, no. That's one of my employees." Another pause. "Is there something I can help you with?"

"Um. Yeah. I…broke my kitchen window and it's going to rain. I definitely need it covered at the very least, and I was wondering how much it would cost to fix it."

"What kind of window?" he asks, and I hear sliding and scraping in the background, and a hammer, and a saw whining and buzzing.

"The kind that slides up and down? It's over my kitchen sink."

"So not a floor-to-ceiling, or anything unique."

"Nope, just your average window."

"Okay, well I think I can have a guy out there in an hour or two. He'll at least be able to board it off to keep the rain out."

I pull the phone away from my ear and glance at

the time: 6:49pm. "He'll come over at eight or nine tonight?"

"He will if I tell him to, because I'm paying him. He's also got no life, so it won't be interrupting anything."

"Hey jackass, I have a life," I hear someone say in the background.

"Pounding pitchers at Billy Bar doesn't count," James replies. "Sorry. He'll be there ASAP, okay? No worries."

"Okay," I say. "Thank you." I hesitate again. "Um, how much will it cost for him to come out?" I hate having to ask, hate the embarrassment of having him know I'm literally counting pennies.

"Quotes are free." Then I hear a crash on his end of the phone. "Watch it, asshole! Put a hole in the drywall and I'm not paying for your time to fix it. Jesus. Clumsy oaf." To me, then. "I gotta go. He'll be by in an hour or two, and don't worry about the cost. Just recommend us to your friends; god knows we need the business. Just text me your address."

He hangs up, I text my address to him, and then set the phone down.

Recommend them to my friends.

Ha. That's a good one.

What friends? I have one friend, Audra, and she lives in a swanky condo where all repairs are part of the building maintenance. So…good luck with that.

Somehow, I've finished half the second glass of wine already. "Screw it," I say out loud, and help myself to the rest of the bottle, and then toss the bottle into the trash so I don't have to look at the evidence of my lush status. I bring the bag of popcorn with me back into the living room, curl back up on the couch, and turn on the Ali Wong special, because god knows I need to laugh.

The hour-long special has five minutes left when I hear tires in the gravel driveway. The engine shuts off, and a minute later a heavy tread pounds on the creaky porch steps.

The knock is four sharp pounds, as if the person on the other end is either impatient, or very strong, or both.

Still clutching my wineglass, I answer the door.

In my scrubs.

Sweaty from the heat.

More than a little tipsy.

Have I mentioned that it's been more than a year since I've had sex?

Hopefully that explains the reaction that follows.

TWO

IF YOU TAKE PURE, RAW, UNFILTERED, MALE SEXUALITY AND boil it down to its essence, and then infuse that with things like *smoldering eyes*, *rugged good looks*, and a *piercing stare*, you'd have a general approximation of the man who stood in my doorway.

HOLY SHIT.

I just blink up at him—and I mean *up*. Way up. Six feet and probably four inches up. And then I scan downward, slowly, blatantly, and probably hungrily—in the way that a starving lioness might stare at a distracted gazelle.

I couldn't begin to guess at his weight, but it's a lot, and it's all solid muscle. Well, mostly solid muscle, at least. He's within a few years of my age, either way. He's wearing dirty, faded blue jeans—the perfect kind, not hipster tight or too baggy, just tight enough that I was antsy for him to come inside so I could get a good look at his butt. His boots are thick black steel-toe work boots, scuffed and stained and faded. He's wearing a black Led Zeppelin T-shirt with the sleeves expertly cut off, showing thick, burly, powerful arms covered in full-sleeve tattoos—I see crossed revolvers and skulls and pinup girls and dragons wrapped around assault rifles and playing cards, the logos of several bands, and what seemed like lyrics in graffiti lettering…it was a jumbled collage of images that would probably tell me a lot about him, if I took the time to study them. Which I'd like to do.

His chest is as thick and bulky as the rest of him and he has an untamed mane of black hair pushed back from his face by a pair of mirrored Oakleys, the hair thick and coarse, tangled, wind-tossed, speckled with flecks of white paint, and he wears a beard to match, a bushy, combed thatch of thick black hair two or three inches long. His eyes, though. Holy moly. Puppy-dog brown, warm and kind and filled with humor. He has a tool belt slung low around his hips, filled with various kinds of tools—hammers and wrenches and screwdrivers and other things I don't know the name of.

He clears his throat, "Evenin', ma'am." He winks at me. "Estimates are free, but staring ain't."

"Sorry—I'm—I'm sorry," I stammer, trying to collect my dignity, get my jaw off the floor, and my libido back in hiding where it's been for so long. "I—it's been…a day."

He laughs. "Wednesday, if you want to be technical about it." He peers past me. "James mentioned you have a broken window?"

"I—yes. Yeah, my kitchen window is broken."

He waits expectantly for several beats, and then clears his throat again. "Um, so—can I come in and take a look?"

I realize I'm still staring, standing in the doorway. Mooning may be a better description.

"Yes. Yeah. Please." I stand aside and extend an arm in invitation.

He sweeps past me, smelling of wood and paint and sweat and man. I took my time shutting the screen door…

I just wanted to see his butt, okay? So sue me.

It's every bit as nice as I'd expected, a denim-clad pair of cannonballs I would like to sink my teeth into.

Whoa, down girl. Rev back that libido of yours.

My front door opens directly into my living room, with the stairs leading to the upper level on the left as you enter, with a half bath under the stairs, and the doorway to the kitchen on the right and the back door beyond that. The man enters my living room, stops in the middle, and pivots in place, his eyes scrutinizing everything, taking it all in. He shifts his weight on the floor, testing the solidity of the floorboards. Peers up at the ceiling—noticing, probably, the lack of crown molding, or maybe the stain where the tub overflowed and leaked. Or maybe the cracks in the plaster. Or…well, any number of hideous flaws in this tumbledown house I never wanted, but am now stuck with.

He finally finishes his inspection and shoots me a glance. "Fixer-upper that got away from you, huh?"

I barely suppress a growl. "Something like that." I move past him into the kitchen—and now it's his turn to watch me, and I distinctly feel his gaze on my backside. Which may or may not have prompted me to sway a little extra, and put a little more spring in my step than normal. "Kitchen is through here."

There's a box fan in the doorway between the kitchen and living room, and another by the back door, which is propped open with an old nursing textbook. He notices all this, too.

In the kitchen he stops and does another full perusal, taking in the aging refrigerator, the warped, cracked laminate floor, the chipped Formica counters, the cabinets—original to the house, but missing some hardware. And, finally, the tiny single stainless steel sink, and the splintered window frame, the broken glass…and the hammer and screwdriver on the counter.

"Wouldn't open?" he surmises, grinning at me.

"No. And it's hot, and I've had a shitty day, and I just wanted the window open. And then it...broke."

He laughs, a good-humored sound. "It broke, huh? The hammer and screwdriver didn't come into play at all?"

I'm not sure which I want more—to kiss the cocky, teasing smirk off his face, or slap it off. "Do you have a name, or should I just call you Tim the Toolman Taylor?"

He does a passable impression of the Tim Allen character's trademark goofy grunt. "I'd answer to that," he says, peeling his sunglasses off to pass a hand through his hair before replacing the Oakleys on his head. "My name's Jesse."

I hold out my hand. "Imogen."

"Imogen," he says, drawing out the syllables: *IHMMM-uh-jen*. "Lovely name." His hand is strong, warm, callused, and gentle as he shakes mine.

I blush. "Thanks."

He doesn't let go right away, and instead his thumb brushes imperceptibly against the web of my thumb. "Nice to meet you."

"You too." He still hasn't let go of my hand, and it's becoming awkward. If only because I haven't let go either. "Do you need your hand back? So you can look at the window?"

He shrugs. "Nah. I can look at it from here."

I yank my hand away and cross my arms over my chest. "Ha, ha. Okay, mister. What can you do for my window?"

He glances at it, smirking again. Amused, perhaps. "Not much, really. I have a piece of plywood in my truck. I can slap that sucker up there and it'll keep the rain out until we can replace the window."

I gulp. "Will you have to replace the whole thing?"

He nods, crossing over to the window. He fingers the frame where it's cracked from top to bottom, and splintered at the point of impact "You fucked this thing up pretty good." He winces. "Screwed it up, I mean. Not supposed to curse on the job. Sorry. Anyway, this is an old window and is beyond repair."

I swallow my own curses. "How—how much do you think a new window will cost?"

He does some mental math, staring at my ceiling for a moment. "I could probably get it done for a couple hundred bucks, say three to five hundred, depending on a few factors."

I fight the urge to cry—I really, really don't have that much to spend on this. "Damn it." I turn away, staring at the stupid window. "It was stuck, and I was hot, and I've had a shitty day."

"I get it. This has been a scorcher of a summer. Today especially." He lifts a tape measure from his tool belt, leans over the sink, and takes a few quick measurements; he pulls a cell phone from his back pocket and taps the measurements into a notepad app. Then, with a wince, he glances at me. "So, a little bad news. This house is old, right?"

I nod. "Around a hundred years old."

"So, back then, window sizes weren't really standard. Getting a window to fit this space is gonna be tricky. You could end up paying more for it, just because of the unusual size. Usually, you pay more for bigger windows, obviously, right? Well, in this case, you're gonna pay more for less. The other option is to get a standard window and widen the opening, but you're gonna pay me the difference in labor. Plus a special order window takes a while to arrive, so you'll be living with a boarded up window longer than you want."

"None of that sounds great," I say, still swallowing hard past my emotions.

"Sorry to be the bearer of bad news." He peers at the window from one side and then the other. Another glance at me. "It was nailed shut, by the way. That's why it wouldn't open."

"But I looked for nails!" I protest, with a shake in my voice.

He reaches up and fingers a spot on the frame, where there's a slight bump in the paint. "They used pretty small nails and then painted over them. Barely noticeable unless you know what to look for."

"Why—why would they do that? Why would anyone nail a window shut and then paint it?" I ask, unable to make sense of it.

He shakes his head. "Who knows? Folks back then did a whole lot of weird shit—stuff, I mean. I've been working on houses most of my life, and I've seen all sorts of goofy things. Bricked-in doors, bricked-in fireplaces, including the original mantle, wacky additions with no adherence to code or even common sense." He glances at the ceiling, at the light fixture that hangs loose from the ceiling, showing a dark gap. "You ever have your electrical looked at? The wiring in some of these old houses can be wonky."

"We did have an inspection done, and the guy said it all looked okay."

He nods. "Well, that's good." He jerked a thumb toward the front door. "I'll grab some stuff and get this boarded up before the rain comes."

"Thank you." I am desperately trying to infuse myself with a sense of calm and collectedness, and only partially succeed.

"Haven't done anything yet except talk." He

gestures at my empty wineglass on the counter. "Sit down, have another glass of wine, and relax. This is taken care of."

Well, put it like that…

I crack open the other bottle, promising myself I'll only have one more LITTLE glass.

A few minutes later, I hear him in the landscaping bed outside the window. Then I see him—he's got on a pair of thick leather work gloves, and he reaches up and pries loose the remaining shards of glass from the window, tossing them in an old, paint-crusted bucket. He then lifts up a ragged section of blue tarp, using an industrial staple gun to fasten it to the outside of the window.

"This won't be pretty, but it'll keep the rain out," he says.

"It's only temporary, anyway, right?" I say, sipping my wine.

He grins at me through the opening. "Exactly! Always look on the bright side of life."

"You're not going to sing Monty Python, are you?"

He throws his head back and laughs. "Well *now* I am!" And he breaks into the chorus of the song, in a surprisingly good voice, and in a British accent to boot.

He surprises me by continuing to sing the song

as he works, stapling the tarp up over the window. And then, singing a Journey song—*the* Journey song, "Don't Stop Believin'"—he nails a piece of plywood up over the tarp. It takes him all of ten minutes, and then he's back inside, stuffing his gloves behind the buckle of his tool belt.

"Normally this is where I say it's good as new, but we're not quite there yet." He tugs at his beard. "So. What do you think? Order a window to fit, or find one and make it work?"

"How long will it take to order one, and how much will it cost?"

"Could take weeks, and with labor, probably over a grand."

Ouch. I *really* don't have that. "And if you just make it work?"

He shrugs. "Same as before. Three to five hundred. I've got some building supply contacts, so I may be able to get you a deal on something. Maybe not perfect, but it'll look nice when I'm done. And it will open."

"You have a really nice voice," I blurt, and then promptly regret it.

"Thanks. I have garage band with some buddies. We play at dive bars in the area, but we've never had anything pan out beyond that, so...here I am fixing windows." He grins. "I don't mind, though. I don't think I'm cut out for the rock star life."

I laugh. "No? Why's that?"

"Well, for one thing, I'm getting too old to act like a twenty-year-old. Besides, this business keeps me pretty busy."

"Well, I guess it's good for me that your musical career never panned out, huh?"

His eyes bore into mine, full of humor and heat. "Yeah, I'm thinking it's working out for both of us."

And then we stare at each other for an awkwardly long time, neither of us saying anything, until he blinks as if coming back to earth from a daydream.

"Um. So. I'll find a window for you and be back to put it in by Friday at the latest."

"Sounds good." Am I whispering? Why am I whispering? I try again, louder, more firmly. "Um. Sounds good. Thanks, Jesse."

"My pleasure, Imogen." He huffs a laugh. "I really like that name. Never met anyone named Imogen before."

"It was my grandmother's name, and her grandmother's."

"Well it's a pretty name." He scuffs a toe. "So, you gonna name your granddaughter that?"

Oh god. Ouch. He can't know the hurt accompanying that question, but still...ouch. "Um. Well, I don't have any kids, so…probably not."

He senses something in my voice, in the way I answered. "Wrong question, huh?"

I frown at his perceptiveness. "I…it's a long story. Don't worry about it."

He tugs at his beard. "I didn't mean to upset you. I'm sorry."

"It was an innocent enough question, and you had no way of knowing—" I cut off abruptly, sighing. "Well, like I said, it's a long story, and I'm too tired to talk about it right now."

He waves a hand, and then hooks his thumb behind his tool belt buckle. "I'll get out of your hair, let you rest. I'll have a window for you ASAP. I'll call you when I have something figured out." He turns to leave, waving at me as he lets himself out the front door. "Have a good night, Imogen."

"You too, Jesse. And thank you for fixing my window."

"Ain't fixed it yet, just patched. But you're welcome. Talk to you later." He grins at me. "And Imogen?"

I hesitate at the humor in his voice. "Yes?"

"It's probably best to keep hammers away from windows."

"Yeah, I think I'll leave the hammering to the professionals in the future."

He quirks an eyebrow and smirks, making my innocent remark a double entendre without saying a word. My face heats, and my thighs involuntarily clench together.

Oh boy.

This guy shows up and suddenly trouble is spelled J-E-S-S-E.

THREE

I N TYPICAL FASHION, WORK THE NEXT DAY IS SLOW. WE'RE booked solid for appointments, but we have very few walk-ins, and there was another scheduling mishap, so we have an extra nurse on duty, which means I spend a lot of time sitting at the nurse's station, playing with a stapler and daydreaming.

One guess as to what—or whom—I'm daydreaming about.

Hint: six-four, big muscles, a sharp, quick sense of humor, and kind eyes.

And a big hammer.

Yeah, Jesse. The man fills my thoughts as I remember our conversation last night. He seems pretty much perfect. And...that ass. I mean, the man's butt is museum quality.

I almost hope for an even hotter day on Friday when he comes to install my window, just so he'll take off his shirt and give me a better look at his body. He's around my age—around forty—so not a young man anymore, but he is clearly in decent shape. Strong, well-built, and fit. There may have been the vaguest hint of a belly—meaning he didn't fit the romance book description of "not an ounce of fat anywhere on him," but men like that don't really exist. Or, if they did, they probably wouldn't want anything to do with a woman approaching middle age, whose body is showing all the effects of gravity and time.

Jesse is sexy as hell and there has to be a line a mile long to get into his bed, and he probably never sees the same girl twice. And they'd all be younger than me, with tighter bodies than me.

Ugh.

Why am I even thinking about him? Why waste my time on this? I'm not in the market for anything with anyone. The ink on my divorce is barely dry.

But Jesse is just…so hot and impossible to ignore.

I was never a bad boy sort of girl—not that having long hair, a beard, and tattoos necessarily mean he's *bad* or a bad boy, mind you. It's just that I usually went for the clean-cut guys. The kind who wore A+F and J. Crew and played soccer or tennis and drove newer used cars they'd bought themselves by being responsible and working on the weekends.

Which had led me to date Nicholas in the first place. We met when I was twenty-eight, and he was thirty-two. He was a guidance counselor, drove a gray Ford Focus he'd bought used, wore polos and button downs even on Saturdays, owned precisely four pairs of shoes—all plain black or brown or tan oxfords, which he shined regularly—and watched CNN and Fox News religiously. He watched both, he said, to get an evenly balanced view of the news. His idea of exercise was walking from the parking lot to the door, and I doubt he knew a socket wrench from a screwdriver anymore than I did. Which made it all the more confusing that he wanted a fixer-upper, but he was insistent and I just went along with it, even though I thought it was a stupid idea.

The real question is, why did I date him in the first place? What had I seen in him? Well, he was steady and reliable, for one. Predictable. Staid. Paid attention to me, at first, at least.

So yeah, maybe I had some issues, but I knew I wanted a man I could rely on, who would be there for me, who I knew would treat me decently. A boring, middle-class, buttoned-up guidance counselor had seemed like a safe bet. And I'd been starved for attention. My last boyfriend before Nicholas had not been a great experience, and the breakup had been worse.

I was feeling bad about myself, when I met Nicholas at…well…Target, as a matter of fact. He was buying towels, and I was buying new bed sheets, because I'd wanted to erase any memory of the guy I'd been dating. We started talking about thread counts, and he asked me on a date, and I said yes.

He had all his hair back then, and no obvious belly. Not that I judge a man's worth based on his hair or belly—I'm not that shallow. If the right guy came along and made me feel like—well, like Jesse made me feel last night…and happened to be balding and a little out of shape, I wouldn't care.

I'd like to spend time with Jesse, though. Feel those hands on my hips…I bet he can dance, too. He probably has amazing rhythm.

"Imogen?" I hear a voice, and for a moment I can't place who is talking to me. Jesse's voice is deep and rough, and this one is rather high-pitched and soft.

"Huh?" I ask, blinking rapidly.

An amused snort greets me, and I see Dr. Bishara standing in front of me. "I have been trying to get your attention for several moments. Are you okay?"

I blink at him, still working on getting my bearings; right—I'm at work, and this is my boss. "Um. Yeah, I'm good, sorry. Just…spacing out, I guess."

Dr. Bishara chuckles softly. "Spacing out, yes. Precisely." He smiles at me. "You did the work of two people yesterday, Imogen. Why don't you go home early?"

I want to, so badly. But I can't. "I need the hours, Dr. Bishara. Why don't you send Kathy home instead?"

"There will not be any more spacing out if I keep you here, will you?" His smile is gentle, but the question is sharp, pointed.

"Nope. I'm good."

"Very well, then."

The rest of the day goes by a bit faster, leaving me little time to spend thinking about Jesse, which is probably for the best.

Once the day is over I head home with plans to hit the shower, make a nice little dinner and chill out in the backyard. It rained a little bit this morning, but then it turned super hot and I'm dying to cool off...in more than one way.

Wait till Audra hears about my new handyman.

My phone rings as I'm getting into my car to head home.

"Hello?"

"Hey, Imogen, this is Jesse." A brief pause. "The contractor from yesterday. I boarded up your window?"

"Yes, of course I remember you," I say. As if I could forget him.

"So, I have a window for you. I could have you all fixed up tonight if you'll be home."

"Already? Yeah, sure. I'm on the way right now, actually."

"Sweet. I'm in the area, as a matter of fact, so I'll see you there in fifteen or twenty minutes?"

Sweet? Is he a prepubescent surfer?

"You got it, dude," I say.

He laughs. "You're mocking me, aren't you?" He says it, once again, in a near-perfect replication of the inflection and tone from the scene in *Toy Story*.

"Oh, no, no, no, no," I say, answering the quote. "Buzz, look! An alien!"

He laughs even harder. "Oh man, I still love that movie. I used to babysit my nieces on Saturday mornings, and they'd literally watch that movie on repeat. I know just about every line."

"I do too, actually," I say. "I worked at a daycare when I was in nursing school, and that was one of about five movies the kids would watch."

I'm in my car by this point and then plug in my earbuds and back out of the parking lot, still chatting with Jesse about our favorite kids' movies—we share an affinity for them, oddly, despite us both being forty-ish and single and without children. His favorite is *The Emperor's New Groove* and mine is *Lilo & Stitch*, and we trade favorite quotes from both movies as I drive home.

I'm home in a few minutes. I pull onto my street,

and see a giant pickup truck sitting at the curb in front of my house. By giant, I mean a heavy-duty black Silverado with massive, knobby, thick-sidewall tires and a lift of several inches, tubular chrome steps, an LED light bar across the top of the cab, a winch at the grill, an oversized, built-in toolbox in the bed, and a back rack with rear-facing work lights.

"Is that you parked in front of my house?" I ask, still on the phone with him.

"Yeah," he says. "When I said I was in the area, I sort of meant in the same neighborhood. So I've just been sitting out here. That's you pulling up?"

"Yep."

He hangs up without warning as I bump into my driveway, which is nothing but a pair of hard packed dirt ruts in the grass beside my house—there's no garage, not even a carport. Another item on the list of things I'd wanted to do to the place—build a garage addition. Parking outside in the Illinois winter sucks.

He's sitting in his truck as I park, all the windows down, an arm hanging out. The engine is off and the radio is on—playing "music" that sounds like someone put a spoon in a garbage disposal and recorded the resulting grinding noise, with a lot of unintelligible shrieking over top of it. He's bobbing his head to the music, and his fingers are fiddling on the outside of his truck door, mimicking the movements of the guitar chords, I realize.

The radio shuts off as he opens the door of his truck and jumps down.

"Hey there," he says. "Long time no talk." His grin is addictive and sexy and easygoing.

"Hi." I gesture at his truck. "What *was* that you were listening to? Your band?"

He laughs as he leans into the cab and withdraws his tool belt, buckling it around his hips—which, holy shit, is a sexy thing to watch. "God, you think I just listen to my own music? I hope I don't come across as that egotistical, Jesus."

"No, I just—I don't know."

He elbows me in the ribs. "I was kidding. Mostly. Number one, I don't listen to my own music. Mainly because we don't have an album or even an EP or any-thing. We're just a dive bar band. We play covers and shit, mostly, with a few of our own originals tossed in now and then, but there are no recordings of us. Number two, that's not the kind of music we play."

I sigh in relief. "Good. Because I'm sorry, but that sounded awful."

He just laughs again. "Eh, it's not for everyone." His eyes twinkle, amusement rife in them. "That's my cousin's band."

I blanch. "Oh. Um. Sorry? I didn't mean to offend you, or—god." I let myself into my house, Jesse on my heels. "I'm sorry. That was rude of me."

He just laughs all the more. "I'm messing with you, Imogen, relax." He shrugs. "I mean, it *is* my cousin's band, though."

I set my purse on the bottom stair and head into the kitchen. "It's definitely not my thing. I didn't mean to insult your cousin's band, though."

He waves a hand. "Oh, he wouldn't care even if you'd said that to his face. He'd think it was funny." Once in the kitchen, his demeanor shifts to business. "So, your window."

"So, my window," I echo. "You found something that will fit?"

He tips his head side to side. "Um, sort of?" He laughs self-consciously, rubbing the back of his neck. "Okay, no, not really."

I wrinkle my brows at him. "I'm confused. I thought you said you have a window."

He nods. "Oh, I do. I have a window. I have the best, most amazing, most beautiful window ever, and it will take this kitchen to eleven out of ten." He shrugs. "It just…doesn't fit—yet. I'll have to do some retrofitting."

"Meaning?"

He holds up an index finger. "Let me go grab it and show you. Maybe it'll make more sense then."

He's gone before I can respond, jogging out the

front door to his truck, leaving my front door wide open. He wrestles a truly mammoth window out of the bed of his pickup and carries it inside to the kitchen, setting it on the sink to show me roughly what it will look like once it's installed.

I gape at him, and then at the window. "That thing is *enormous*, Jesse."

He grins at me. "Sure as hell is."

"There's no way something that big will fit in my tiny little space."

His grin widens, and an eyebrow quirks up. "It will if you're as good at fitting big things into little spaces as I am."

My cheeks flame, my gut spins, and my thighs clench. "That's—that's not what I meant."

"It's not?"

"No!" I protest. "I was talking about the window."

He just smirks at me, his expression teasing and lascivious at once. "So was I. What were *you* talking about?"

I suck in a deep breath and try to compose myself. "Nothing. Never mind." I move closer to the window he's holding in place for me. "Seriously, though. I don't understand your plan. What kind of window is this?"

"It's a casement window," Jesse explains, pointing at a little rotating handle-and-knob near the base of the window. "Turn that clockwise."

I rotate the knob clockwise and the entire window panel opens outward; I rotate counter-clockwise and the window closes again. "The whole thing opens?"

He grins at me. "Yep. This will let in a whole bunch of airflow. Plus, this window is seriously energy efficient." He sets the window flat on the floor to one side and withdraws a tape measure from his tool belt.

He extends it a few feet and measures the frame of the window, and then lays that measurement against the space over my sink between the cabinets. From what I can tell, the window will just barely fit. Maybe.

"It looks like it'll be a close fit," I say.

He nods. "There'll be just enough room to put in the window and fit some molding around it. I'll have to open the space up almost all the way though." He eyes me. "It'll be a pretty major upgrade. This window is top of the line."

"I can't afford top of the line, Jesse."

He just winks and clicks his tongue. "Got you covered, sweetheart. James is doing a custom build in the neighborhood, a few streets over, and the folks we're building it for wanted all these sweet casement windows throughout the whole house, right? Well, we measure and count and order them all, get them in, install most of them, and the wife is like, um hold up, I want this whole wall to open so our backyard is indoor-outdoor. Cool, right? Well, she's already paid for the windows and doesn't want them anymore. James told her we couldn't refund her the price of the windows and she just waved it off. They're loaded, and apparently don't really care, so James told us to make use of them if we could. So, I snagged one. And since I'm not paying for it, neither are you. One top-of-the-line casement window for free. Win-win."

"What if she changes her mind again?" I ask. "It would be a nightmare if you installed this and then she wanted it back."

He waves a hand. "Nah. We're already almost done building the new patio door area, and she loves it."

"If you're sure this is on the up-and-up, then that would be pretty exciting. I do love this window."

He frowns at me for the first time. "Don't let the tattoos fool you, Imogen. I take my job seriously, and I'd never do anything dishonest."

"Oh god, no, Jesse—it's not like that. I didn't mean it like that." I rest a hand on his forearm, on the inked skin. "I like your tattoos."

He only stares at me for a long moment, scrutinizing. "People tend to be kinda judgy sometimes."

"Like being a forty-year-old divorcée with no kids?"

He nods. "Yeah, maybe something like that." He leaves the window on the floor and goes out into my living room. There are two windows in my living room, facing each other. He eyes me inquisitively. "Can I take a quick peek at your bedroom window?"

I blush, for some reason. "Um. Sure?" I lead him up the stairs to my room, and then promptly shove him backward out of the room. "Just—just give me a second. It's—um…just—just hold on."

He laughs. "What, you got something hidden in there?"

"Yeah, a mess." I hold up a hand. "Just let me pick up a few things, okay?"

He laughs. "You do realize I've seen women's underwear before, don't you? I'm just going to look at your window real quick."

I squeeze into my room. "Yeah, I'm sure you've seen tons of underwear. You probably have a collection or something. But you haven't seen mine, and I intend to keep it that way."

His smirk makes my core heat. "I haven't seen yours…*yet*."

"Nor will you."

"We'll see." His smirk is at once teasing and cocky, which does things to me.

I shut the door between us and scurry around my room picking up piles of dirty underwear, and scrubs, and jeans with one leg inside out, and T-shirts, and bras hanging off my bedposts and closet knobs, shoving it all into a laundry basket which I then shove into my closet, slamming the door shut. Finally, with my bedroom something close to neat and not embarrassing, I let Jesse in.

He goes to my window and measures it, and the space around it, and then glances at me. "So there were more windows she didn't want and, as of this morning, none of the other guys had a use for them. As far as I know, they're all still available. I could probably cut you a deal on the labor and install all of them for you."

"If it's three hundred minimum to install one window, that'd be more than I have to get done. And, as sad as it is, I don't have that to spend right now." I shrug. "I'd love a bunch of beautiful new casement windows, trust me, I really would. I just…things are tight at the moment."

He nods. "Well, let me at least get this one in, see how long it will take. Maybe we can work something out."

He turns to leave, and pauses at the tiny vanity I have up against the wall beside my bed—it's an antique I rescued from a garage sale, a beautiful piece

I've been meaning to strip and repaint. And there's a bra hanging off the corner of the chair. Jesse hooks a fingertip under the strap and lifts the undergarment up. Embarrassingly, it's a plain white utilitarian one, and not one of my fancy lacy lingerie numbers I sometimes wear when I need to feel secretly sexy.

"Missed one," he says, with a hot, wicked grin.

I snatch it from him and toss it under my bed. "Don't be a pervert."

He just laughs. "It's not like I sniffed it, Imogen. Relax. I'm teasing."

I'm blushing again—I'm a forty-year-old woman, long past the blushing stage—or so I'd thought. "You tease a lot."

"I like to have fun," he says, exiting the room. "Does it bother you?"

"No, it doesn't bother me," I say. "I just…I don't come from a teasing sort of background."

"Well, you should try it sometime. It's liberating." He heads down the stairs. "Point is, don't take anything I say too seriously, unless it's about my work."

"So I should just ignore all the innuendos you keep throwing my way?" I ask, following him downstairs.

He pauses at the landing, his hand on the front door. "I mean, yeah, you could ignore them if you want." He turns back to tower over me, standing just a little too close for innocence. "But where's the fun in that?"

He's out the door, then, leaving me smelling his scent in the air and feeling his lingering body heat and seeing his deep brown eyes burning with promise and intent.

Oh my.

This is definitely becoming a thing.

A dangerous, problematic thing I'm simply not ready for.

I shake away the strange, powerful stirrings I feel in my gut—and further south—as I head upstairs to change out of my scrubs.

Or at least I try to shake away the stirrings. I swear, I try. But, as I strip out of my scrubs and toss them into the laundry basket, I can almost feel his presence in my room. He leaves his clean, delicious, masculine scent everywhere he goes, and that scent has a way of burrowing into my awareness, into my gut—and into my whole being. I'm in trouble.

I hear the sound of a saw screeching, so I know he's occupied in the kitchen; I traipse naked from my bedroom into the bathroom, which isn't en suite. I crank the shower on and pull my hair out of the tight bun I wear at work, and then examine myself critically in the full-length mirror on the back of my bathroom door.

My hair is brown—almost auburn if the sun hits it just right, but usually a deep, rich, brunette—and loose like this it hangs past my shoulders in thick, shimmery waves. My eyes are green—the shade of grass in the summer sun. I'm five-seven, and tend to be on the curvy side. No reason to mention my weight, but let's just say most of it sits on my bust and hips, and I'll admit since the divorce I haven't been as faithful about the gym as I used to be, so things aren't as tight as I once prided myself on. I have naturally tan skin and since I have a ten-foot-high privacy fence around the backyard, I've been known to indulge in some nude sunbathing to darken the tan a little, but mostly because nude sunbathing feels indulgent and luxurious and a little naughty, and I need to feel that way. Especially after Nicholas stopped paying attention to me, and even more so now that I'm alone.

My breasts aren't enormous, not like those saline-filled melons Nicholas's secretary carries around on her chest—flaunting them with every movement and accentuating them with inappropriately low-cut tops, which is most of the reason Nicholas is such a popular figure with the kids at his school, primarily the boys...

Anyway. *My* breasts? I cup them, lift them, let them fall, prop them up, let them sway, turn this way and that to examine them from different angles. If I'm fitting for comfort, I'm a D-cup, but if I want to prop these puppies up for maximum effect, I'd do a C, and I'd spill out of them. The number around is slowly increasing, again due to the effects of the divorce. They're still pretty perky, though, I must say. I admire them in the mirror, playing with them. Smooth and perky, still in defiance of gravity despite the fact that I'm forty. They have some decent bounce to them, too.

I run my hands down my waist to my hips, and then turn to the side to check out the rear view. A little more juice back there than there used to be. I used to have a tight little ass, and I kept it that way with regular workouts that tended to feature a lot of leg and butt focus. These days, there are a few dimples back there, and on my thighs…and I have some stretch marks. Put on some Spanx and a tight dress, though? I can still work it.

Between my thighs? I'd have to say things have stayed nice and tight in that area. No kids, so…you know. I avoid that line of thought, though. I could use a trim, probably. I've been alone or effectively alone for nearly two years now, so the landscaping could use some updating, you could say. No one's seeing that, so what reason is there to spend a lot of time on upkeep?

Time to take care of that.

I step into the shower and go through the motions of washing and conditioning my hair, washing my body, and then I shave my legs. And use my trimmer for the first time in…well, a while…to prune the shrubbery, so to speak. And by prune, I mean all but shave.

Just because it's time, though.

It has nothing to do with the man downstairs.

I have no reason to think he'd ever be getting a peek at my *shrubbery*, or any other part of me.

None at all.

He's here to fix my window.

That's it.

It can't hurt to daydream, though, right? A girl has needs, after all. Even childless, forty-year-old divorcées—*especially* childless forty-year-old divorcées.

Clean, shaved, and trimmed, I dry off and wrap a towel around my hair and another around my body, and dart back into my room. I hear noises in the kitchen, so I know Jesse is still where he's supposed to be.

Instead of getting dressed, though, I perch on the edge of my bed, unwrap my hair from the towel, and idly pat and squeeze it with the towel, letting my mind wander to the sexy hunk of man downstairs.

What would he do if I went down there like this, in my towel? Would he look at me as if he couldn't believe his eyes? As if he couldn't take his eyes off me? Would he be tempted to rip the towel off? Where would he look first? What would he touch first?

A man like Jesse? I imagine him to be a tits guy. His big strong callused hands would go to my breasts first. Cup them, thumbs brushing over my nipples. He'd probably tease me with kisses, never quite putting his mouth where I want it, not until I was crazy with need.

Which I am, right now.

He'd make quick work of the towel. After paying long, lavish attention to my breasts, his attention would finally wander south. As do my fingers, thinking about him.

God, I shouldn't.

But I can't help it, and a girl has to get her relief where she can find it, right?

It's a matter of seconds before I'm wondering what he could do with his mouth besides tease me verbally, and while I imagine that, I find my trusty friend Miss Clitoral Stimulator and bring myself to release. I have to bite down hard on my lower lip to keep quiet, only remembering at the last second that the very man I'm thinking naughty thoughts about is downstairs, and that these floors and walls are thin.

When I can breathe normally again, I wash and put away my friend. I run a brush through my damp hair, and put on a little lip gloss.

But now I have a problem. If I were home by myself in this heat I would slip on my favorite summer lounging outfit: a tiny pair of bikini bottoms and my Bulls tank top that my tits don't quite fit into. But that might be a bit much under the circumstances. I think for a moment and come up with something that will be cool, but a little less overt: my old thin red cotton shorts that are short but not too skanky, and the Bulls tank top, no bra.

I hesitate at the door of my room, insecurities bubbling inside me.

I should put on underwear.

And makeup.

And do my hair

Forget underwear—I should put on Spanx.

I shouldn't let this man I don't know from Adam—this hot, sexy, funny man I'm super attracted to—see me like this.

I rarely wore something like this around Nicholas, and I was married to the man for ten years.

Anyway, that's old news.

This outfit was my little secret. Well, one of my little secrets. My other was that I read erotic romance and pretended I was the heroine, and daydreamed more frequently than I liked to admit about plot lines from those stories happening to me—a secret I'd indulged in even when married, because Nicholas had stopped even trying to fulfill me after the third year of our marriage, and had started cheating by the fourth or fifth year, I think.

I shake myself. Why am I thinking about stupid asshole Nicholas? I'm done with the bastard. Let him have his silly secretary and her fake tits and annoying giggle. Let her have *him*—god knows I got little enough use out of him even when we were married.

Downstairs is a sexy man who seems, despite all odds, to be interested in me. Attracted to me to at least some degree. Enough that he flirts with me and offers either thinly veiled or open insinuations and innuendos.

A man who would be perfectly at home as the hero of one of my romance novels.

So.

Am I going to go down there dressed like this?

Yep.

You bet I am. And I'm going to pretend with all my heart that I'm not terrified out of my mind, that I'm not intensely self-conscious about the size and sag of my ass, of the fact that even though they're relatively perky still, my tits are definitely showing signs of gravity—swaying a lot closer to my navel than they used to. I'm going to act like I traipse around in this outfit all the time, regardless of who's around.

I'm going to make myself some dinner, and watch Jesse work, and I'm going to flirt back with him, and pretend I have the courage to do more than flirt.

That's a joke. I definitely don't have the courage to do more than flirt.

But I can do that much at least, right?

FOUR

I SWALLOW MY NERVES AND SUMMON MY COURAGE. My knees shake as I descend the stairs, and butterflies flutter wildly in my stomach. I pause on the bottom of the stairs, just before I turn the corner and become visible from the kitchen.

"I'm crazy," I whisper to myself. "This is crazy. I should go put real clothes on."

But I don't.

Why?

Some urge, some instinct, some surge of daring. I don't know. I don't know what I hope to accomplish. If nothing else, perhaps I'll feel brave. At worst, foolish.

No, at worst he'll take one look at me and show zero interest—actually, the worst would be for him to show disgust or disapproval, and then I'd be crushed.

But this is nuts, though. I mean, the first time a man shows even the slightest hint of interest in me,

I'm prancing around my house in front of him in a skimpy outfit, hoping for confirmation that a man can still find me even remotely attractive.

I let out a shaky breath and enter the kitchen, raking my fingers through my loose, damp hair.

Jesse is outside, doing something to the newly widened opening. There's sawdust everywhere, a pungent, pleasant smell. Bits of wood and plaster and paint litter my sink, and the new opening seems enormous, stretching from cabinet to cabinet on either side of the sink, and from countertop to ceiling.

Jesse looks up through the open window as I enter the kitchen, and freezes in the act of whatever it is he's doing. His eyes lock on me, and then rake slowly, deliberately downward, pausing at chest and hips, and then rake upward just as slowly—openly ogling me.

"Have *mercy*," he murmurs under his breath.

The open, honest heat in his gaze arrests me as I pause in the doorway. The intensity in his voice freezes my muscles and heats my blood. He still hasn't looked away, and the tool in his hand drops, forgotten, to the ground at his feet with a thump.

"Uh…hi," I mutter.

He blinks, remembering he's staring, and bends to grab his tool from the ground—and whacks his head on the wall on the way down. "Ow—shit!" He straightens, rubbing his head with one hand and clutching the tool with the other. "Hi. You, um. You changed."

"Yeah, I needed a shower, you know?" Awkward, awkward, Jesus, so awkward. "I hope that's okay." Why wouldn't it be okay for me to shower and change in my own home? I'm acting like a twelve-year-old.

"Okay?" He licks his lips, his eyes raking over me yet again. "Yeah, I don't mind. At *all.*"

What to say to that? I have no idea. Flirting is so much harder than it sounds…than it should be…than I remember it being. Because at what point does it stop being flirting and start being overtly hitting on him, or him hitting on me? Do I want him to hit on me? Should I use my ol' womanly wiles? Bend over just a little to allow a bit of cleavage to spill out? Or stretch to get something from a high shelf so my shorts ride up a certain way? Or should I just play it straight and see what happens?

I have no idea what to do next.

Do something. Say something.

"That's a big hole," I blurt, and then immediately wince. "I mean. Um. You widened it a lot."

He smirks. "Yeah, well, it's a big window, so you need a pretty sizable opening." He winks at me. "Don't worry, though, I always measure three times and cut once. It'll fit like a glove and look like a million bucks."

"It looks great so far. There's so much more light in the kitchen now."

Really? It looks great so far? It's a hole in my wall. I growl under my breath at my own stupidity and start pulling out the fixings for dinner. I put some frozen ground beef in the fridge yesterday, thinking I'd make myself a fancy dinner tonight—I have some red and yellow peppers, and some minute rice which, for a single lady, counts as fancy, these days. I try to ignore Jesse as I brown the beef, but it's not easy.

I feel his eyes on me every single moment. My fridge faces the window, so when I go to retrieve the peppers from the crisper drawer, I have to bend over. It's a nerve-racking experience. Do I keep my knees together? Should I just crouch? Crouching would be unnatural and awkward. Why did I put these in the bottom-most drawer? I have to bend way over to get them. What's he doing back there? I don't dare look—if I look, it'll be obvious that I'm after his attention. I bet my butt is going to look huge when I bend over. God, this is dumb. Just get the peppers and be done with it, you silly woman.

I've never been so self-conscious about doing something as simple and everyday as bending over to get something out of a fridge. But I can feel his gaze; I can feel him watching me. I guarantee he's not missing a single jiggle or shake as I move around the kitchen preparing this meal. I just wish I knew what he's thinking. Does he like women built like me? Or is he one of those guys who goes for the stick-thin, fitness model type? If that's the case, I'm out of luck, because that's never been me, even at my fittest. Even when I was in the gym three or four days a week lifting and running and doing yoga, I always carried a little extra around the bust, waist, and hips. That extra hit me my senior year of high school and never really left, no matter what I ate or how I worked out, and eventually I just accepted it along with the label "curvy girl."

I just wish I knew how Jesse likes his women.

I lean over, open the drawer, and pull out the bag of peppers—and I feel the shorts riding up. I feel them sliding between the cheeks of my butt, and I feel the air on my backside, telling me there's quite a lot of bare skin showing, and that it's probably obvious what I'm *not* wearing under the shorts.

I hear a soft groan from behind me, which shifts abruptly into a cough, and when I straighten, Jesse is red in the face.

"You okay?" I ask.

"Yeah," he says, his voice hoarse, his eyes darting everywhere except my face. "I'm—just—um. Sawdust. Choked on some sawdust."

There's no sawdust in the air at all. Was that

groan I heard before he started coughing one of appreciation and desire? A girl can dream.

I start dicing the peppers, pausing to stir the meat every now and then, and keeping an eye on the rice as it boils. I'm halfway done with the peppers when Jesse comes back inside. He critically examines the opening, measures it, measures the window again, and then nods to himself.

"Time to mount this bitch," he says, half to himself, half to me.

My eyes widen, and I almost cut my finger off as I shoot him a glance. "Excuse me?"

He blinks, and then pales. "Ah—um. I—the window. I'm going to install the window now…is…what I meant."

"Oh." I stand there at the counter, awkwardly holding the knife in one hand and a yellow pepper in the other. "I thought you were talking to me."

"I was." he stammers, backtracking. "Um. I mean. I was talking *to* you, not *about* you. I'd never say—ah… I was referring to the window, not you. Time to mount the window. I shouldn't have—um. I mean." He slaps his forehead. "I'm sorry. I hope I didn't offend you."

I try to lighten the mood, go for a joke. "Well, I certainly hope that's not how you talk to women."

"I never refer to women as bitches unless it's in

reference to my ex, and I sure as hell never use the term 'mount'," he says, indignant.

"Well, that's good to know. It's not an attractive term."

He's back on more solid footing. "No, it definitely lacks sexiness." He's silent a moment. "Unlike you." He says this to me with his eyes on mine, his hands idly toying with the edge of the window.

"Oh, yeah?" I say, a little disingenuously.

"Yeah. The term 'mount' is decidedly unsexy." He pauses again for emphasis. "Unlike you."

"Unlike me?" Is he calling me sexy?

"Yeah. You don't lack sexiness."

I decide it's probably safest to put the knife down for now. "I—I don't?" I sound even more shocked than I feel, and endeavor to sound…something like confident. "I mean. Neither do you, if we're on the subject of sexiness."

Jesse runs a finger along the upper edge of the window frame. "I don't think I'll ever see a Bull's tank top quite the same way, now that I've seen the way you wear one."

I glance down as if I have no idea what he's talking about. "Oh, this old thing? It's comfy, and I've had it forever, so I guess it has some sentimental value. It doesn't quite fit anymore."

His gaze wanders from mine southward, to my

cleavage, lingers there, and then travels back up to mine. "Oh, I don't know about that. I'd say it fits you just fine."

I grin, because I can't help it. His words make me a little giddy with flattered excitement and anticipation. "It does cling in certain places, doesn't it?"

He hesitates over his reply. "Ah, yeah. Cling is a good way to put it." He steals a glance at my hips. "Those shorts come with the tank top?"

I twist away a little, straighten one leg behind me, and look back over my shoulder at my own butt. "Oh, these? Um…? No, I think I bought them as workout shorts when I was in college, back when I had both the courage and the body to wear them out of my own house."

"Well, I can't speak to courage, but I'd say, for my part, that you definitely still have the body to wear those shorts wherever the hell you feel like."

I laugh, a genuine bark of humor. "That's awful nice of you, Jesse, but I was raised to think shorts ought to at least cover all of my butt to be considered acceptable to wear out of the house." I tap the undersides of my buttocks, which hang below the edge of the shorts. "As you can clearly see, I've outgrown that particular stipulation."

Once again, he doesn't hide the blatant way his eyes roam my backside. "Well, it's working in my favor, that's for damn sure." He clears his throat, turns to the window. "I—um. I'll get this in and get out of your hair."

"Oh, you're fine," I say. "You're not in my hair."

"Not yet I'm not," he says, but it's under his breath and I don't think I was meant to hear it.

I pretend I don't hear it, and go back to cutting up the peppers. The meat is browned now, so I drain it, add the diced peppers, a packet of taco seasoning, and a little extra garlic and cayenne for a kick. A few minutes of tossing that over the heat and it's done. The rice has been done for a while, so all I have to do now is put together a little salad. Some greens, some cucumbers, celery, tomatoes, baby carrots, some cheese, and it'll be good to go.

By now, Jesse has the window in and is crouched on the sink fastening it into the space with a screw gun. He has pieces of molding stacked on the counter nearby, and uses a nail gun to fasten molding around the edges, then takes some outside and does the same around the exterior.

Done outside, he returns to the kitchen with a small shop vac, which he uses to suck up all the sawdust and mess, and makes quick work of cleaning up his tools and supplies, returning my kitchen to its original state, plus one new window. This done, he stands in the middle of the kitchen eyeing his handiwork.

"What do you think, Imogen?" he asks, glancing at me. "How do you like your new window?"

I turn the stove off, cover the pan with a lid, and stand beside him. The window is...huge. It lets in acres of daylight, making my little kitchen feel larger, airier, and just...lighter. He reaches forward and rotates the knob to open the window all the way, and immediately a gentle breeze floats through, catching the draft from the open back door and front door.

I just stare at it for a moment, bathing in the cool breeze. My kitchen is utterly transformed, and I'm bizarrely emotional about it.

I try to breathe past it, but I can't I'm choked up. My eyes are tearing.

"I know it's just a stupid window," I manage, "but you don't know how long I've wanted this. Just a little breeze while I'm in here." I laugh at my own tears. "Sorry, I'm being emotional."

"It's more than just the window, I'm guessing." He bumps his shoulder against mine, as if he wants to comfort me but isn't sure how or what's appropriate.

I laugh, sniffle, and wipe at my eyes. "Yeah, you could say that." I glance at him, and then opt for some of the truth. "When you first came over, you asked if this was a fixer-upper that got away from me."

"I sure did."

"That's fairly close to the truth." I tug my shorts

a little lower and my top a little higher. "My ex-husband had the brilliant idea of buying an older house that needed a little TLC with the idea we could spend our weekends and summers fixing it up. He's an associate principal at the high school, so he's got summers off. He's not exactly a handyman or construction expert, but his idea was that we'd learn together."

Jesse snorts. "Yeah, that never works."

"So I discovered." I sigh. "I wasn't thrilled with the idea, myself. It seemed like a lot of work, and I'd always had a hard time even getting Nicholas to change a light bulb or fix the leaky sink. Ripping out the linoleum floor and retiling? New windows? New front porch? Sand and restain the hardwood floors? Yeah, good luck. I knew better, but…" I trail off with a shrug.

"But you let him convince you anyway, because you loved him, and nothing ever got done, and finally you divorced his lazy ass?" Jesse guesses.

I laugh. "Pretty close, yeah. Factor in him banging the science teacher *and* his secretary, consistently telling me I've put on a few pounds since we got married…stuff like that. I wouldn't divorce him just for being lazy. I mean, he worked a lot, but once he got home he turned into a couch potato."

Jesse's glare is scary. "He told you you've put on weight? He actually said that to you out loud?"

I shrug. "Yeah. A couple times."

"Is he, like, a super-fit, health-food, gym-rat sort of a guy?"

I laugh until I have to hold my stomach. "Oh my god. Oh my god." I get myself under control, and try to speak without laughing. "Yeah, no, Nicholas is... he's Mr. Belding, but thirty-some pounds overweight."

"But *you're* the one who changed?" He shook his head. "The science teacher and the secretary...were they, like, hard up for sex?"

I laugh again, but it's strained with old pain. "Nope. That's the hell of it all. The science teacher, the first person he cheated on me with, is thirty, married, and teaches a spin class on Sunday mornings. She's fit and pretty and her husband is pretty good-looking himself. She has *kids*, for shit's sake." I shake my head and growl. "The secretary is even harder to understand. She's not even thirty, is a size two, and she has these *enormous* fake breasts. She could be a contestant on *The Bachelor*, is what I'm saying. One of the ones who gets voted out in the first two episodes."

"Is your ex good-looking despite being overweight?" Jesse asks, sounding genuinely baffled. "Like, what is it?"

My laugh is even more pained and forced. "No, not really. Average in pretty much every way. I mean, he's not downright ugly, but no, he's not especially good-looking." I laugh again. "Really makes me wonder what's wrong with me, and what I was thinking."

Shit. Self-pity is *not* attractive.

Jesse winces. "I'm an asshole. I'm sorry. None of this is my business, and I clearly stepped in a pile of painful crap."

I touch his bicep. "You're not an asshole."

"If you married him, you clearly saw something in him, and I was calling that into question."

"As well you should. I've called it into question myself any number of times."

"Still, it's none of my business, and I've got no call asking you questions like that." He gestures at me, a sweep of his hand from head to toe. "I just—I don't get it. I look at you, and I can't for the life of me figure out how the hell he justified cheating on you. He's got all *this*—" another gesture at me, this time an angry or frustrated stab of his hand, "—waiting for him at home, and he's banging married women and skanky secretaries?"

I lean against the counter, back to the window, facing Jesse. "Look, I don't like labeling people. Just because she has fake tits and fucked my husband doesn't make her a skank. They do seem to actually have a thing, honestly, because they've been dating for a while now. Maybe there's something about her I don't see—I don't know. It's not like I've ever tried to get to know her, obviously, I just...I don't like name-calling or labels, unless I'm talking about Nicholas."

He shook his head, frowning at me. "You've got more grace than I do, if you can say that about the girl who fucked your husband."

"I just...I'm trying to be the better person. I was loyal. I stayed with him until it was obviously no longer going to work, until it was clear it wasn't just an indiscretion or two, but an ongoing choice. And yeah, those girls made the choice to sleep with a married man, so they're not innocent, but the real blame lies with him." I sigh. "Him, I give a lot less grace to."

"Don't blame you there." He smiles at me. "Not only is he a lazy, stupid, useless son of a bitch who took on a project he didn't have the skills or balls to see through, he bought a fixer-upper he couldn't fix up."

I laugh, but can't quite meet his eyes. "That's funny and sweet of you to say. I'm sure I wasn't innocent in the situation, though."

He blows a raspberry. "Oh bullshit. I mean sure, none of us is ever totally innocent. There's always something we could have said or done or been better at, or something we missed, but in situations like you're describing, there's just no excuse. There's nothing you could ever do to justify or excuse the way that deep-fried bull testicle of an ex of yours treated you."

"Maybe you're right." I turn around and look at my new window. "I love my window, Jesse. I can't thank you enough. Really, it's...it's too much." I laugh. "Now I have to figure out how to fix the rest of my windows to match."

"You're welcome."

We stand in silence, which Jesse eventually breaks. "I, um—your food is getting cold, and it smells pretty good." At that moment, his stomach rumbles loudly, and he laughs to cover it. "Sorry, I didn't have time to stop for lunch today, and my stomach is letting me know it doesn't appreciate it."

I would like to say I hesitated, that I thought it out, that I asked myself if I was really in a place to be doing this, but...I can't honestly say that's the truth.

The moment his tummy rumbled and he murmured his excuse, I was formulating in my head how to ask him to stay.

I gesture at the pan. "I, uh...I have more than I can eat by myself." It's true, although I'd done it on purpose out of habit, so I'd have leftovers during the week; I meet his eyes, tendering a hesitant, nervous smile. "Do you want to stay and eat with me?"

He blinks. "I—" he broke off, hesitating.

"If you don't have other plans, I mean. I, um—I guess you have other plans, huh? A hot single guy like you is probably on a waitlist for dates," I stammer, fumbling to cover my nerves. "I mean, it's nothing special, but you're—you know. You're more than welcome to eat me. Eat *with* me! Shit. I mean—I mean eat *with* me." Mortification rolls through me. "God, shoot me."

Jesse is laughing. "Imogen—Jesus. You're too much. Number one, I would love to stay and eat *with* you. I don't have plans, or a waitlist for dates, or a little black book, for that matter. The food you made looks and smells amazing, and it's special because you made it. Number...three? Four? Whatever. I would also absolutely eat you, because, Imogen, honey, I have no doubt that you taste fucking delicious. Last, I won't shoot you, because I like you, and, in the words of The Man in Black, 'there's a shortage of perfect breasts in this world—it would be a pity to damage yours.'"

"Oh god, you're quoting *Princess Bride*." I hold the back of my hand to my forehead and sway backward. "Swoon."

He laughs. "The movie quotes really get you, don't they?"

I laugh and nod. "They really do. I'd drop quotes to my ex all the time, and he'd never get them, and I was always like, what? How do you not know what that's from? It's just part of how I communicate."

"Well that's something I understand," Jesse says, reaching for the buckle of his tool belt. "I'm the same way."

Just as I'm in the process of pulling two plates out of the cabinet, my mind becomes distracted. I've become so used to seeing him with that tool belt on that I momentarily forgot it was separate from his actual pants. So, when he reached for that buckle and started loosening it, I maybe sort of panicked a little.

Excited, horny, frantic panic.

The thought of this hot, masculine, sexy, helpful man unbuckling his jeans is just...too much for my poor libido.

I drop the plates.

They smash on the floor with a deafening crash, shards and chunks flying in every direction. A shard of ceramic slices the outside of my calf, drawing a long but shallow gash.

"Shit!" I glance down at my leg, which is already welling with blood. Damn it. "Okay, hold on. Let me get the broom."

Jesse finishes removing his tool belt, sets it on the counter, and reaches for me, stopping me from moving. "Just stay where you are. You're bleeding and you're barefoot, and there are pieces everywhere. You take a step in any direction and you'll cut your feet all up." He keeps hold of my arms with both hands, smiling reassuringly at me. "Just tell me where the broom is and I'll handle it."

I point at the little closet between the stove and the far wall. "In there."

He retrieves the broom and dustpan. "Paper bag?"

I point at the sink. "Under there."

He finds a paper grocery bag, opens it, tosses the largest chunks into it, and then makes swift, efficient work of sweeping the floor from side to side, corner to corner. After dumping the shards into the bag, he sweeps again, just to be sure, and then sets the bag aside and puts the broom away.

He turns to me. "Now you."

I frown in confusion. "Now me, what?"

He gestures at my leg. "Gotta tend to your war wound."

I laugh. "You mean my utterly insignificant little cut I received from my own clumsiness?"

He shrugs. "Po-*tay*-to, po-*tah*-to."

"Nobody, not even an English person, says po-*tah*-to," I point out.

He indicates the counter beside the sink. "Hop up there."

I shake my head. "It's fine, really. I just need to wet a paper towel. It doesn't even hurt." That was a lie—it stung like a bitch, but I didn't want to seem weak or squeamish on top of all the other dumb shit I'd done around this guy.

I'm moving toward the sink as I say this, but I only get a few steps. And then I feel a pair of big, strong hands on my waist. He spins me around and backs me up to the counter. Before I have any clue what he's intending to do, he dips down, wraps those powerful, huge, callused hands around the backs of my thighs—and with only the slightest hint of effort, he lifts me up and deposits me on the countertop. I gasp, a shrill in-breath of surprise, and then my lungs squeeze and my heart slams in my chest and my core tightens and heats, and my thighs clench, and heat pools and desire seeps through me. Jesse is inches away from me, standing between my thighs, his hard, broad chest and massive shoulders a wall in front of me, his trim hips wedging my legs apart. His hands are on my waist again, just above my hips, and his eyes are warm and Labrador puppy brown and twinkling with humor and sparking with what I desperately want to believe is desire.

"I—okay. I guess I'm sitting on the counter," I say, trying not to sound breathless.

"Yeah, guess you are." He backs up, leaving the enclosure of my legs—I'm sorely tempted to hook my feet together around his back to keep him there, but I don't. "You have any first aid stuff?"

"I don't need first aid, Jesse," I breathe. "It's barely even bleeding."

He cradles my foot in his hand and lifts my leg to take a look at the cut. I'm not breathing. I'm shaking all over. The gusset of my shorts has nowhere near enough fabric to provide any decent modesty, not with my leg lifted like this. Oh god. If he looks, he'll see my hoo-ha. When was the last time I shaved? Oh yeah, just a few minutes ago, upstairs. I keep my eyes on his, watching him, watching where his eyes go.

I try to swallow but my throat is dry, unlike certain other areas.

Will he see that? Will he smell it? Oh fuck, he probably smells me.

And holy mother of all hells, am I aroused right now.

Jesse's eyes start at my face. Watching for demurral or any hint that I'm upset—which he won't find. Then, seeing nothing but my lip caught between my teeth and my eyes wide, he drags his eyes downward. I'm sporting a serious pair of headlights—my nipples are, shall we say, not small, and have a tendency to react aggressively to the slightest provocation or drop in temperature. And this shirt is, as I've said, so thin from age and wear and washings that it's nearly sheer. With Jesse's touch and attention and my own arousal, my nipples are the hardest they've ever been, standing out so thick and long and hard that I could cut twin holes in a pane of glass.

He groans again. It's a growl, a low, almost inaudible rumble, so deep on the register that I feel it more than hear it. "Have *mercy*," he murmurs to himself rather than to me.

After spending a moment blatantly ogling the protruding nubs of my hardened nipples, and the round weight of my breasts straining the fabric of my tank top, Jesse's gaze rakes downward. Pauses at my navel, my belly. His gaze there is a brief blast of cold water on my libido as self-consciousness slices through me—I've always been weird about my stomach, and never more so than this stage of my life, when stress makes me eat more than usual, busyness keeps me out of the gym and into the unhealthy aisles of the store. My belly used to be flat and toned. I never had visible abs or anything, but I could rock the hell out of a midriff-baring crop top back in the day. Nowadays? Not so much.

I squirm, hating his gaze on what is, to me, my ugliest and least beautiful area. I'm good with my cleavage—having big tits has its drawbacks for sure—running hurts, jumping is dangerous, stairs are my enemy, and button-down shirts are a joke—but they also are weapons I can and have used to my benefit. I'm also fine with having a juicy booty. It's maybe a little juicier these days than it used to be for the afore-mentioned reasons, but for the most part, possessing a curvy, jiggly butt is more of an asset than a problem. I'm just not cool with my belly.

Stop looking at it. God, please stop looking at my belly. Look at my thighs, look at my hips, look at my tits—anywhere but there.

"Stop it," Jesse growls.

I gulp. "Stop what?"

"Doubting yourself."

I stare hard at him. "How did you—ummmm, I mean—what?"

His eyes fix on mine. "You just…shut down. I felt it. Don't do that. Don't ever doubt yourself."

I snort. "Yeah, because it's just that easy."

"No, it's probably not, but you're a beautiful woman, Imogen. You have no reason to doubt your-self, or to be self-conscious about any part of your body."

I'm deeply uncomfortable with the abrupt turn of events, and try to pull my foot away. "Jesse, I just—"

He holds on to my foot, refusing to relinquish it. "I get it, though," he says.

He leans over me, his weight against my leg as he reaches for a strip of paper towel, wets it, folds it, and then straightens. As he does so, I feel his eyes on me again this time sliding sensuously up my leg, from my calf to my thigh. I tense all over, fighting the urge to clamp my thighs together. It's what I'd normally do, how I've always reacted in situations like this, even with someone I've been intimate with. It's not that I'm shy or that I lack adventurousness sexually—it's just…well, it's complicated, and Jesse's gaze is moving upward, destroying my train of thought.

Oh god.

I force myself to remain still—stock-still, not even breathing—as his eyes trail and traipse and dance up my thighs, my skin pebbling under his gaze. I swallow loudly, feeling faint, shaking all over.

Look at me.

Don't look at me.

Touch me.

Don't touch me.

I'm terrified and mortified.

I'm excited and thrilled and horny as hell.

His eyes halt at my core. I look where he's looking—and yeah, there's not a lot left to the imagination. I can't breathe. Shit, I actually can't breathe. Am I having an asthma attack? I don't have asthma, but my lungs aren't working.

I hear a deep, low snarl, and I realize it's coming from him, from Jesse, as he stares at my core. He has no qualms about what he's doing—there's no apology or attempt to hide it or cover it up. I'm not pulling away or stopping him, so I can't be mad about it, and honestly, his open, daring, greedy gaze is a hell of a turn-on.

I don't know what that says about who I am, or rather who I've become.

And I don't care.

It feels so naughty and almost dirty to let him stare at me like this. I barely know him—less than barely. We don't even know each other's last names. And here I am, sitting on my counter in an outfit a Hooter's waitress wouldn't wear, letting a man I literally just met stare at my lady parts. And I *like* it.

I really do.

What the hell is wrong with me?

I watch him carefully. His eyes widen, and his jaw clenches. His hands curl into claws and then into fists, and his forearms and biceps bunch and flex as he squeezes his fists tight. And then, with a ragged huff, he loosens his fists and wiggles his fingers. Using the wet paper towel, he wipes gently at the long, shallow cut to the outside of my calf. His touch is so gentle, so careful, I barely feel it as he dabs and wipes the cut clean.

"There." He cups my Achilles in one hand and lowers my leg. With an almost reluctant sigh, he presses my knees inward, closing my thighs, and steps away, tossing the paper towel in the trash by the fridge. "You were right. It's not bad at all."

"Thank you," I whisper.

He's in the middle of the kitchen, hands shoved into his pockets. "Yeah."

I hop down from the counter—a movement that sends my cleavage bouncing, a fact he doesn't miss—and grab another pair of plates.

I dish out the food, hand him a plate and a fork and say, "I don't have a dining room, and the kitchen is a little dusty, so in nice weather I eat out back."

I've got a little round glass table and two chairs in the backyard, and it's my favorite place in the world. I sit here in the mornings as weather allows and drink my coffee, and just breathe. The closest thing to peace is what I feel here, at this little table. It's my place.

Inviting Jesse to share my favorite place feels deeply personal in an odd, intimate, scary way. This table and chairs were a purchase I made after the divorce was finalized, because I'd always wanted a table out here and Nicholas would never get me one and, at the time, I was saving all my money for the renovations. The day the judge signed the papers, I drove from the courthouse to an antique store, bought this set, brought it home, and promptly sat down with a glass of wine and cried.

Now it's *my* place.

So why oh why did I invite Jesse to eat here with

me? He's sitting in the delicate wrought-iron chair, looking like an adult sitting in one of those miniature chairs in a kindergarten classroom. He's too big for the chair, too big for the table, too big for the backyard. He just fills the whole space with his presence.

I set my plate on the table and take a bite—I smile, pleased with myself for making a yummy meal.

Jesse has eaten half his food before I get done with two bites, and then I realize there's nothing to drink. I set my fork down and speak around a mouthful. "You want something to drink?"

He nods, fork halfway to his mouth. "Yeah, please. Whatever you have is fine. I'm not picky

"I have sparkling water and...wine, and that's pretty much it, unless you want me to make coffee."

He laughs. "Water, wine, whatever you want."

"No coffee?"

Another laugh. "At seven at night? I don't think so. I'd be up till next week." A self-conscious grin. "I used to be able to drink coffee all day and all night and never think twice, but nowadays? Coffee past, like, four in the afternoon keeps me up for hours. Getting older sucks."

"It sure does."

He eyes me. "Yeah, and what would you know about getting older? You're just a kid."

I snort. "Okay, if you count forty as a kid."

"I'm forty-four, so I win."

"I didn't realize this was a competition."

"I can turn everything into a competition," he says. "I'm sort of competitive."

I get up and decide to screw it, I'm pouring wine. So I uncork a bottle, pour two big glasses, and bring them back outside. Jesse has his phone out as I enter the backyard, but as soon as he sees me, he powers it all the way off, and shoves it back into his pocket.

"Sorry, just checking my email. James tends to rely on email for all his important communication."

"It's no big deal." Actually, I'm impressed by his courtesy.

Nicholas was always on his phone. What's the term I read about? Phubbing. Snubbing someone by talking on your phone. That's Nicholas. Yet another way he proved how little he cared about me.

Jesse, on the other hand, even on an impromptu means-nothing dinner like this, is showing more courtesy than Nicholas ever did.

It feels good.

"You didn't have to turn it off," I said.

He shrugs as I hand him the glass of wine. His eyes are hot and intense on mine. "My mama raised me to have manners, and in my book, staring at your phone instead of a sexy woman is just bad manners all around."

"I thought you'd had your fill of staring a few minutes ago," I say, the words spilling out unbidden.

He snorts sarcastically. "Got my fill? Imogen, have you looked in a mirror lately?"

"Um, yeah, just before I came down after my shower."

"Haha, okay Miss Literal. What I mean is, no, I definitely did *not* get my fill of staring at you." His gaze stays fixed on mine, and is so intense that I have a hard time holding it. "That's not a thing, Imogen."

"What's not a thing?"

"Getting my fill of looking at you."

Oh god. Swoon.

Instead of swooning gracefully, however, what I end up doing is choking on my wine. Is this guy real?

"Did Audra send you?" I ask, another blurt I have no control over and didn't intend to say.

"Audra? Who's Audra?" He shakes his head. "No, I work for James Bod and I have no idea what Audra has to do with anything."

"Audra is my best friend," I say, "and she's been after me before the ink was dry on my divorce papers to meet someone. She's tried fixing me up a dozen times in a dozen ways with a dozen different kinds of guys. I thought maybe this whole thing was an elaborate ploy of hers."

He frowns. "How could she have arranged for

you to smash your own window? Is she a Time Lord or something?" He shakes his head, laughing. "I mean, seriously. And why would you think that in the first place?"

"Because you're too good to be true."

He leans close to me, so close I can smell the wine on his breath, the utterly masculine scent of sawdust and sweat. "Good? Have you not seen the big truck and the tattoos and the long hair?"

"Yeah, but that doesn't make you bad. Just…a certain kind of man. You're kind, and considerate, and generous, and skilled." I hesitate over the next words, but again my mouth betrays me. "And hot as fuck."

"Hot as fuck, huh?" His smirk is heated and humorous.

"Um. Sexy as sin?"

"I'm not a romance novel hero, so I'll stick with hot as fuck, if you don't mind."

"My point is that yeah, actually, you *are* a sort of romance novel hero."

He frowns. "How do you mean?"

"You show up looking the way you look, and you fix my window, and you flirt with me, and you say things that make me literally and figuratively swoon." I shrug. "Ergo, you are a romance novel hero."

"I'm not flirting with you, Imogen."

My heart sinks. "You're—you're not?" God, have I just totally read this whole thing wrong?

He leans even closer, so close we could kiss, if either of were so inclined. "Nope. I'm hitting on you."

Hope blooms, desire blossoms, and need burns sun-hot. "Oh. I see."

At that moment, a horn blares, and then a few seconds later, a fist pounds on my front door. Puzzled as to who it could be and what they would need so urgently, I trot to the front door and crack it open.

The man on the other side of the screen door is even taller than Jesse, with arms the size of my waist. His hair and his beard are neatly cut and combed, and both are brown sprinkled with silver. He has a pair of Oakleys on his face, and his phone is clutched in one hand, and he looks furious.

"Um, can I help you?" I ask.

"Where the fuck is Jesse? His truck's here and his phone is off."

"Who are you?" I demand, not opening the door further than a small sliver.

"James Bod," the man says through gritted, grinding teeth. "His boss."

I hear Jesse's tread behind me. "Yo, James, what up?"

"Why's your phone off, you fuckin' tool?" James demands, his voice an angry bark.

"Whoa, back off, James," Jesse says, sounding taken aback. "Take a breath, man. What's crawled up your ass?"

"The plumber fucked up at the Thompson job. The whole fucking basement is flooded! I need all hands so we can save the project, and my top employee has his goddamn phone turned off!"

Jesse shoulders past me and opens the door all the way, talking to James through the screen door. "Okay, well sorry for actually having a fucking life, James. Jesus."

"The basement is *flooded*, Jesse. Waist deep." James runs his hand through his hair. "It's a cluster-fuck, buddy. It's gonna mean a total redo on the entire basement."

Jesse groans. "Fuck, man. Seriously? We were damn near done with the basement. All but paint and switch plates."

"Right, which is why I need you to get your ass over there."

"I'll be there in five."

James turns around on a heel and trots down the steps, but then halts at the bottom and trots back up. "Sorry I was a dick," he says to me, looking sheepish. "It was unprofessional of me, and I apologize."

I smile at him. "Thank you for the apology, Mr. Bod. I accept. And it's fine. Emergencies are like that."

He juts his chin at the interior of the house. "My brother-in-law fix you up all right?"

I frown. "Your brother-in-law?"

James jerks a thumb at Jesse, who had jogged into my kitchen to retrieve his tool belt. "That joker. My brother-in-law."

"Jesse is your brother-in-law?"

Jesse nods at me as he pauses by the door. "Yep. Fortunately or unfortunately, depending on the day and his mood." He turns to face me. "Sorry about this. Thanks for dinner."

"It's okay. Duty calls, right?" I smile up at him, feeling a stupid, annoying, persistent flutter in my belly—and regions southward—at the smile on his lips and the promise in his eyes. "Maybe I'll find some thing else for you to fix."

Jesse laughs. "Imogen, babe—trust me, there's *plenty* around here for me to fix."

"Hey, Don Juan, let's *go*," James growls. "Flirt with the clientele on your own time. Or better yet, *don't* flirt with the clientele at all."

Jesse nudges open the screen door, giving me a brilliant grin and a sly wink. "The job's done, Jamie. So she's not a client at the moment, just a *former* client. And don't be a dick."

James shakes his head as the two of them jog toward their trucks, still bantering. "I'll show you a dick if you don't get your ass in your truck."

"Yeah, and I'd need a scanning electron micro-scope to even see the damn thing, you fuckin' mi-cro-peen chump." Jesse whacks James upside the head. "Douche."

"Hey, asshole. I can fire you, you know. Brother-in-law or not, best friend or not, I *will* fire your ass." James reaches his truck—it's almost a match for Jesse's, being huge and black with every accent chromed out, sporting huge knobby tires and a lift kit, a back rack, and toolbox.

Jesse just laughs. "I'd love to see you fire me. Your little company would fall apart in ten seconds without me."

James snorts, yanking open his truck door. "Funny, cause I seem to remember it was going just fine without you."

"Oh yeah? And who, pray tell, found you your CPA to sort out your messy-ass books?" Jesse de-mands, climbing up into his own truck. "And who has the supply contacts at Pella *and* Kohler, hmm?"

James starts his engine, and then leans through the open window, shouting, "One word, asshole: Lunchbox!"

"That was second grade! Let it go already!" Jesse shouts back.

I laugh at their banter, which continues even as

they drive away. When they're gone, I head back inside, clean up dinner, put the leftovers in the fridge, and pour the rest of the wine into my glass.

Feeling at loose ends, I wander around my house, sipping wine and mooning about Jesse like a lovesick teenager.

He's just so *dreamy*!

FIVE

M**Y PHONE RINGS WHILE I'M IN A ROOM WITH A** patient. I'm happy and mad all at once. Happy because it seems to be working, and mad because I'm with a patient. My luck being what it is, it was in the back pocket of my scrub pants this morning, when I pulled my pants down to go pee and my poor phone took a swim. I fished it out within seconds of it hitting the water. I blew it dry and stuck it in rice in an effort to get it working. It still works…sort of. But it won't go to silent, the screen is marbled and watery, and it won't charge. So now, with my phone ringing in my pocket, it sounds like it's…well…still at the bottom of the toilet bowl.

I'm in the middle of checking my patient's blood pressure.

"You need to answer that?" he asks. The patient is a seventy-five-year-old man, a regular, and a mild hypochondriac. And a serious crank.

"No, it's okay. I dropped it in the toilet this morning and now it won't go into silent mode. Sorry, Mr. Christensen."

"Shoulda left it at home, then, or in the car," he grumbles as I write down his blood pressure. "Unprofessional, is what it is. Damn cell phones ringin' all the damn time. Everybody staring at a screen insteada interacting with folks."

"Your blood pressure is still pretty high, Mr. Christensen," I said. "It's one-thirty over eighty-seven. You've really gotta work on getting that under control."

"Oh, save it for the real doctor," he grouses "Don't need a lecture from some damn nurse."

I roll my eyes at him, but go through the rest of the visit in silence.

After I'm done with Mr. Christensen, I stop by the desk and shove my phone at the bottom of my purse—because he was right about it being unprofessional to have my phone ringing in the room with a patient. Then I have three more patients—an embarrassed high school senior with a gnarly STD, a toddler with a cold and a helicopter mommy, and a middle-aged woman with swimmer's ear.

By the time I'm done with all of them, Dr. Bishara is finished with Cranky Christensen.

"Imogen, a word with you please?" Dr. Bishara

says, indicating his office.

I sigh. Here we go.

I follow him in, close the door, and lean against it, refusing to play his power game, the one where he sits on the corner of his desk and tries to intimidate me.

"Sit, please," he says.

I smile. "I'm fine, thanks. I have patients to get to. What's up, Dr. Bishara?"

He glares at me through his thick glasses. "Mr. Christensen said your phone rang while you were with him. We have a very clear policy regarding cellular devices, I do believe."

"Yes, Dr. Bishara, I'm aware. But I dropped it in the toilet and now it won't go on silent mode. It's in my purse, now."

"If your phone cannot be silenced, it should remain at home."

"I have aging parents who live in Florida, Dr. Bishara. I can't just not have my phone." Which is true enough.

"Then replace it."

"I can't afford to, at the moment." I hesitate, and then go for it. "Which does lead me to think...I've worked for you for *ten years*, Dr. Bishara. I've never been late, never called off, and I cover more shifts than anyone else. I've also never asked for a raise."

Dr. Bishara removes his glasses. "Imogen, I do not think this is the right time for this conversation. I am in the middle of reprimanding you for violating our cell phone policy and you ask for a raise? What kind of logic is this?"

"Reprimanding me?" Oh—now I'm pissed. *"Reprimanding me?* I'm your best employee! How many other times has this happened? What about Tiffany? She's literally always on her phone! She answered a call while she was *with a patient*, and you said nothing. But my phone goes off *one time*—something I can't fix right now because my phone is broken and I can't afford a new one because I haven't had a raise in *six years*—and you reprimand *me?*"

"Now wait a moment—"

I roll my eyes and sigh. "You know what? No. Seriously?" Don't be dumb, I tell myself; but it's too late. My ire is up. Time to do something stupid. "Dr. Bishara—I quit."

"Imogen, don't be ridiculous."

I remove the stethoscope from around my neck and set it on his desk. "What's ridiculous is that I haven't quit before now. I can make double at the hospital doing the same thing I do here. At this point, I'll take the extra hours and extra stress." I give him a sarcastic, cutesy finger wave and fake smile. "Good luck without me, Dr. Bishara. You'll need it."

I shove the door open, ignoring his protests. I grab my purse, and walk past the front desk. Amber hurriedly puts a call on hold and chases after me.

"Did he seriously just fire you?" she asks, following me out to the parking lot. "For your phone going off?"

I laugh, feeling slightly hysterical. "No, I quit."

Amber halts in place. "You—you *quit*?" Her voice rises about an octave on the last word. "You can't quit! You're the only reason this entire office is able to function!"

"I know," I say. "But I'm done." I pause with my hand on the handle of my ghetto-ass car. "Also, Amber, you should know your husband is cheating on you. Tiffany saw him at a restaurant with some other woman, making out and stuff. I told her she should tell you, but she didn't. So...there you go. Sorry."

Amber sniffs. "Dammit. I suspected, but I haven't been sure."

"Tiffany has pictures, actually. But she said you were a bitch to her about covering for her that one time she got wasted and no-call-no-showed, so she wasn't going to tell you." I laugh, not at all kindly. "Good luck with her. She's a real treat."

And with that, I climb into my car and drive away. Instead of going home, though, I go to the nearest cellular service provider and buy a new phone.

Apparently I was due for an upgrade anyway, so it didn't actually end up costing me a full arm and a leg. Then, with shiny new phone in my hand, I decide to keep splurging. Nothing like quitting your job to make you feel like celebrating.

I decide on Mexican. Chips and guac and margs and a smothered burrito.

My phone rings halfway through my second margarita. This time, I can see the screen, so I know who it is: Jesse.

I make him wait—make myself wait—before answering. Don't want to seem too eager.

"Hello?" I say, as if I don't know who it is.

"Hey, Imogen. It's Jesse."

"Oh, hey." I try for breezy and end up sounding overly breathy. "What's up?"

"I tried calling you a bit ago, but your voicemail is full and you weren't answering messages."

"Oh, yeah, sorry. I was at work. I dropped my phone in the toilet." I laugh. "My voicemail is full because my douche of an ex-husband left a bunch of messages on it right after we got divorced. He got drunk and drunk-dialed me, I guess. Nobody ever calls me, and nobody ever leaves voicemail, either, so I never thought about deleting them."

"Dropped your phone in the toilet, huh?" His voice crackles with humor. "Let me guess—it was in your back pocket?"

"Shut up."

"They should have back pocket insurance specifically for women."

"Is there a reason you're calling, other than to make fun of me?" I ask. "Because I'm busy celebrating, here."

"Celebrating? Celebrating what?"

"I quit my job, and got a new phone."

A long silence. "Congratulations? What are you going to do now?"

"Be able to use my phone, for one thing. The screen has been shattered for like two months."

"I meant about work."

"Oh." I sigh. "I don't know. Probably apply at the hospital. It's a higher stress environment, but they pay more than an office. I took the office job because I wanted less stress. With my experience and my RN credentials, it shouldn't be a problem."

"Why'd you quit?"

"I don't know. I probably shouldn't have, but I was pissed. I dropped my phone in the toilet, like I said, and the ringer wouldn't go off, it wouldn't switch to silent, so when you called I was with a patient. My boss, Dr. Bishara, has a very strict no cell phone policy, but it appears he's okay with other people violating it, just not me. I've worked for him longer than any of the other nurses, and he reprimands *me* for my phone accidentally ringing one time—once! I've worked for him for almost ten years! So I just...I quit."

"Because of my call?" he asks, sounding worried.

"No!" I say. "Well, yes, but it was time. I like being a nurse, but that place was driving me crazy."

He sighs. "I'm sorry my call came at an inopportune time, regardless." He pauses. "So, the reason I'm calling is because I wanted to know if you'd be okay with me swinging by your house today while you're gone. I have something I want to do, and I want to surprise you with it."

"You're calling to tell me you want to surprise me?" I ask, laughing.

"Yes, I need your permission. And access inside."

"What are you doing?"

He chuckles. "Um, well, if I told you that, it wouldn't be a surprise, would it? Just...trust me, okay?"

I consider. For all of, like, fifteen seconds. "There's a spare key."

"Let me guess—under the welcome mat?"

"Nope."

"In the flower pot by the front door?"

I laugh. "No! I'm not that stupid, Jesse. There's a little equipment shed in the backyard."

"I see it," he says.

I sit in silence for a beat. "Wait, you're there now?"

"Well...yeah. No time to get shit done like the present, amiright?"

"I guess. So, in the shed there's a shelf on the back wall, near the ceiling. Way high up."

"I see it."

"There's an old box of strike-anywhere matches on the left side of the shelf. Inside that is a spare key lockbox..."

I hesitate, because giving a man who is, truthfully, still an unknown—a stranger, if you will—the key to my house...? Am I dumb? Naive? Too trusting? Yes, perhaps. But I just have this feeling about him. An innate instinct that I can trust him.

"Um." His voice breaks my silence. "The code?"

"Sorry, I just..."

"You know, if you're not comfortable with me being in your house when you're not there, I totally get it. Just say so." He waits a beat or two. "I do hope you feel like you can trust me, though. I know we haven't known each other long, but—"

"Six-six-oh-eight," I blurt. "My anniversary. God, I need to change that."

"Yeah, you do. How about you change it to eight-one-one-eight?"

I frown, not recognizing the date as anything

significant to me. "Why? What does that signify?"

"I'm hurt, Imogen. Deeply wounded." He laughs. "It's the date we met."

"Oh." I'm blushing hard, now, for some dumb-ass reason. "Yeah, that's a good one."

"I'm teasing," he says, still laughing. "Okay, I'm inside. So, can you stay away from the house for a few hours?"

I hesitate. I was thinking of going home after this and changing into a bikini and sunning in the back-yard. But why not give him a chance to surprise me? God knows that hasn't happened enough in my life. Well, good surprises, at least.

"Sure," I say. "I'm out of a job now, so I've got nothing but time on my hands."

I hear tools clanking, and a rustling as if he's shifting the phone to clutch it between ear and shoul-der. "You're an RN, right?"

"Yeah, why?"

"Well, our big project we're doing? That custom build in your neighborhood? The wife is a doctor, and she's actually a department head. The ICU, I think. I could give her a call for you."

"Not that I doubt a call from you would do any good with her, but—"

"But I'm a construction worker building her house, and why would I have any sway with the department head of a hospital?"

I laugh. "Exactly."

"She's mentioned several times how understaffed her department is, just in the course of making small talk while she's on-site." I can almost hear the shrug in his voice. "It's worth a shot, right? If you can get a new job right away without having to go through rounds of submitting your resume, that'd be a good thing, right?"

"It would be amazing," I say with a sigh. "Sure, give her a call."

"You're an RN, with what kind of experience?"

"I've worked for the same private practice for the last ten years, and I worked in the ICU in the University of Illinois Hospital for eight years before that."

"Damn, girl. You've been nursing for a minute, haven't you?"

I blush even harder. "I, um…I started taking college courses during my sophomore year of high school. I worked with counselors at the community college and my high school so I could work out how to take all the prerequisites in the right order so by the time graduated…" I trail off. "No need to explain all that. Point is, yeah, I knew early on that I wanted to be a nurse and went after it."

"You know you literally cannot bore me, right?

Like, it wouldn't be possible for you to ever bore me."

I laugh. "I'm pretty sure me talking about how I took anatomy and microbiology and developmental psych and all that would bore you to actual tears. Manly tears, but tears nonetheless."

I hear tools being set down. "You'd be surprised." A long, significant pause. "I may not be interested in nursing or whatever, but I'm interested in *you*, so, therefore, I'm interested in nursing degree prerequisites."

"Are you sure you're a real person?"

"'If you prick us, do we not bleed?'" he says.

I frown. "Did you just...did you just quote Shakespeare?"

"Who'd'a thunk it, right?" He chuckles ruefully. "A dumb ol' blue collar construction bro quoting Shakespeare?"

"No! That's not—I mean—Jesse, that's not what I meant."

He laughs even harder. "Why not? It's true enough. I didn't exactly ace my high school English classes. My sister was the book nerd. She was in a production of Merchant of Venice her senior year, and for some reason that particular line has always stuck with me. It's not like I can sit here and quote Shakespearean sonnets to you or anything, so don't get too excited."

"You don't give yourself enough credit."

"Nah, it's not that. I just get put into a particular box pretty frequently. And, for the most part, that *is* where I fit. It's just…it's not totally and *only* who I am as a person." He laughs again. "Anyway, I'm gonna let you go. I wanna get this little project finished."

"Okay. Thanks."

"Don't thank me yet—you haven't seen what I'm doing!"

"Okay, okay, well…I'll talk to you later, then?" I think of something. "Wait—did you guys get your emergency flood situation under control?"

H sighs deeply. "We worked until like four in the morning, but yeah, we did."

"That's good," I say. "I'm glad you got it sorted it out."

"Me too." A pause. "Anyway, I'll call Dr. Waverley and then call you. Have a nice day off."

"I'll try. You too. Bye." I hang up, and my food arrives, and I lose myself in wondering what he could possibly be doing to my house.

After lunch—and cutting myself off at three margaritas, because it's just too early to get sloppy—I decide to take myself to a movie. There's a new romantic comedy out, and the theater is just down the road. I splurge on popcorn and a bottle of water, and enjoy some much-needed laughs.

Of course, the romantic element of the movie isn't doing my overactive imagination any favors. On the way out of the theater, a ridiculous fantasy runs through my head. I have this vision of arriving at home and seeing Jesse in my living room, covered in sawdust, shirtless, sweaty, wearing nothing but a pair of tight jeans and a tool belt. He'd be ecstatic to see me, and he'd push me up against the fireplace and kiss me, and his big strong hands would go to the tie of my scrubs—

Down girl. Rawr. Seriously, I need to get this libido of mine under control. I haven't been this worked up since...well, ever. Those first few months after I lost my virginity in high school, I was a horny little thing. And there were a few boyfriends between that first guy and Nicholas, who could get me going, but these last few years with Nicholas I was half-dead. Just switched off. Like he'd lost interest in me, and thus I stopped thinking about myself as a sexual creature, stopped thinking about my needs. He lost interest in me, and I lost interest in myself. And now, suddenly, I'm alive again. I'm remembering that I have wants and needs again.

And my sex drive is coming back.

I wasn't a hookup or a fling sort of girl, but when I was dating a guy, I tended to be pretty uninhibited. Adventurous, even. Sitting in my car, I think back to those days. Specifically, a certain college sophomore named Lee. All-State soccer, ended up being vale-dictorian at graduation, med school student...surfer blond hair, freckles on his nose—and on his ass—with a charming smile and an easy confidence that I couldn't resist. Lee also had a preternaturally pow-erful sex drive. The boy was insatiable in a way I've never known, before or since, and that was infectious. I don't think I've ever been as wild, kinky, or voracious as I was with Lee.

And just being around Jesse is making me feel like I did when I was with Lee; like I'm a starved monster, a creature who simply cannot get enough. I want, *want*, *WANT*.

Gah. It's infuriating.

Because back then, I was innocent, with an intact heart and a willingness to trust, a willingness to take chances.

Nowadays? My heart ain't exactly intact, and neither is my ability or willingness to trust and take chances on a guy.

Let him into my house to fix it? Sure. I can change the locks, or even move, if it came to that—but it won't, because I think Jesse really is a good guy, honest and trustworthy.

Doesn't mean I'm willing to let anything happen, though, because I'm just...well...scared, I guess.

My phone rings—it's Jesse. My heart leaps, and my cheeks heat.

"Hello?" I answer.

"Hey, it's Jesse."

I laugh. "Yeah, I know. There's this little thing called caller ID."

"Smart-ass."

"Better than being a dumbass, as my dad used to say," I say, laughing.

"I'm not sure where that leaves me, then. My dad used to say I was the dumbest smart-ass he ever met." I hear him take a drink of something, and then he's back on the phone. "So, what'd you do with the last couple hours?"

"Ate lunch and saw a movie. I actually just got out of the movie."

"Oh? What'd you see?"

"Just some romantic comedy. Nothing you'd like."

"There you go making assumptions about me again, Imogen. What if I like romantic comedies…in a very straight, very manly sort of way?"

"Then you'd be a frickin' unicorn among men."

He does a very, *very* bad impression of a neighing horse, and I lose my shit, cackling until my ribs hurt.

"I didn't think it was that funny," he says.

"Oh god, it was hysterical. That was so bad it was

good, Jesse." I sigh. "So. What's the reason for your call?"

"I can't just want to hear your lovely voice?"

I'm melting. "No. You can't."

"Oh." He hesitates. "Too bad, because it's true."

"Careful, Jesse, you keep talking to me like that, you'll end up trapping yourself a lonely forty-year-old divorcée with a broken heart and an overactive imagination." And a sex drive that's currently stuck on turbo, but I manage to keep that part to myself.

"Maybe that's what I'm after."

"Maybe you'd be biting off more than you can chew."

"Maybe I can take really, *really* big bites."

I have to actually fan my face. "Jesse. What do you want?"

"You, here, in those booty shorts and that tank top." A pause. "Or even less. I'd settle for less, in this case."

"*Jesse.*"

"Hey, you're not the only one with an overactive imagination. You'd have to spend a week in church to make up for the things I've imagined about you."

"*Holy shit,*" I breathe. Oops; I didn't mean to say that. "You have no idea," I say, louder.

"Maybe we should get together for drinks and compare fantasies," he murmurs.

"Compare, or act out?" Shit, shit, shit, shit, shit. Did I SERIOUSLY just say that to him?

He growls, and I hear a thump, as if he slammed his fist against the wall. "You're gonna be the death of me, Imogen. For real."

I struggle to bring this dangerous conversation back to safe, solid ground. "You didn't call me just to verbally torture me, did you?"

"Who's torturing who, here, Imogen?" he asks. "But no. I talked to Dr. Waverley a few minutes ago."

"And?"

"And, if you have time, she wants you come in for an interview."

"She *what?*" I squeak. "When?"

"I was under the impression that she meant right away. Like now-ish."

"I'm still in my scrubs and I don't have my resume ready."

"I think she just wants to meet you, have a little conversation. Nothing formal. She told me to give you her direct number so you can give her a call if you're able to come in."

"Um. Okay."

"I'll text you the number after we hang up."

"Okay." My throat is thick. "Jesse, I—"

"Thank me later," he interrupts. "Hint—visual stimulus counts as thanks, in my book."

I laugh. "Okay, okay, message received."

So, I hang up with Jesse, spend a few moments calming my nerves, and then call the number Jesse sent through.

It rings four times, and then a high, firm, authoritative female voice answers. "This is Dr. Waverley."

"Hi Dr. Waverley, this Imogen Irving. My friend Jesse said he spoke to you?"

Her voice softens immediately. "Ah, Miss Irving, yes. A lovely young man, that Jesse."

"He sure is."

Dr. Waverley laughs. "Oh, I *bet* you agree! I don't mind admitting that I hired James and his crew based on what may be less than professional reasons."

"Having met both James and Jesse, I can see why."

Her tone goes back to businesslike. "So. You have a BSN from the University of Illinois, and experience in the U-I-H ICU, I understand?"

"Yes ma'am. I did my residency in the ICU there, and stayed on for seven years after that, before transitioning to a private practice."

"May I ask why you left the ICU?"

I only barely hold back a sigh of resentment. "I got married. The hours were pretty intense, it was a lot of stress, and I wanted kids."

A pause on the other end. "Something tells me this is a sensitive subject, so I'll hold the rest of my questions. What I really want to know is, would you be willing to return to the ICU?"

"I think I would, yes." I think back to the bustle and the chaos and the intensity of the ICU, and feel a little thrill run through me. "What I mean is yes, ma'am, I definitely would."

"I understand you recently left your employer."

"Ah, yes, I did."

"Suddenly?"

"Yes, I must admit it was sudden. But I just—it was something that I'd needed to do for a long time."

Another pause. "Well, Miss Irving, I'm in desperate need of experienced nurses in my ICU, and I happen to have a block of time free at the moment. Would you be able to come in for a more in-depth conversation?"

"Right now?"

"Yes, right now."

"I'm not—I mean—I'm still wearing scrubs, and I haven't updated my résumé in years. I quit this morning, if you'd like the honest truth."

She chuckles. "All the better. I've found it's best to interview people when they're not ready for it. You get more of a person's true self, rather than a nervous, practiced facade. Just come in, we'll have a chat, and barring any kind of unexpected surprises, you'll be newly employed before the day is done."

"Um—that sounds amazing. I'll be there in fifteen minutes."

After the routine goodbye pleasantries, I hang up.

And now I have to calm my nerves all over again.

I drive to the hospital and sit in the parking lot for a moment, still trying to collect myself.

It can't really be this easy, can it?

Apparently it can.

Dr. Waverley and I spend over an hour together, talking. She's a wonderful woman: wise, kind, firm, knowledgeable, and personable. I have the feeling she'll be a dream to work for—authoritative and in charge, but not a micromanager or power tripper. She'll expect the best, expect results, but will also be reasonable. I have a packet of paperwork, my official scrub color code, and a start date of the following Monday—which gives me a few days off to fill out my paperwork and buy a few sets of ICU color-coded scrubs.

I drive home, and for once I'm so caught up in excitement about my new job that I momentarily forget how I got the job in the first place.

Then I get home, and Jesse's truck is in my

driveway, backed in, and full of construction detritus. There's also another truck parked on my curb. Unlike Jesse's and James's, this one is more subdued. It's silver, with normal tires at the normal height, and one of those body-color-matched bed caps. The tailgate and cap windows are both open, revealing a dizzying array of power tools, bins, containers, toolboxes, ladders of all sizes, tarps...who knows what all. Coming from within the house—the front door of which is propped open—are the sounds of a nail gun and a vacuum.

I park at the curb behind the truck and approach the front door, eyeing Jesse's truck and the mess inside it, but I can't divine what he's done from the contents.

I enter hesitantly, unsure of what I'll find. I pause at the entryway and call in. "Hello? Jesse?"

The sounds halt, and I hear the clomp of booted feet.

My jaw literally drops open.

Hello, fantasy made real.

SIX

MY GAZE TRAVELS FROM FLOOR UPWARD, SLOWLY, twice. He's wearing his usual boots, stained and scuffed and well-worn, with jeans so faded they're almost white. Tight, but not too tight. There's a rip in the left knee, showing tanned skin.

He's shirtless, his tool belt slung low around his hips.

Covered in sawdust and sweat.

He has a Blackhawks hat on backward, with his Oakleys perched on top.

God—holy god. He's so hot it's mind-boggling.

His body, though?

I'm literally speechless.

His chest is heavy with muscle, thick and tanned and solid. His arms are python-thick, and his waist trim. His jeans hang just below his hips, showing the band of his underwear and a hint of those V-shaped lines. His tattoos cover his chest as well. He has a hint of a belly—not a beer belly, just a slight layer over a rock-hard abdomen. He likes food, and likes working out in equal proportion, and he's not a twenty-year-old kid anymore either. He's all man, hard and muscular. His chest isn't fitness model smooth and hairless, either, but is rather hairy. Not wookie/werewolf hairy, just...masculine and manly.

And then another pair of boots clomps across my floor. My jaw can't drop any further, so my voice squeaks in protest of the sudden emptiness of my lungs.

"Uh—huh? Who?" My voice is a breathless squeak. "Ahem. Who—who are you?"

The man standing beside Jesse is...well...nearly his equal in terms of sexiness, although his opposite in build and appearance.

Five-eleven or six feet, lean as a whip, and built like Brad Pitt in *Fight Club*. Blond hair pulled back in a neat ponytail, sunglasses on top of his head. No shirt—all abs and pecs in razor-sharp definition. Shaven jaw, no tattoos or piercings, with icy blue eyes. God, he's beautiful.

Jesse grins. "Imogen, this is my buddy, Franco. He works at Dad Bod with me."

"Hi—um. Hi." I'm still a little shell-shocked at the excess of male hotness in my house.

Jesse pokes Franco in the belly—which doesn't

give even a millimeter. "It's annoying isn't it? The bastard is a year older than me, we eat the same and work out the same, and the fucker has an eight-pack while I'm packing on a keg."

Franco snorts derisively. "First, I'm ten months older than you, not a full year. Second, we may eat the same *kinds* of food, but you eat twice the amount, and third, we may work out at the same time and do the same things, but you lift twice what I do."

"Yeah, well, that's 'cause you're a twink," Jesse says, laughing.

Franco just rolls his eyes and turns away. "Which makes you something that it'd be offensive for me to say out loud and, unlike *you*, I have *manners*." He shoots me a grin. "I should warn you about Jesse. He's a big ugly roughneck with no manners and less class. Give him an inch and he'll take a mile. He's like a stray dog, actually. Feed him, and you'll never be rid of him."

Jesse reaches into a pouch of his tool belt, withdraws a nail, and flings it at Franco's retreating back, pegging him square between the shoulder blades, leaving a red welt.

"Ow! You asshole!" Franco says, pawing at his back and spinning. "You better watch it, buddy boy. I'll staple your hand to your dick while you're sleeping, and don't think I'm kidding."

I can't help laughing. "You guys are ridiculous."

"*He's* ridiculous," Franco says, winking at me as he vanishes into the kitchen. "*I'm* amazing."

I mean, I'd have to agree.

"I'm amazing," Jesse echoes in a sarcastic tone of voice. "Get outta here, twink. I don't need you anymore."

"Don't lie to yourself, Jess," Franco says, re-emerging from the kitchen with a toolbox in one hand and a shirt with the other, "you'll always need me. For one thing, I can count to twenty without taking off my boots."

"Fuck you, pretty boy," Jesse shoots back, grinning.

The two men bump fists, and Franco heads for the door, requiring me to move out of the way.

"Thanks for your help, Franco."

"You're welcome." He aims this at me. "Meaning *you're* welcome. Jess, you owe me a few rounds at the bar."

I slide inside so Franco can leave, and I smell him—sweat and man. Makes me dizzy.

And there's still Jesse to deal with. I put my back to door post and try to keep my knees from buckling. Why am I so weak right now? Hot guy overload? My poor libido has probably short-circuited.

"Imogen?" Jesse asks, his voice worried.

I blink at him, and realize he's standing in front of me, frowning. "Huh? What?"

"Are you…okay? You were spacing out, or something. I was talking to you."

I'm still all…woo-hoo. So my verbal filter, which isn't the best around Jesse to begin with, is totally kaput. "Oh. Yeah. Sorry. Just…a little overwhelmed. You and Franco both in my house with your shirts off is a little much for my poor underserved libido to deal with."

Jesse smirks. "Underserved libido?"

I curse mentally. "Um. You know. I—I didn't mean to say that out loud."

His smirk widens into a shit-eating grin. "But you did, and now I'm curious as to what that means." He swaggers a few inches closer to me, so his big frame occludes the house, the whole world, everything. "'Cause I think it means you haven't had sex for a long time."

"You'd be correct in that assumption," I whisper.

"How long?" he murmurs, filling my universe with his scent, his masculine aura of dominance and confidence and sexuality and strength. "Couple weeks? Couple months?"

I laugh bitterly, an unattractive snort/raspberry combination. "Try over a year."

"Jesus," he mutters, wincing. "How are you even alive?"

"I wonder the same thing sometimes."

"How long have you been divorced, if you don't mind me asking?"

"A little over a month," I tell him. "The proceedings took three months, and we'd been having death-knell marriage problems for...oh god, almost a year before that. At least a year. But the warning signs were there long before that, I just—" I stop. "You don't want to hear about my shitty-ass marriage or my even shittier divorce."

"No, not really," he says, "but I *am* sorry you went through all that. You deserve better."

"Oh? And how do you know that?"

"I can tell. I'm a good judge of people."

"And what does your judgment of people tell you about me?"

He stares down at me for a long moment before answering. "That you're an amazing woman who settled for an asshole who wasn't worth even five minutes of your time."

"You got at least half of that right," I say. "Nicholas...was a mistake."

He frowns at me. "You don't think you're amazing."

"My house is falling apart and I can't afford to

fix what's broken much less improve it, my car is a piece of shit with no A/C and no radio, and I haven't so much as kissed a man in almost a year and a half."

I laugh again, more bitterly than ever.

"So, no," I say. "I don't really feel all that amazing, most days."

He closes in even further. "I can help with some of that."

"You can?"

"You are…absolutely perfect in every conceivable way. The whole package that is you…you're stunning."

I swallow hard and blink harder. "Thank you, Jesse."

He smiles at me. "I know hearing that from me once isn't going to undo the months and years of shit your ex put on you, but it's a start, right?"

I sniff. "Right." I try a smile back at him, and it's easier than I expected it to summon a genuine smile for Jesse. "Once from you actually does do a lot to erase all that. So, you know, don't be shy with the flattery. In my case, it'll probably get you pretty far."

He laughs. "It's not flattery, it's truth." He sidles closer, and his hips nudge mine and his chest brushes against the tips of my breasts. "I can turn this place into a beautiful, cozy, attractive home for you—we'll just take it one step at a time. Like what I did in here today, which you haven't even seen yet."

"I'm basically broke, Jesse."

He does the smirk again. "Yeah, but you just got a new job, didn't you?"

"How'd you know?"

"Because Dr. Waverley called me to tell me thanks for sending you her way."

"Yes, I did get a new job, and I'll be making double what I was. So I owe you a big thanks, too."

He smiles. "You're welcome." His smile widens, heats, turns mischievous, almost wicked. "There's one other way I might be able to help you out."

"With my underserved libido?" I breathe.

His laugh is an amused, aroused rumble. "That wasn't what I was going to say, but yes, I'd love to help rectify your underserved libido." He lifts his hands and cups my cheeks. "What I was going to say was that it's a sin a perfect pair of lips like yours haven't been kissed in so long, and I volunteer my services."

"Oh...you mean..." I begin, my voice breathy.

"Meaning I'm going to kiss the hell out of you right now, unless you stop me."

"I'm not stopping you," I say, a little too quickly.

His laugh is knowing. His palms are warm and rough against my cheeks, and his thumbs scrape over my cheekbones, and I'm not breathing, and he's everything in front of me, all around me, blocking me in with his big body. And then his lips brush mine, a slow, hesitant, questing touch—a warning. I barely have time to register this is happening—that he's kissing me—and then the kiss is changing, and I'm struggling to keep up. His mouth firms against mine, and his tongue flicks against my lips—my mouth opens at that request, and then his lips are pliant and demanding and hungry and—

I've never been kissed like this. Not ever.

I can't breathe, but I don't need to. He's all the oxygen I need. I'm dizzy, spinning. Leaning against him. My hands are flat on his chest, and now my fingers claw into his pecs, and I'm lifting up on my toes going for more, tasting his tongue and twining mine with his and exploring his mouth and hungering for him.

My thighs clench and my core heats, weeps. God I need this. I need him. I need more.

Holy shit.

He's still kissing me, like he can't get enough, like he's carried away by this as much as I am. Oh god, I can feel the weight of *more* towering behind this kiss, laced through it. There's so much more than just this kiss and I want it all, but right now, this kiss is all I can handle.

All too soon he's pulling away, and he's breathing hard.

"Oh god," I whimper. "Why'd you stop?"

"Because I want to show you what Franco and I did in here today." He backs away, raking a hand through his unruly hair. "And because if I didn't stop, I wouldn't be able to stop at all."

"Would that be such a bad thing?"

"If we go there together, Imogen, it won't be quick or sudden or unexpected, and it won't be up against your front door." His eyes burn, bright hot intense brown. "If we go there together, Imogen, it'll be goddamned magical. It'll be something you'll never forget as long as you fucking live."

I close my eyes and breathe carefully. "Show me what you did, Jesse," I say, after I've opened my eyes and can function something close to normal

He backs away a little further, staring at me hard. "Yeah."

He turns away, but not before I see the bulge against his zipper is very large, and very prominent evidence that he's as affected by the kiss as I am. Which doesn't do much for my resolve. I tighten my jaw and clench my fists, making a concerted effort to not stare at his ass as he leads me out of the front hallway into the living room.

"Take a look," he says, gesturing at the front window.

I stop in my tracks, halfway into the living room.

"What? How? Why?"

There were a total of four windows in my living room, two facing the front, two facing the back. These four windows and the amount of natural light they let in were one of the selling points of this house for me. But those had been small, narrow and short, with thick glass panes and lots of heavy lead crosses. Even so, they'd let in a lot of light…they'd also let in a lot of drafts in the winter.

Jesse had replaced all four windows with ones to match the brand new window in the kitchen, so now my walls on both sides of the living room were entirely glass. The room felt like it had been expanded several dozen square feet, and with them cranked open like they were, there was a beautiful cross-breeze— enough wind to not just ruffle my hair a little, but to actually cool the room off considerably.

Tears sprang into my eyes unbidden. "Jesse, you—I—"

"Before you say a word, you're not paying a cent for these windows." He was behind me so I couldn't see him, but I heard the grin and the pride in his voice. "Nobody else at the Waverley job wanted them, so I snagged all the windows."

"All of them? How many were there?" I ask.

He didn't answer right away, and I turned around to face him, and saw his grin spread. "Well…how many windows do you have in your house?"

I blinked. "Um. Four here, three in the kitchen, two in the master bedroom, and two in the spare bedroom." I have to count. "Eleven?"

He grinned even wider. "There were a total of twelve windows."

I was incredulous. "And she just ate the cost of them? That's…"

He waves a hand with a snort. "Don't even try to imagine how much. A fucking lot. When we explained how long the return and refund process would take and how long it would delay the project, she was just like, I'm not waiting, order the doors and be done. We're already so far over budget it's ridiculous, but I guess they don't care. I don't know. I don't get rich people sometimes, man."

"Yeah, me neither." I frown at him. "But Jesse… you're not saying you replaced *all* of my windows, are you?"

He nods solemnly. "That's exactly what I'm saying. I replaced all of your windows…plus one."

"What do you mean, plus one?" I asked, warily.

"You'll see. For now, check out the kitchen." I circle out of the hallway toward the kitchen, Jesse following behind me. "You ever think about taking those walls down? I checked it out, and the one wall *is* load bearing, but it's not a huge space to cross, so you could pretty easily put a beam up across it. It'd feel like a whole different home."

I stop in the hallway, trying to picture it. "*All* the walls? Like this whole floor would be open plan?"

He nods, grinning. "I can't say it'd be a cheap project, but if I was gonna remodel this house, that'd be the first thing I'd do. The floors are in good shape, the kitchen is cute. You'll need a new roof eventually, and central A/C, fresh paint all around…some new sinks and vanities and other details like that, but on the whole, this place isn't actually that bad. New tile or marble in the kitchen, new countertops, that's pretty big ticket stuff, obviously. But opening the floor plan would be first."

"You're talking thousands of dollars, though," I point out. "I can't even afford to fix the A/C on my damn car at the moment."

"Couple grand sounds about right to knock down the walls and put load-bearing beams up." He shrugs. "Just a thought."

"It sounds lovely, Jesse," I say, sighing. "I'd love to. And as soon as I have a few extra thousand dollars just sitting around, you'll be the first person I call."

"Just don't wait until then to call me. There's lots of little, relatively inexpensive stuff we can do that'll improve things around here." He pushes past me, grabs me by the hand, and pulls me into the kitchen.

"We'll talk about that later. For now, take a look."

Once again, I'm left speechless. Two more new windows—facing the front yard and the backyard. Huge casement windows replace the old tiny ones, and the room feels enormous now, breathing and full of sunlight.

"My god, Jesse. It's amazing." I turn to face him. "I can't—I just can't."

He grins. "You haven't seen everything, yet," he says, sounding excited. "Come on upstairs."

I follow him up, failing to restrain my gaze from his taut, hard butt as it wiggles and shifts up the stairs.

How can he be so hot *and* so kind and generous? It should be impossible. I'd thought it *was* impossible.

I stop halfway up the stairs, ripping my gaze away from his delectable ass, realizing something is different on the stairs.

More light.

Breeze flowing upward, through the open front door.

I look upward. Jesse is leaning against the wall at the top of the stairs—next to him is another enormous casement window. The plus one. There was no window here, before, just blank wall.

"This was wasted space, before," he says. "It was just begging for a window, so I obliged." He glances at me, looking and sounding nervous. "I know I should have asked before adding a whole new window like this, but…it's just—I *knew* without a doubt that it would improve the light up here and the airflow over-all. So I trusted my gut and hoped you wouldn't hate it."

He just cut a hole in the side of my house—with-out asking or informing me first—and put a brand new window in.

Theoretically I should be *pissed*. I barely know the man. I have no contract with him, no references to previous work besides the window he did in my kitchen. But god, this window works wonders on the stairs and the landing area in general. I move the rest of the way up the stairs and stand at the window—I can see most of the neighborhood from here. The air-flow brings the temperature down, lets in light…god, it's amazing. I think I've used that word too many times already, but…

I shake my head. "Your gamble paid off, Jesse." I smile at him. "I love it. Thank you."

He jerks his head toward the master bedroom. "Check out your room."

I enter my room, blinking at the staggering amount of light coming in. It feels like a whole new room.

More tears.

I can't breathe, can't speak. Who knew a person

could get so emotional over some windows? But they just make me so happy.

"How—how did you and Franco get all this done in an afternoon?" I ask. "I mean, I know you probably work fast, but this seems like a lot even for the two of you."

He just shrugs. "Eh...I called in some favors with the guys. And I actually got my start in construction installing windows back in high school, so it's something I happen to be able to do pretty fast."

"You called in favors? For...me?" My voice breaks.

He just smiles at me. "Sure did. But it's how we work. It's not a big deal."

"It is to me, Jesse." I look around at my room, and fight to get myself under control. "Good thing I didn't have time to let my room get messy again, huh?"

Jesse laughs. "Yeah, no bras or panties left out this time...sadly."

I chuckle. "It's literally just underwear, Jesse. It doesn't actually turn you on, does it? Seeing my bra or underwear?"

He shrugs. "The garment itself, no. The mental image of *you* in it? Yeah, it sure as hell does."

"You've never seen me in my underwear."

He is silent a moment, chewing on his lower lip. "Yeah, well, I have a really good imagination." His gaze is rife with promise. "And a whole lot of hope."

"Hope?"

"That I'll get to see you in your underwear."

"I *am* broke," I whisper. "That could be your payment."

"Don't tempt me," he growls.

"Too late?" I breathe. "Why shouldn't I tempt you? What if I want to? What if I want—"

"Imogen," he rumbles, interrupting me. "You want to start something with me, you won't have to try very hard."

I do want to start something with him.

Don't I?

A worm of doubt wiggles through my skull, though. Do I want to start something with him? So soon after my divorce?

I push the thought away and gaze up at him. "What if I'm not really even trying, yet?"

"What if I'm not either?"

"You're not?" I ask, my voice in a squeak. "You said you were hitting on me."

"I am," Jesse murmurs, not breaking our gazes. "But I'm not seducing you yet."

"You won't have to try very hard to do that."

At that moment his phone blares, a deafening foghorn sound that makes me just about jump out of my skin.

"Sorry, that's my ringer for James. He typically only calls me when it's important or an emergency." He answers the call. "What's up, James?" He listens for a moment, responds with a growled, "Yeah, I'll be there in a minute." And then he hangs up without another word.

"Duty calls, huh?" I ask, more disappointed than I should be that he's leaving.

"Yeah. Dr. Waverley and her husband—both of them—are at the project, and they have…concerns."

"Oh dear."

"Yeah. They weren't happy about the flooded basement, understandably. So when we got it cleaned up and fixed, they decided to expand on their original plan, and because it was our guy that screwed up, we're basically eating the cost difference."

"Sounds like this job is a pain in the butt," I say.

He shrugs. "They all are in one way or another. Good thing about the Waverleys is that they agree on everything, so it's not a fight for every little detail. Those jobs are the worst. We've seen custom builds like this wreck marriages."

"I can imagine," I say. "So, what do I owe you and Franco for all this?"

He rubs the back of his neck. "James will kill me and then fire me if I don't charge you for my time at least."

"I wouldn't let you do all this for free, Jesse. Your time and skill are valuable."

He grins. "I think so too, for the most part. But I like you a lot, and I don't want you to think I'm saying or doing anything just for the money or the work."

"I don't think that."

"Then you're not suspicious enough," he growls.

"Probably true," I say, thinking about the way Nicholas played me for months.

He steps close to me. "Look, I gotta go. But I'll drop by with an invoice once I figure out how little I can get away with charging you without pissing off my boss, best friend, and brother-in-law." He grins. "The bastard is a stickler for little details like financial solvency and orderly accounting."

I laugh. "Silly James, getting caught up in such petty minutiae."

"I'll see you later?" he says, making it a question.

"I hope so," I say, as he waves and heads down the stairs. "Jesse?" I call after him, and he stops half-way down, glancing up at me. "Thank you. From the bottom of my heart...thank you."

"It was my pleasure, Imogen," he says, his voice warm and genuine and pleased.

I watch him take his tools over to the truck as I stand in my new bedroom window.

He tosses his tool belt on the passenger seat

through the open window, sets his toolbox in the bed, and then bungee cords a tarp over the detritus in his truck bed. Sliding into the driver's seat, he turns over the engine, which kicks to life with a throaty diesel rumble. I watch him plug his phone in, scroll a moment, and then the grinding, thrashing, churning sound of the heavy metal music he likes so much drifts up to me at the window, partially muffled but still loud.

As he backs out, his eyes look for me.

A bolt of daring slams through me; I don't give myself time to second-guess or doubt myself.

I grasp the hem of my shirt and lift it up. For a reason I couldn't have explained, when I got dressed this morning I put on my favorite, fanciest, raciest bra, a barely there demi bra in vivid red lace. I don't stop at just lifting my scrub shirt up for a quick flash, though—oh no. When I do something rash and possibly stupid, I go all the way.

I take my shirt off completely.

And then, just because I'm the way I am, I tug the knot of my scrub pants, which promptly fall into a pool around my ankles, revealing the fact that I'm wearing the matching red thong.

Jesse, still backing out, is looking at me rather than where he's going and almost crashes into a car passing behind him—it honks its horn angrily and

Jesse slams on his brakes just in time.

I cringe at having almost caused him to wreck but, at the same time, I'm pleased I had that effect on him.

And then, with a crunch of gears, he throws his truck into park, leaves it running, shoves open his door, and storms back toward my house.

His expression isn't angry, it's...

I don't know what it is, because he's through my front door and stomping up the stairs before I have time to register what's happening.

And he's in my bedroom doorway, filling the frame, shoulders heaving, eyes sparking, fists clenched.

"I'm—I'm sorry," I breathe, "I didn't mean to almost cause a wreck."

"Imogen, you can't pull a stunt like that and think there won't be consequences," he growls.

SEVEN

"I—I—"

That's all I get out before he's across the room, his bulk pinning me back against the wall beside the window, his lips slanting across mine, slamming roughly, tongue eagerly, forcefully demanding mine. I give in to him, give him my tongue, give him my lips, and press my body up against his. His zipper presses hard against me, the bulge behind it even harder.

I throb.

My core is damp, slick, and hot.

I pulsate with need, every vessel and molecule and pore of my body demanding *more*.

His hands cup my waist, gently at first, and then when I respond so voraciously to his kiss, his fingers tighten into claws. They scrape down and latch onto my hips, dimpling the flesh. His fingers walk around to grasp my buttocks, taking a palmful of each cheek and pulling against him, grinding himself against me.

I whimper.

Moan.

"Jesse," I breathe. "Please."

I don't know what I'm asking for. What I even want.

My voice, the whimper, his name, my plea—it seems to shake him out of a trance. He abruptly releases me, staggering backward. His jeans are tented at the zipper, his chest is heaving, his eyes are narrowed and full of fire.

"I have to go," he snarls. "I—have to go."

"Jesse, I—"

He shakes his head, backing away from me. "Don't. Not a word. I *have* to go, and you are far too tempting to be good for either of us right now."

I just stand there, returning his stare, trying not to feel rejected. I'm in my bra and underwear, wanting him, kissing him, and he's walking away.

He hesitates at the door. Wipes his lips with the back of his hand as if to wipe away the residue of my kiss. And then with a wordless growl, stalks back over to me. "Fuck it," he says, and kisses me again.

This time, I put all I have into the kiss. I do the one thing I've wanted to do since the moment I laid eyes on him—well, the two things, in a particular order: I run my hands through his thick glossy unruly black hair, slide my palms down his broad hard back, and take a double handful of his butt.

It's every bit as rock hard as I thought it would be.

I don't want to let go.

He breaks the kiss but doesn't pull away. "Imogen. I *have* to go. I can't blow off our biggest clients."

"I know."

He rubs a thumb across my lip. "But don't think it's easy for me to walk away."

"It's not?"

He laughs, a bark of sarcasm. "Don't you feel how *hard* it is for me?"

I grind against him. "Boy, do I ever."

He growls. "Don't do that. I'm barely controlling myself right now, Imogen." He sighs. "It can't be like this, rushed out of desperation."

"I don't mind admitting I feel a little desperate, Jesse," I say, reluctantly letting go of his amazing ass.

"Yeah, me too." He laughs. "Okay, I've got to go. For real."

I wait, but he doesn't move, his hands still resting on my waist, just above my hips. "Jesse?"

He growls, backing away. "Go hide in the bathroom or something."

I laugh. "Really?"

"Absolutely." He steps backward and waves a

hand at me, gesturing from head to toe. "You, in *that*? How the hell am I supposed to voluntarily walk away when you're standing there looking like that and all but begging me to do all sorts of dirty, wicked things to you?"

I feel a thrill bolt through me—flattered pride and renewed confidence. I have a pink terrycloth bathrobe hanging on a hook on the back of my bedroom door; I take the robe off the hook and put it on, cinching it tight, obscuring my body from throat to calves.

"There. Better?" I ask, gripping the edges of the robe to keep from grabbing him again.

He snorts. "No, of course not. Covering up your beautiful body is a goddamn travesty, but at least now I can make myself leave." He turns to leave, but once again halts in the doorway; this time, though, he stays facing away from me. "Next time you feel compelled to tease me like that, you'd better be prepared for me to lose all my control. Because I just used every last ounce of self-control I have where you're concerned."

"Maybe next time I won't be wearing anything under the scrubs," I hear myself say.

"Goddammit, Imogen," he growls. "What are you trying to do, woman? Kill me?"

"Sorry, sorry," I say. "You seem to bring out the worst in me."

His eyes narrow. "I haven't even fucking *started*

bringing out the worst in you."

"Go," I breathe, "before I do anything else rash."

And so he goes.

And when he's gone—really gone, his truck rumbling around the corner and out of sight—I strip off the robe and the underwear and throw myself onto my bed.

What the hell has gotten into me? What the hell is wrong with me?

I'm never this bold, never. Even with Lee, I wasn't like this. I would go along with what he wanted, but it was always his idea, I just went along with it. Eagerly, willingly, voraciously—but none of the wild or daring stuff was ever my idea or at my instigation.

God, I have to be losing my mind.

I've clearly gone too long without sex and it's warped my mind and rotted out my inhibitions and better sense.

I DO NOT KNOW JESSE AT ALL, I remind myself.

Yet I've stuck my tongue down his throat, he's had a glimpse at my bare hoo-ha, I strip-teased for him down to my underwear, let him grab my ass, and grabbed his. I really have all but begged him to…

Well…

Fuck me six ways to Sunday, that's what.

And I don't know him.

Do I even know his last name? I don't think I do.

I'm crazy.

This is stupid and crazy and irresponsible and reckless and even if I am officially divorced and single, getting involved with a guy right now is probably a bad idea.

A really, really bad idea.

If I had any sense I would call Audra and get her to talk some sense into me. Although, to be honest, she'd probably tell me I hadn't gone far enough.

But, back to Jesse. Jesse is…

Too much.

There has to be a flaw somewhere.

Because, honestly, I've never met anyone so hot, so skilled, so kind and generous, and so funny and easy to hang around with, and a great kisser, and his hands are so strong and… I'd put up with a whole lot of things for a guy like him.

That sends a blast of cold water through me.

Because that thought was a long-term kind of thought. A getting attached kind of thought.

But…how can I not get attached when he does the things he does for me, when he says the things he says to me, when he kisses me the way he just kissed me?

Not once, but twice.

Those hands on my butt? His hands are big

and strong, so even my big juicy ass fits perfectly in them. I wonder where else his hands fit?

Sliding up my stomach, cupping my breasts? Thumbs flicking my nipples?

I let my hands be guided by my imagination, pretending my hands are Jesse's. I cup my tits, flick my nipples until they're hard as diamonds and sending bolts of intense sensation through my whole body. And then I let one hand drift down between my thighs, to my tense, wet core. God, I'm so turned on I don't even need my vibrator. Half a dozen slow circles of my fingers around my clit and I'm gasping, wishing they were his hands, his fingers. Better yet, his tongue...

Oh god—I come hard, immediately, thinking of Jesse's beard rasping against my thighs and his tongue slicking against my opening—

Even as I come, I reach for the stimulator and crank it all the way up, press it to myself, and slide two fingers inside, wishing and pretending it's him, and that he's here in all his masculine, muscular glory. I come a second time imagining him touching me, licking me, kissing me, moving over me to fill me...

But even when I've come twice and I'm too overstimulated to come again, I'm not sated. The tension and the need are still there.

If anything, getting myself off thinking about Jesse is only making it worse.

Two days later, as I'm retrieving my mail, I find an envelope with my name scrawled on it in thick black Sharpie. Inside is an invoice printed on a Dad Bod Contracting header. It's a very neat, professional invoice, breaking down the labor for the window installations.

Twelve hundred dollars. I go faint at first, but then after thinking about it, I realize that twelve hundred dollars to remove eleven old windows, widen the openings, install new windows, and create a whole new opening on the stairs is…well, it's all but thievery on my part.

A hundred bucks per window, essentially.

I don't have the money, since the mortgage is due soon and I don't get my last check from Dr. Bishara for another week, but I write a check for the exact amount anyway and put it in an envelope, copy the address listed on the invoice, and put a stamp on it. It's not until after I've put the check in the mailbox, lifted the flag, and gone back inside that I realize Jesse wrote a note on the back of the invoice:

Imogen,

I wish James would let me not charge you, but he's a tightwad like that. I really have had an amazing time working on your house (and getting to know you!) and I hope, selfishly, that you have something else on your Honey-Do list just so I can come back over and fix it.

Or, just call me. Or text me.

Even if something isn't broken, if you're so inclined.

Hope to talk to you again soon,

Jesse O'Neill

PS: don't be too surprised if I just show up at some point. I may not be able to help myself.

I have his number in my phone, so I bring up a new thread and try to figure out what to say to him.

Me: *I have a check in the mail for you. Thanks for being so cheap! You deserve so much more than what you charged me for the amazing work you did. Say thanks to Franco and the others for me.*

Jesse: *You could have waited to send the check. No rush. And you're welcome. Wish it could have been less, or free. I feel wrong about charging you. Franco says if you want to thank him, meet us at Billy Bar. It's our favorite local watering hole. He'll buy you drinks as thanks.*

Me: *Him buying me drinks as thanks makes no*

sense. I do know where Billy Bar is, but I have to work early in the morning, so I'll have to take a rain check on that tonight. Thanks for the invite, though.

Jesse: *Consider it a standing invitation. We're there pretty much every night after work. Not late, and we don't go hard...not anymore at least. Just a few buddies having a few drinks. Low key.*

Jesse: *If you ever do come, I'll buy you a few shots of tequila and hope tequila works on you like it does the girl in the Joe Nichols song.*

Me: *LOL. Didn't peg you for a country music fan.*

Jesse: *I'm not, but James is, and if we have to ride together in his truck, country is all he'll listen to. Gag.*

Jesse: *Does it, though?*

Me: *Does it what?*

Jesse: *Make your clothes fall off.*

Me: *at this point in my life, Jesse, pretty much any alcohol will make my clothes fall off. A slight breeze, for that matter. Hell, just say please.*

Jesse: *Please?*

I laugh out loud.

Me: *You're with Franco. If I send you a pic right now, he'll see it.*

Jesse: *You think I'd let that tool see it? Not a chance! I'd guard it with my life.*

Am I really considering doing this?

God, I'm pathetic.

I can't send him a full nude, though—I need to leave him something to want. I can't give it all away all at once.

An idea strikes me, and I race upstairs to my bedroom. In the closet of my bedroom is a single box of things from my life with Nicholas that I didn't throw away—mostly photos from our wedding, simply because there are some great, nostalgic photos of me with my parents, and me with Audra. Also in the box are the envelopes I sent the invitations in, and the large, pink, heart-shaped stickers I used to seal the envelopes. I'd bought a huge quantity of them simply because it was cheaper, and never threw the extras away because they're pretty, and I've actually used the stickers for various things in the past.

Never anything like this, though.

I toss a packet of stickers on my bed, close my blinds, and then strip out of my clothes. Naked, I ask myself again if I'm really going to do this. It's rash, irresponsible, and crazy. It's not the kind of thing a divorced forty-year-old woman is supposed to do.

Or maybe it is.

I don't know.

But I'm doing it.

I place a sticker on each of my nipples—the stickers are just barely large enough to cover my nipples, and I mean *barely*. If my nipples were to get hard, the stickers would probably pop off. I make sure my bed is neatly made, and there's nothing on the floor around the bed, and then climb on the bed and try a few poses with my phone in selfie mode.

God, this is hard.

Why am I doing this?

Because I'm dumb, and horny, and desperately want him to like me.

Because I desperately need his approval and compliments; the affirmation that I'm still attractive to someone is addictive.

Yeah, I realize all this, objectively.

Still doing it.

I snap a few photos. The picture I end up liking best is of me sitting up, weight on one arm, with one leg curled under me and the other bent up and crossed over to hide my core, with my torso twisted to face forward, chest pushed forward, shoulders back. The expression on my face is the hardest part to get right, I find. Try too hard to look sultry and I just look constipated. Can't be a blank look either, or a typical selfie grin. And not too serious.

Finally, after about thirty deleted tries, I have one I feel is decent. I've edited it a tiny bit, just to brush out some wrinkles and work some magic on the lighting, but I'm pleased with it, for my first and only nude selfie.

My tits look good—big, firm, perky. The stickers are coming loose in the photo, which even sort of adds to the sexiness of it, because you can almost but not quite get a glimpse of my nipples.

Before I send the photo, I text Jesse: *I'm going to send you something. You have to promise me no one will ever see it except you.*

His reply is instantaneous: *I'm actually alone in the bathroom at the moment. And I promise on my life, and on my honor as a man.*

Me: *Okay, well...I'm probably crazy for sending you this, but...here you go.*

Before I can second-guess my recklessness, I send the photo.

And immediately panic.

Oh dear god—what did I just do? I just sent a man a topless photo of myself.

He'll show it to Franco and James and everyone he knows.

He'll post it online.

Worse yet, he won't like it and he'll ghost on me.

He texts me back a few seconds later: *Holy shit, Imogen! I have no words. None.*

Me: *that is, very literally the only nude I've ever sent anyone.*

Jesse: *Really?*

Me: *Absolutely. Like I said, you bring out the worst*

in me. Or, to be fair, not the worst, just...the craziest. You make me do crazy shit I have no business doing. Like sending you a nude.

Jesse: *I see nothing crazy about it.*

Jesse: *You're incredible. I have to stay in the bathroom and not look at the pic just so I can go back out without embarrassing myself. My buddies are probably wondering what the hell is wrong with me.*

Me: *You like it that much?*

Jesse: *Imogen. Legit, I'm fighting the urge to whack off in the bathroom of this fucking bar. That's how much I like it.*

Me: *I'm not sure I believe you're that turned on. I might need photographic proof.*

Jesse: *Are you soliciting a dick pic from me?*

Me: **blinks innocently* why, no. That would be positively salacious of me.*

Jesse: *Can't say I've ever actually taken a picture of my own dick before.*

Me: *You can be...creative about it. Also, you don't have to. I was just being silly.*

Jesse: *Don't walk it back now, Imogen. Never apologize for what you want, and never hesitate to ask for what you want. With me, and in life. You deserve everything you want and more.*

Me: *Don't ruin our witty banter with your damned heartfelt saccharine bullshit. ;-)*

Jesse: *I'm locking the men's room and taking a photo for you.*

Jesse: *And now I feel even more respect for the guts it took to send that to me. This is awkward and embarrassing and difficult.*

Me: *I took and deleted about thirty before I got the one I liked.*

Jesse: *Yeah, I've taken like fifty and there's someone banging on the door. This one is okay, I think. Not as good as yours, but then, you're a goddamn goddess and I'm just a scruffy nerfherder.*

Me: *You're gorgeous, and I love that you just quoted Star Wars to me.*

A few seconds later a photo pops up in the thread, and I immediately tap it to make it full screen.

My jaw drops, and my core immediately begins weeping with joy.

He took off his jeans and shirt, stood in front of the mirror of the bathroom, and took a mirror selfie in just his underwear. Tight black boxer briefs. He must have zoomed a little, because it's a bit grainy, but worth it because I can see his entire package outlined by the stretch black fabric.

And holy mother of all fucks, is he well-endowed.

My heart crashes in my chest, and my core tightens, and my nipples go so hard the pink heart stickers fall off. The thing in his underwear is ENORMOUS.

So long, and so thick. I enlarge the photo, shameless-ly, hoping for more detail or something. What I see makes me whimper out loud: at the very top of his underwear, just beneath his navel, is a hint of pink. As if his underwear weren't quite up to job of totally containing him.

God, oh god.

There's no doubt. I stare at that photo long enough that I'm absolutely certain the tip of his penis is visible.

Why that drives me so nuts, I don't know.

But it does.

So nuts that I don't hesitate to whip out my little friend and set it to work between my thighs. I stare at the picture he sent, at his enormous chest and thick arms and hard stomach, at his broad shoulders and trim waist and powerful thighs, at his rugged features and incredible hair. And yeah, at his package, at the erection only barely hidden by his underwear…

An erection caused by *me*.

I'm in the middle of my orgasm when he texts back.

Jesse: *So? What do you think? It's been like five minutes and not a word from you.*

I can't quite bite back the half-scream of my or-gasm, which is, for some reason, heightened by the fact that he's texting me as I'm coming.

And then…my phone rings.

It's him.

I answer it. "H-h-hello?" I whisper, breathless.

"You can't just not text back after I send you that. Gonna give me a complex. Or a panic attack."

I'm gasping, still shivering and trembling from the aftershocks. "Sorry. I was…um…just…enjoying your photo."

His voice goes deep and raspy. "Imogen. No. *Please*, no. Don't tell me I called you in the middle of what I think you're in the middle of."

I hold my little friend up to the phone, so he can hear the buzzing. And then I replace it between my thighs, and immediately a whimper is torn out of me.

God, there has to be something wrong with me. Did getting divorced short-circuit *all* of my inhibitions? Like, what is actually wrong with me that I'm doing this?

"Fuck, fuck, fuck," Jesse growls. "You are. You're seriously—" His voice drops, and I hear background noise fade away, as if he'd gone outside into the parking lot. A moment later I hear a car door open and thunk shut. "You're seriously doing that, right now?"

I let another whimper escape, as answer, holding the phone up to my ear. "Jesse…"

"You're close, aren't you?" he murmurs.

"God, yeah. I've already come once."

"Shit. Why'd you answer?"

"I—I don't know. Oh god. Oh god…"

"You're looking at the photo?" His voice is strained, tense.

"So hot," I say. "The little hint of the tip sticking out the top is what put me over the edge."

And then I groan, a long, low sound of impending release, and I hear rustling on the other end. "I'm gonna get arrested, but fuck, I can't help myself. If I don't come right now, I'm gonna go haywire."

"Do it," I urge. "Right now."

"In my truck, in the parking lot of Billy Bar."

"While on the phone with me."

"Then hold off."

I groan. "I can't. Not for long."

I hear him hiss, and then growl. "I'm doing it."

"Doing what?" I ask. I don't know who I am, right now. The words coming out of me are some other person. Some other Imogen who has phone sex with men I barely know.

"Touching myself."

"Looking at the photo?"

"Yeah," he says, through grated teeth. "And picturing that little glimpse of your pussy that I got the other day. That little glimpse has haunted my dreams ever since."

"Have you done this before?" I ask. "Jerked off

thinking about me?"

"Have you?"

"I asked first, but...yeah, I have. A couple times, actually."

"I have too. I tried not to, but—after that day in your kitchen, you in that goddamned outfit? I couldn't help it. I felt like a dirty jackass for using you like that, but god, you turn me on in a way I've never been turned on before." He groans again, low and ragged.

"It doesn't make you a dirty jackass, not if I don't mind. And I don't." I've slowed the stimulator, but I'm still riding the edge. "Jesse, I need to—I can't hold off much longer." I hear a slick sound, and the knowledge of what that is makes me squirm and pant. "Now, Jesse. I need to come."

He moans, and then snarls. "Now, Imogen. Right now. I'm coming."

I hear him groan, a long sustained animal snarl, and I wrap my own breathy scream of release around his growls, and then there's silence between us.

"Jesse?" I say. "Where—if you're in your truck, where'd you...you know, put your...cum?"

He laughs, still out of breath. "Empty bottle."

I laugh, somewhat hysterically. "I can't believe we just did that."

"Yeah, me neither," he says, chuckling nervously. "It's a first for me."

"Me too." I hesitate. "Is this whole thing a little crazy?"

"Yeah, maybe a little. Or a lot." I hear a knock on his window. "But I'm okay with crazy." Another knock. "Look, that's my buddies giving me shit for vanishing. If they see this bottle and what's in it…"

I laugh. "Go. But…call me later, okay?"

"You bet your ass I will."

He hangs up, and I promptly scream into my pillow in equal parts excitement, thrill, embarrassment, and euphoria.

And then several days go by, and I don't hear from him.

EIGHT

I REFUSE TO CALL HIM OR TEXT HIM FIRST, JUST TO RETAIN at least a sliver of my dignity.

Then I start my new job—and I love every second of it. It's amazing. Challenging and intense and difficult and rewarding, and it pays *really* well, considering what I'm used to. I'm so busy that first week that I barely have time to turn around.

After my shift that first Friday, I go out with Audra. She immediately notices that I'm off, somehow, and demands an explanation, but I adamantly refuse to admit there's anything weird going on with me. Audra being Audra—meaning a bloodhound for gossip—doesn't believe a word of it.

Audra Donovan has been my best friend for twenty-five years. We met in a YMCA pool the summer we both turned fifteen, and have been inseparable since. We have a weird relationship, though—we don't see each other every day, and we don't even talk or text

every day. We get together a few times a month, and
get tipsy together, and catch up on what's happened
since we last saw one another. We're both super busy,
and Audra has a crazy social life on top of a demanding job, and it's just the way we do things.

She's five feet six ("and a half," she insists on em-
phasizing, to this day), keeps her naturally platinum
blonde hair in a pixie cut, and has a body a twenty-
five-year-old would be jealous of—breasts most people wrongly assume are fake, an ass that doesn't quit,
and taut, toned, firm everything. But then, she's a
personal trainer at a national gym chain—she's the
top trainer for the region, so she travels from gym to
gym, training clients and supervising the other train-
ers and working out like a fiend. It's kind of an addic-
tion for her, I think. But it clearly works, on a physical
level, because at forty, she's in better shape than most
women—and men—half her age.

We're at our usual place—the Mexican restaurant
I went to by myself the other day; we've been coming
here for burritos and margs for at least ten years, if
not longer. We split a pitcher of margaritas and each
of us orders the house special—an enormous burrito
stuffed with beef and rice and cheese, smothered in
sauce and sour cream and drowning in a sea of refried
beans. After we eat, we drink more margaritas, and
finally, after two hours of wheedling, Audra manages

to get me to admit that there just may be something going on.

But that's all she's getting.

I'm not talking about Jesse.

Nope, nope, nope.

"Dammit all to hell, Imogen Catherine Irving!" Audra screeches, leaning over the table and gripping my forearm with clawed fingers. "Tell me what the *hell* is going on with you! You never keep secrets from me!"

I shake my head, sipping water. "Audra, please, just give it a rest. I'm not ready to talk about it yet."

She sits back, sighing. "You're no fun. You clearly have juicy gossip, but you're not sharing."

"It's not gossip, it's my *life*." I meet her sky-blue gaze, trying to communicate assurance. "I'll tell you everything, I swear. I just need a bit more time, that's all."

"It's a man," she mutters. "I *know* it's something to do with a man. That's the only thing you'd ever keep from me."

If I say another word, she'll have it all out of me. She'll guess, correctly, and because I can't ever lie to her, I'll corroborate her guesses. And I'm really not ready to hear what Audra would have to say to me. Because I already know—she'd ask why I haven't slept with him yet, and then ask if I've even seen his dick.

Yeah, she's a little crazy, but I love her.

She narrows her eyes at me, and I can feel the guesses coming. "You're all hung up on a guy, aren't you? He's got you flustered and confused, and you're too stubborn to do anything about it, because of *feelings*." She somehow manages to turn that last word into a swear word and a caustic mockery at the same time.

"Shut up and have another drink," I say, pouring more margarita into her glass, hoping it'll distract her from the truth in her guess.

"How about I have another drink and *don't* shut up?" she says, taking a long gulp. "I'm onto it, aren't I? Is he hot? A brick would be hotter than that ugly blobfish of an ex of yours, so it can't be hard to find someone hotter than him. He's gotta be pretty hot if you're not willing to talk to your best friend of twenty-five years about him."

Doesn't she just wish she knew Jesse? She'd stop talking to me for a month just so she wouldn't be tempted to steal him from me, if I let her meet him.

Which is why I'm not telling her about him, and why she won't ever meet him. At least not until things are more solidified.

Wait. Solidified? Things aren't going to be solidified. There's nothing there but attraction. I'm sex-starved and horny, and he's a willing target for my desperation. That's all it is.

Audra is watching me like a hawk. "You're thinking about him right now, aren't you? I can tell. You're trying to talk yourself out of whatever it is, because you're scared and your divorce was just finalized, and you think there has to be some kind of waiting period before you move on, emotionally and physically. Which is bullshit. The best way to move on is to live your best life. And that involves letting yourself have something you want, just because you want it. Not everything has to *mean* something."

I sigh. "Audra, you're lecturing me based on your own guesswork. I'm neither confirming nor denying anything."

She shrugs. "I know I'm right, and I'm lecturing you based on that."

I pinch the bridge of my nose. "Audra Roslyn Donovan. I said I'm not ready to talk about it yet. Can you just...*please*...give it a rest?"

She sticks her lower lip out in a faux-pout. "I just want you to be happy, and you haven't been happy for a very, very, *very* long time."

"I know."

"I only act like this because I love you," she says.

"I know. And also because you can't handle not knowing every last detail about everyone and everything."

"This is true." She eyes me. "But when you do tell me, I'm going to freak out, right?"

"Audra."

"Fine." She wakes her phone to glance at the time: 9:55pm. "Shit. I should go. I have a meeting half-way across the damn state at seven tomorrow morning, so I should get to bed."

"Yeah, I've got an early shift tomorrow too."

It's my turn to pay the bill, and then we hug it out at our cars.

"Don't wait too long to tell me," Audra says, letting me go. "You know how I get."

"I know, I know."

"Whatever it is, go for it."

"What if I'm considering hard drugs and unprotected sex with homeless men?'"

Audra cackles. "You're way too straitlaced to even have protected sex with a man you *do* know, and the one time you tried pot in college you freaked the fuck out and swore off everything harder than wine and margaritas."

"Maybe getting divorced has brought out my wild side."

She doesn't cackle, this time. "I'd say it's about time, in that case. You're smart, and you're careful, both of which are good things, but sometimes, babe, we need to be dumb and reckless." She boops my nose with her forefinger. "Even at forty."

"*Especially* at forty."

"Truth. I'm going now," she says, getting into her car, a beautiful white, convertible, two-year-old Mercedes E-Class, which I'm not at all jealous of. "Be bad, Imogen. You've more than earned it."

I laugh. "I'll try, but I'll never be as slutty as you."

"You could be, with practice and training! Squad goals!" she shouts out her open window.

I laugh even harder. "Two people can't be a squad, Audra!"

"Semantics! Be bad!"

I drive home on mental autopilot, considering Audra's advice. Generally speaking, I try to do the opposite of whatever she advises me. She's a cut-and-dried commitment-phobe—her dating life is somewhere between serial monogamy and hookup artistry. She rarely sees the same guy more than a few months, never lets them get to know the deep-down, really-real her. My relationship and subsequent divorce from Nicholas only served to confirm her bias against commitment, and I very seriously worry she'll never let herself feel anything deeper than casual affection. The why of it all, for Audra, is a very long story and one best left untold, but suffice to say she's got her reasons.

But it doesn't stop me from worrying. Just like

she worries about me, for the diametric opposite reason.

What if, in this one instance, she's right? What if I should just be bad this one time?

Take what I want and consequences be damned?

I don't know if I'm capable of that, which is the root problem.

What if I try, and it backfires? I'm fragile enough as it is right now—another heartbreak would put me beyond any capability of repair, I think.

Would it be worth the risk?

With Jesse, just possibly.

I turn onto my street and then, half a block from my house, I slam on the brakes so hard my tires squeal. My front yard is brilliantly illuminated, shining from the back rack spotlights on Jesse's truck, which is backed up part way onto my lawn on a diagonal, the front tires on the street. I pull into my driveway, exit my car, and stand there, stupefied.

He has completely rebuilt my front porch. Before, it was three too-short, too-narrow steps leading up to a landing just big enough to stand on as you enter the front door. Now, the front porch spans the entire width of the home, with the steps properly sized and spaced for a natural tread. As I stand there, gaping, he presses his nail gun into the bottom-most tread at the front left corner, squeezes the trigger to send in a nail with a pneumatic *thwack*. And then he sinks back on his knees and tosses the nail gun aside.

He turns to me, wiping sweat off his forehead with the back of his wrist, grinning. "Hey." He gestures at the new porch. "Surprise!"

I open my mouth, and close it again without making a sound. "Um." I have to try twice to even get that much out. "Why?"

"Well, I sort of vanished on you, and I came by this afternoon to talk in person, and my foot went right through the step." He shrugs. "So, I ran over to the lumber mill and got down to business. I started out thinking I was just gonna do another porch like you had, but then said nah, fuckit, might as well go whole hog, you know? I was done for the weekend, so this is all on my own personal time."

I step away from my car and sit on the edge of the porch a few feet away from Jesse. "I don't know what to say or how to even begin thanking you."

"Well, 'thanks' is a pretty good start." He gives me his trademark cocky smirk. "I can probably think of a few other ways, if you're really determined to thank me properly, though."

"You drive a hard bargain, Mr. O'Neill," I say, smiling coyly up at him.

"I drive a hard something, all right," he murmurs, standing up to tower over me. "Not sure if 'bargain' is the right word, though."

"Would you like to come in for a glass of wine?" I ask. "I have to work early in the morning, so I can't stay up super late, but if you wanted to talk, we could do it over some wine."

He nods, wiping his brow again. "Sounds good. Let me put my tools away and I'll be right in."

I just nod and smile, and head inside. Usually the first thing I do is change out of my scrubs and into my pajamas, but I find myself resisting that idea, instead choosing to put together a snack plate of cheese and lunch meat and nuts, and pouring the wine. If I change into *that outfit*, it'll spark a sexual chemistry conflagration I'm not sure I have the wherewithal to resist, and until I'm sure of what I want and what to do about Jesse and this thing, I need to back things off a little.

Audra told me to be bad, to be dumb and reckless, but I'm not the type of person who can entirely just throw all caution to the wind all at once. I have to be smart about being stupid. And so far, all I've been is stupid, letting my libido rule over my sense and sensibility: "If I could but know his heart, everything would become easy."

Ha—Jane Austen, you were far too wise for your own good, lady.

Jesse clomps in the front door and into my

kitchen, lifting the bottom of his shirt up to wipe his face, baring his hard, tanned stomach. He goes right to the sink and washes his hands and face—automatically, without even thinking, I hand him paper towel to dry his face.

He tosses the wadded paper towel in the trashcan and glances at me. "Awww. I was hoping you'd change into something a little more comfortable."

I can't help grinning at him. "I know. I'm sorry. But I think for right now this probably safer."

He nods seriously. "You in those pajamas? Yeah, you wouldn't be safe around me."

I carry the snack plate out into the backyard, and Jesse follows me with the glasses of wine, and the bottle. When we've settled into our seats and have taken a few exploratory sips and bites, I glance at him. "So. You were going to explain why you didn't call or text for almost a week?"

He nods, tossing a couple macadamias in his mouth. "Yeah, so what happened was, James got an emergency call from his cousin over in Indiana. Apparently their basement flooded and they had to gut the entire basement. James's cousin called a local contractor to do the gut and remodel, and the guy fucked something up. I'm not sure how, but he compromised the integrity of the subfloor between the basement and the main level. I think he most likely took out a post that was load bearing. The whole living room floor started to cave in, so Aaron called James to come fix it, and in a hurry. James grabbed me and Ryder and we hopped in his truck and hauled ass over to Aaron's house, some five and a half hours away in Evansville. We left directly from the Waverley site within ten minutes of the call. I had my phone in my pocket, but nothing else. Well, halfway to Aaron's house, my phone dies. Not a big deal, right? James has a car charger. Only, it breaks. Kaput. So James's phone dies too. Neither of us know your number by heart, and Ryder doesn't have it. And then we get to Aaron's house and get right to work. We literally worked around the clock, because that floor was about to go down like Humpty Dumpty." He pauses for a sip of wine and to wolf down some cheese and meat.

"So. To make matters worse, James and I left both our phones in his truck, with the windows open. Aaron doesn't live in the best neighborhood, and when we came out to grab something from his truck, both of our phones were gone. We worked around the clock for damn near seventy-two hours, barely stopping to sleep and eat. The second we got back, we both went to figure out our phone situation, and instead of calling you, like I said, I figured I'd stop by. I've been back from Indiana for less than a day." He shrugs, eyeing me warily. "And *that* is why I didn't call for you almost a week."

I ruminate on his story. "Sounds plausible enough," I say, keeping my voice neutral and my expression blank.

He frowns. "Why would I make it up? That's what happened. I wouldn't just vanish like that. I have a vested interest in keeping in touch with you."

I can't keep the smirk off my face. "I believe you—I'm just messing with you."

"Ha ha frickin' ha," he says, sarcastically. "Got me."

"So, what's your vested interest?"

He lifts an eyebrow. "Um...I like you? I want to see you? Hang out with you? Maybe even get you to go on a date with me?"

I nod. "I see." I meet his gaze. "A date, huh?"

He nods. "A date. We could have dinner and go mini-golfing or something."

I give him a baffled look. "Mini-golfing? What are we, sixteen?"

He looks sheepish. "I dunno, I don't really do dates a whole lot."

This sparks a load of questions and a hot bolt of suspicion. "Meaning?"

He shrugs, but he's not looking at me. Instead he's focused on the plate, where he's a little too carefully rolling a piece of cheese into a slice of salami.

"Meaning dates, like with flowers and manners and meticulously orchestrated events—that kinda stuff doesn't factor into the way I do things."

"So, in plain English, you don't date." I frown at him over the rim of my wineglass. "What do you do, then?"

He rolls a peanut across the plate with a forefinger, still not looking at me. "Um. Go to bars, usually. Find a good lookin' gal, chat her up, and…you know. Have some fun."

"So you hook up, and that's it."

He meets my gaze steadily. "Yeah, basically. It's always worked out for me. I'm busy with Dad Bod Contracting and the occasional gig with my band, and don't really have time for dating and all the BS that comes with it. Never saw the point, you know?"

"But you want to go on a date with me?

He nods. "I didn't meet you in a bar, and you're not that kind of girl." He takes a long gulp of wine. "Look, Imogen—it's obvious that the fact that I don't date has thrown you for a loop, and I get it. But I've always made sure expectations are set out firmly in the beginning, so there's no confusion later."

"I see."

"I keep things clear, you know?" He tosses a few more peanuts into his mouth. "I don't do heartbreak."

Oooh, ouch. That one stings.

I'm one big messy ball of heartbreak. I'm currently heartbroken, and on top of that, I'm lonely and desperate for attention and validation, which makes me ripe for even more heartbreak.

And Jesse is exactly the type of guy who would, unintentionally, break my heart even further.

I don't know what to say; or rather, what I *should* say. What comes out is a probing personal question I had no intention of asking, but there it is, tumbling out of my traitorous mouth. "So you've never had a girlfriend?"

He doesn't answer for a conspicuously long time. "I, uh…sort of. But that's—I don't—" He's squirming, clearly not wanting to talk about it, but not wanting to say so.

I sigh. "It's fine. I shouldn't have asked."

He crushes a peanut between his thumb and the plate, and then grinds it into dust. "Nah, it was just a weird thing, and talking about it is…"

"A no-go?"

He nods, seeming pathetically grateful that I'm not pushing it. "Yeah. It's not a big secret or anything ugly, I just…it was a weird situation."

"I get it. This whole divorce with Nicholas is pretty new still, so it tends to just kind of pop out at the most inappropriate times. I wouldn't normally, and don't normally, lead with it like I have with you."

I don't know where to go from here. I'm weirded out by this whole exchange, and feeling off-kilter, unsure. I was already unsure if this thing was something it'd be smart to keep pursuing, and now I'm even more unsure.

Jesse senses this, and shoots me a look of resignation. "The whole hound dog thing is a problem for you, huh?"

"It's not entirely that, it's just…everything in my life is tricky and touchy right now, and getting involved in anything seems like a less than brilliant idea, I guess." I sigh, hating how little sense that made. "I'm just feeling weird right now. About a lot of things, not just you."

He nods, and pushes back his chair. "I get that. You've been through a lot, and I don't want to add to it."

"Jesse, I just—"

He smiles gamely. "I get it, Imogen. I do. I don't like it, but I get it." He stands up. "I hope you like your new front porch."

He's almost to the front door before I get myself into motion. I catch up to him as he's opening the front door.

"Jesse," I say, halting him with his hand on the knob. "I'm not saying I don't want…something. I just don't know what that is, and I don't want to lead you

on or jump into something I'm not ready for. So…
maybe you could…" I don't know what I'm trying to
say, and trail off awkwardly, hoping he'll finish it.

He does. "Be content to stay on the back burner
until you figure your shit out?"

It hurts hearing him put it like that. "Just give me
a little time."

"That I can do," he says.

I sigh. "And for what it's worth, I'm sorry I'm
such a disaster."

He laughs, lets go of the knob, and turns back to
me. "Imogen, honey…you're allowed to be a disaster.
You're also allowed to not know what you want." He
leans in close, takes my face in his hands, and kisses
me with tenderness and gentility that almost breaks
my heart—and my resolve.

And then he's gone.

I stay standing where he left me, eyes closed, face
tilted up, trying to hold on to the feeling of his lips on
mine.

Eventually, long after the rumble of his diesel engine has faded into the night, I turn and go to bed.

But sleep is a long time coming, and my dreams
are filled with almost-kisses and not-quite embraces
and images of Jesse unzipping his jeans.

NINE

I N A BREAK WITH TRADITION, I CALL AUDRA FROM MY CAR after my shift the next Saturday, while I'm still in the parking lot.

She answers on the third ring, out of breath, the sound of clanking weights in the background and the muffled thumping of music. "Hey, what's up? Has it been a week already?"

I don't even know where to start. "I...he...I can't—I don't know how to—"

Audra responds as only Audra can. "I'll grab Chinese on the way over. You just make sure you have plenty of wine on hand. I don't work tomorrow, so we can party it up, and you can spill everything."

"Okay," I say, barely whispering. "Thanks."

"Well, duh, that's what best friends are for, dummy."

"I love you."

"Love you too. Be there in thirty."

Forty minutes later, she's bustling into my kitch-
en with three bags full of carryout Chinese, wearing
a perplexed expression. "Did you grow a set of skills
I don't know about?" she asks, setting down the food
and withdrawing cartons of rice and Styrofoam boxes
of sweet and sour chicken and General Tso's.

I shake my head, handing her a glass of wine.
"No. It's somewhat more complicated than that." I
gesture at the bottle, which is… not as full as it should
be. "I'm a glass ahead of you, so chug-a-lug, bug."

Audra takes me literally, and chugs her glass of
wine before pouring more. "There, now we're caught
up." She finds my paper plates and a serving spoon,
gesturing at me with the spoon. "I'll dish the food,
you dish the news. Who's the guy that's got you so
mixed up? And how the hell did you afford this many
pimp-ass windows? And a new porch?"

I laugh. "It's all part of the story. His name is Jesse,
and he's a contractor." I take my plate from Audra
and we move to my couch, setting our glasses of wine
on the floor at our feet. "Remember when I broke my
kitchen window and had to have it repaired?"

Audra nods as she takes a bite of food.

"I saw this ad for a company that claimed to be
willing to do any project small or large, and look good
doing it, so I called them. Dad Bod Contracting. The
owner sends his guy out, and he shows up at, like,

nine at night."

Audra blinks in surprise. "That's nuts. No contractor ever shows up before noon or after five."

I nod. "I know. But this guy did." I make eye contact so she knows how serious I am with my next words. "He's the sexiest man I've ever met, Audra. I can't even explain it. He's big and muscular, but not a bodybuilder, or the vain gym rat type. Rugged, but still handsome. Funny, and nice…and way too generous for his own good." I sigh.

"The company he works for, which is owned by his best friend and brother-in-law, is building a house for my new boss, which is how I got my new job in the first place." I pause for a sip of wine. "And the wife, my boss, Dr. Waverley, she decided after she'd bought and paid for a whole bunch of windows that she didn't want them, and ordered something else entirely, so the windows were just…free. So Jesse came and boarded up my window, and then came by the next day with one of those extra windows and installed it. And then, a few days later, he calls me and asks if he can have access to my house, because he has a surprise. I tell him where my spare key is, and when I get home, he and his buddies have replaced literally all my windows, as well as adding a new one over my stairs. All for twelve hundred dollars. Fifteen hundred, including the original kitchen window replacement.

And then—and *then* when I tell him I quit my job, he makes a call to Dr. Waverley, for whom he's building a house, gets me an interview, I get the job, and *then*—"

"There's *more*?"

I laugh, nodding. "That's not even the half of it, Audra! He ghosted on me, but it was an accident and misunderstanding, so he came over to talk, and his foot went through the front step, and—"

"Those stairs were a hazard, so I'm not surprised," Audra puts in.

"I know, now quit interrupting, dammit. So he just went out and bought a bunch of wood and nails, tore down my old porch and built this new one, all while waiting for me to get home from work. Just because."

"I feel like I'm missing a lot of details, here." Audra takes both our plates and dishes up more food for us, and brings the bottle of wine to top off our glasses. "You need to go back and go over a few things."

"No, Audra, you don't understand." I lean close to her, eyes wide. "He kisses like a god. He kisses like…like kissing was invented just for him."

Audra's eyes bug out. "You *kissed* him?" she asks, incredulous, around a mouthful of food.

"It was…he kissed me, and then it was us kissing each other." Even now, my lips tingle in memory.

"But you didn't fuck him yet, right?" She washes her food down with a huge swallow of red wine. "I mean, that would be so far out of character I don't think I'd believe you even if you said yes."

"Do you have to be so crude about it?" I ask, crankily—this is an old argument between us. "And no, we haven't slept together.

"Yet."

I take time to eat a few bites before answering. "I…that's the issue, Audra. I don't know if I could. Or should."

She stares at me, chopsticks halfway to her mouth. "Um. You're kidding, yes?"

I frown. "Do I sound like I'm kidding? I drank almost an entire bottle of wine in less than an hour, waiting for you. When was the last time I drank that much that fast? College, I bet."

"No, there was the time when you first suspected Douche-Canoe was cheating on you. You called me on a Tuesday and told me to bring hard liquor."

I frown even harder. "True. I don't really remember that night very well, though."

Audra cackles. "Well, no shit you don't remember! You had like ten shots and four beers—and you don't ever drink anything but wine or margaritas. You were hammered. Like, whoa hammered. As in, more wasted than I think we ever even got in college."

I wave a hand. "The point *is*, Audra, I don't know what to do."

Audra shakes her head. "You make no sense, woman. What should you do? Ride that dick, girlfriend!"

"Audra!" I scold.

She cackles again. "Do you expect anything less from me? Do you know me? Have you met me? I'm the least appropriate person on the planet, and you know it." She goes serious. "For real, though. You should totally sleep with him. Why wouldn't you?"

"I'm scared?"

"Of the size of his dick? Have you seen it?"

I snort, and almost choke on the wine I was in the middle of swallowing. "God, no!" I glance at the ceiling and shrug. "Well, sort of. I kinda, sorta sent him a topless photo. I had pasties on, but still. Well, not pasties, exactly. Those big pink heart stickers I used for my wedding invitations. I sent him that, and he sent me a pic he took in the public bathroom of his favorite dive bar—of him in his underwear. So…I got a *sort of* glimpse at what he's rocking. And yeah, I'm a little afraid."

"Show me! I wanna see!" Again, she says this while trying to chew a mouthful of food, making it muffled.

"Um, no!"

"I've shown you pics guys have sent me," she whines.

"Yeah, but you don't really care about them. It's all about riding the dick for you, slutty-buns."

For once, Audra seems to take real offense. "Hey now, that's not fair. I do care about them. I just…don't believe in love."

"I'm sorry, that was rude."

She seems somewhat mollified, but not all the way. "You *have* to show me, now. Otherwise I'll be offended for at least two weeks. And then who will you have wet burritos and margaritas with?"

I sigh. "If he'd sent me an actual nude, I'd say no. But it's just underwear, so…fine."

I pull out my phone, bring up the photo, and show it to her. She blinks at the photo in admiration for a moment, and then pulls the screen closer to her face. "Wait—is that…" She touches the screen with thumb and forefinger and spreads them apart to zoom in. "It is! He's actually peeking out of those tighty blackies."

Her comment blasts a laugh out of me, spraying rice and chicken everywhere. "Tighty blackies? Really, Audra?"

She's still staring at the phone. "Jeee-*sus*, Imogen. You weren't lying—the man is gorgeous, in a rugged, rough-hewn sort of way." She glances up at me.

"Does he have any hot friends?"

I grin. "Actually, I did meet one of the guys he works with, and yeah, he's…um…yeah. He's hot, too."

"I demand an introduction, in that case," she says, handing the phone back to me finally, but then immediately snatches it back. "Wait—I need to see the photo you sent him."

I reach for the phone, trying to take it from her. "NO! It's embarrassing!"

Audra tosses her plate onto the coffee table and hops over the back of the couch with enviable agility. "Just let me look! It's not like I've never seen you naked before, dummy. We used to go skinny-dipping together all the time in the lake at my parents' cottage up north."

I sink back to the couch in defeat. "If you make fun of me, we'll be fighting for real."

While I clean up the mess I made, Audra scrolls through my phone to find the photo, looks at it for a moment or two, and then lifts her eyes to me. "Why are you embarrassed by this, Imogen?" Her voice is uncharacteristically serious. "It's a beautiful, tasteful, sensual photo. You're beautiful. He's a lucky man."

I shake my head and snort, but inside I'm fighting a lump in my throat. "Sending that was terrifying. And I felt awkward as hell taking it. I think I took like fifty before I got that one that felt right."

Audra is not fooled. "Why does it feel like you're about to cry?"

I duck my head. "Feeling good about how I look is…difficult. Nicholas made sure of that."

Audra is back over the couch and sitting next to me in an instant. "That's why you need this, Imogen. This guy makes you feel beautiful?"

I nod, swallowing hard. "Yeah, he really does."

"And he's gorgeous, has a big package, he's muscular, and you said he's nice and funny, *and* he's got skills, *and* he's willing to go out of his way to do things for you." She gives me a look that says, *what are you, stupid?* "I don't see the downside, here. What's holding you back?"

"I'm scared, Audra."

"Again—of what?"

"I really, really like him. And I really, *really* want him."

"But…?" she prompts.

"It's not a but, it's a…it's that I like him maybe too much. He's a player." I bob my head to one side. "Not a player—that's not fair to him. He just doesn't date."

"So he's like me?"

I nod. "And you know I love you. But if you slept with a guy, and he started falling for you, what would you do?"

Audra sighs. "I'd ghost on him."

"Exactly."

"But what if he ends up wanting something besides the same old same old with you?" She shrugs. "It's not impossible. Maybe he's just been waiting for the right one, and you're it? How would he know if you're it unless you try him out?"

I snort. "Try him out? He's not a car, Audra, he's a person. God, you're so tactless sometimes."

Audra props her feet up on the coffee table, crosses her arms under her breasts, and stares at the ceiling—I wait, knowing that this posture means she's thinking through something she wants to phrase just right. Finally, she tucks her feet under her thighs and twists to face me.

"Okay, so answer me this: how long has it been since you've had really truly *amazing* sex? Not just okay married couple boring sex, but world-rocking, earth-shaking, hard-core fucking that you know you won't ever forget?"

I have to give this some thought, and the answer that emerges is one I don't like. "Lee, in college." It comes out as a whisper.

"Never once with Nicholas was it like that?"

I shake my head. "No, not really. It wasn't bad, but it wasn't amazing. Not like that."

She frowns at me. "So then…what was the point of being with him?"

I shrug. "It wasn't that kind of relationship. It was comforting. Stable. Easy. The sex was good enough for the first few years, and while I knew it wouldn't shake my world or anything, it was enough to keep me…not satisfied exactly, but not so dissatisfied I'd wander, I guess. Not that I ever would cheat—I'd have left him before I did that."

"I think I understand that, to a degree." Audra dishes herself more food as she answers. "And I mean, I know sex isn't everything in a relationship, but I've never been interested in a relationship, and you know why. But it *is* an important part of things."

"What does this have to do with Jesse?"

"I'll get to that," she says. "But first, another question. The first time you suspected Douche-Canoe was cheating on you, who was there to get you drunk, clean you up, and help you pick up the pieces?"

I blink hard. "You."

"And when you found out for sure, who was there?"

"You," I repeat.

"And when your divorce was finalized, who took you out for a celebration?"

"Audra—"

"Who was there for you, Imogen?"

"You, but—"

She takes my hands in hers. "So if you get involved with this guy, and you get in too deep and he ends up hurting you—which, I grant, is a possibility—do you really think I won't be there to help you through it?"

"I know you will," I whisper.

"Okay, so yeah, you stand a chance of getting hurt. You wear your heart on your sleeve and you get attached fast, I know this. And if this guy is a commitment-phobe like me, yeah, he could vanish on you if things get to a place he's scared of going." She taps her chest. "But if that happens, I'll be there to do what best friends do—love you, and get you back on your feet, and make sure you don't gain a million pounds through heartbreak eating."

I laugh. "And you know I would."

Audra isn't done yet. "Next thing I want to say—You're divorced, now. No kids—I know, I know, touchy subject, and I'm sorry—but it also means you have no commitments besides your job. Nothing holding you back from doing whatever you want. This is your chance to reinvent yourself, Imogen! It's hard to not fall into the *Real Housewives* clichés about turning a new page and fresh starts and all that, because that's really what you have now that you're free from Douche-Canoe. You can do whatever you want!

Be whoever you want. This isn't a time in your life to let fear hold you back, this is the time to try new things, do things you would never do—" and here she taps my phone, sitting on my thigh, "—like sending topless photos to a hot guy you're interested in. Be bold, be bad."

"Look—after Nicholas, I'm afraid if Jesse hurts me, I'll never recover, and I'll die a lonely old maid because I'm too afraid to let myself find anyone."

"That logic cuts both ways, babe," she says. "Anyone you meet has the potential to hurt you. The only way to know if a relationship—whether it's sexual or romantic or friendship—is safe and that you won't get hurt is to give it a chance."

"Which is why you're the way you are?" I ask, the question pointed.

She winces. "Yeah, well…I'm great at giving advice, not so great at following it myself." She sighs. "We're talking about you, not me. And I'm telling you, as your best friend, as the person who knows you better than literally anyone on the planet, I'm *telling* you to go for it with Jesse. If it's nothing but a one-night stand, great. You'll have a night I doubt you'll forget. If it ends up being more, even better. If it's something in between, like just a temporary thing to scratch an itch you both have, that's great too. There's no wrong answer here. You have to move on, Imogen.

Your marriage to Douche-Canoe was over a long time ago—the divorce was just the final nail in the coffin. This is *your* time. You're not getting any younger, babe, so, you know…seize the day, and all that."

"You just may be right," I admit.

Audra laughs. "Of course I'm right!"

"Okay, okay," I say. "I'll try."

"You'll try?" She echoes, faintly.

I nod. "I'll try."

She shakes her head. "Wrong—this isn't something you *try*. You just let whatever happens happen, and you go into it without any expectations. Just enjoy yourself. That's it. Super simple."

"Whatever happens, happens," I repeat, "and no expectations."

"And tell Audra every last dirty, sordid detail, the moment he leaves."

I laugh. "And tell Audra every last dirty, sordid detail the moment he leaves," I repeat.

We drink more wine, and eat too much Chinese food, and then too much ice cream, and watch half of the latest season of *The Bachelor* on my laptop. Audra falls asleep on my couch—a regular occurrence on our nights in.

I'm half-asleep myself as I head upstairs, but when I get into bed, I can't sleep from the excitement I feel. There's trepidation, too—the fear of getting hurt hasn't gone away or lessened, but I know Audra will help me through it if that happens. And Audra is right—I have to get back out there, or I never will.

And besides—everything I've experienced with Jesse so far tells me that regardless of how things end up with him, it'll be worth it.

Earth-shaking, world-rocking, hard-core fucking? Yes, please.

I fall asleep trying to picture what that might feel like.

TEN

I'M NOWHERE NEAR BOLD ENOUGH TO SIMPLY ASK JESSE TO come over so we can sleep together, so I'm oddly relieved when my kitchen sink starts leaking the next day.

I text him immediately, but have to edit my text several times before I'm comfortable with the wording: *Hey, so my kitchen sink is leaking, both from where the faucet attaches to the sink and around the edges where it's supposed to be sealed to the countertop. Any chance you have a pretty porcelain farmhouse sink just laying around?*

The bubbles pop up immediately, and a text bloops in a second later: *You just want me for my skill with power tools.*

I let my fingers do the talking, and don't edit or filter my reply. *Yep. No ulterior motives here. Just pure opportunism.*

Jesse: *I can't tell if you're being sarcastic or not.*

Me: *that's the tricky thing about text messages, it's hard to infer stuff like that.*

Jesse: *Ryder is doing the electric for a remodel an old farmhouse remodel, and I think they're actually doing a total gut job and going super modern on the inside, so there's a possibility I may be able to score one.*

Me: *I was totally kidding about that. I'll gladly pay for a new sink. I mean, you may even be able to fix the one I have, but I've always wanted a farmhouse sink. You don't have to go scavenging for me.*

Jesse: *Hey, why pay for something if I can easily find it for free? I'm not promising anything, but I'll swing by the job and look. Either way, I'll get you fixed up ASAP.*

Me: *You're the best.*

Jesse: *Don't forget you said that when you're trying to come up with ways to thank me. My previously stated methods of acceptable thanks still apply. ;-)*

I laugh out loud at that, because, it being a day off with nowhere to go, I'm in my pajamas. I decide to "thank" him a little right away.

I stand in front of my full-length mirror in my bedroom and take a full-body selfie, making sure to twist and lift and work all the magic for the best pose—showing off cleavage and thigh and making my waist look smaller than it is.

I leave it unedited, and send it to him with a

caption: *here's a little down payment on my thank you. :-**

I second-guess the kissing-face emoticon the moment I send it, but it's too late to take it back.

He texts back instantly: *Have mercy!*

Me: *fine. Here's a little extra...mercy.*

I face the mirror again and tug the neck of the shirt down a little, showing a bit more cleavage, snap a photo, and send it.

Jesse: *I meant that as an epithet, but I'll take the extra mercy. The only problem is now I'm installing cabinet hardware with a hard-on, which I can't very well just disappear to take care of, if you know what I mean.*

Me: *Poor Jesse. Should I apologize?*

Jesse: *Hell no. Just saying. That's what you do to me.*

Me: *It's not even that hot. Just a little tugging on the shirt.*

Jesse: *It doesn't take much where you're concerned. I have to go, though. James is getting pissy that I'm texting instead of working. He's a real slave driver. I'll let you know what I come up with regarding the sink.*

Me: *Okay, thanks. See you soon?*

Jesse: *Not soon enough, but yeah.*

Me: *You're sweet.*

Jesse: *and you're hot. GTG. Bye for now.*

I'm grinning like a fool, and vibrating with

excitement. And trepidation. But mostly excitement.

I spend the rest of the day cleaning house, mowing the backyard, and weeding the beds.

Once I'm done with my chores, I decide to sun myself a little in the backyard and do some reading, so I fix myself a little drink—some red wine mixed with soda water—and stretch out on my lounge chair. I'm only out there a few minutes when I figure, what the hell, may as well get some real sun. So I wiggle out of my shorts and peel my tank off, and enjoy some naked rays—with proper sunblock, of course, because skin cancer would suck, and so do sunburns. I flip to my stomach after an hour or two, and then, simply because I'm so relaxed, I end up falling asleep.

I'm startled awake by the sound of my front door opening, and Jesse's voice calling a hello.

I wriggle back into my shorts and tank top in record time, and I'm still tugging the shirt down when he appears in my kitchen, carrying a huge sink in his arms. He glances through the window and sees me, catching me just as I finish rolling the tank down over my breasts, and his eyes go wide. He sets the sink down and sidles outside. I remain on the lounge chair, trying to stay calm.

"Hey, you," he says, grinning. "Did I interrupt something?"

I don't know how to respond. "I…um. No. I was

just…sunbathing."

His smirk is knowing. "Making use of that privacy fence, huh?"

I stand up and meet his gaze. "Yes, Jesse, I was sunbathing in the nude. I actually fell asleep, so you startled me."

"I did knock like, twenty times," he says. "And you know, next time you don't have to be quite so quick to get dressed."

I roll my eyes. "You'd like that, wouldn't you?"

He nods, not a trace of humor on his face. "Sure as hell would. Those stupid pink heart stickers are driving me crazy."

I laugh. "I wasn't quite daring enough to do it without them."

"I get it. But I'm going crazy not knowing what's beneath them."

I snort. "Nipples, Jesse. Just nipples. Seen one pair, you've seen them all."

"I know that, intellectually." He steps a little closer, and the items in question tighten, harden—a fact his gaze doesn't miss. "That doesn't change the fact that I desperately want to see yours." His smirk shifts into a full-on smolder. "Or better yet, taste them."

I clench my thighs together and fight the urge to moan. "Taste…them?"

He nods, his voice dropping to a whisper so low

and intimate I have to strain to hear him, have to lean into him. "Taste them. Lick them all over. Kiss them, rub them against my face, devour them until you're begging me to stop."

"That's stupid," I breathe.

"Which part?"

"The part where you think I'd beg you to stop." I can't believe the words coming out of my mouth. "I'd beg, but not for you to stop."

"You change your mind about me, then?"

"It was never about that, Jesse. Not entirely, at least."

He's staring down at me, his eyes firmly on mine rather than the generous view he certainly would have down my shirt, from that angle. "Last time we saw each other, you shut things down pretty firmly. Now you're singing the opposite tune."

"Yeah, I've been kind of back and forth about things." I'm not going to apologize for it, and I don't.

He just lets the silence between us breathe for a moment, and then backs away. "Want to see your new sink?"

"Yes, please."

He heads into the kitchen, and I gasp at the sink he's brought. It's huge, two deep tubs, made of spotless porcelain. On the floor next to it was a box with a photograph of an antique-style double-knob, high-arch faucet.

I crouch and stroke the porcelain. "It's lovely, Jesse. Absolutely perfect. Exactly what I've always pictured." I glance up at my current sink, which is significantly smaller than this one. "But will it fit?"

"What did I tell you about my skill at fitting big things into small spaces?" he says with a lopsided grin.

I blush. "Jesse!"

He just laughs and whips out a tape measure, lays it across the sink lengthwise and widthwise, and then the space between the lower cabinets. "Like the windows, it'll *just* fit. You'll lose a few inches of counter space on either side, though."

"For a sink like this, I'll happily trade the counter space."

He slaps the counter. "Well, I'll get started. Shouldn't be too labor intensive."

"I'm gonna get some dinner going," I say, heart in my throat. "Um. Do you...want to stay? Have dinner with me?"

"You know I do." He wiggles his phone out. "And we're in luck—James is up at his hunting cabin in Wisconsin, so there won't be any emergencies from *el jefe*."

"Good, because it seems like every time we get a few minutes alone, your boss has an emergency."

He rolls his eyes. "No kidding. Who knew

construction involved so many emergencies, huh?"

"Right?"

We each begin our work, him removing the old sink, and me putting together a meal. Fortunately, I have chicken thawed, so it's a matter of pan-frying some breasts while water is on the boil for pasta, with some broccoli steaming.

Jesse sniffs the air as he marks where to cut the countertop away. "You're a really good cook, you know that?"

"According to my ex-husband, I'm a utilitarian cook. I can do the basics pretty well, but—"

"Your ex was a dick," Jesse cuts in. "Not to put too fine a point on it, but he was a grade-A dick who clearly had no clue what a treasure he had in you."

"Thank you for that," I say, focusing on dicing the chicken.

When that's done and the pasta has been boiled and the broccoli steamed, I mix it all together in a casserole dish, mix in a few cans of cream of chicken, cover it, and put it in the preheated oven to bake.

I wash my hands, and then lean against the counter. "I'm going to go up and rinse off before we eat. I'm all greasy from sunblock."

"Can I help?" he says, grinning, "I'm great at rinsing."

I'm sorely tempted to say yes, but I don't. "I think

I can manage on my own."

He snaps his fingers. "Damn. Way to ruin all my hopes and dreams."

"Ruined? Or delayed?" I tease, sashaying toward the hallway.

He twirls his chalk marker between his fingers. "The way I'm feeling right now, they're the same thing."

I have no answer for that—at least not one that doesn't involve jumping his beautiful bones right there in the kitchen. So I just shoot him a smile over my shoulder as I head for the stairs. In my room, I strip out of my clothes and rinse off quickly, taking a few extra minutes to make sure everything down south is trimmed and that my legs are smooth. What to wear is a conundrum, though. I don't want to look like I'm trying too hard, so it can't be fancy, but I want to look nice, so it can't be grubby, either.

I end up wearing a blue and white silk romper, barefoot, no jewelry, minimal makeup, and just a spritz of perfume. I twist my hair up in a simple chignon with a few loose wisps draped casually down my cheeks. Underneath the romper, I'm wearing the same red lace set of lingerie that had almost caused the wreck, because while I'm not positive anything is going to happen tonight, I want to be ready if it does.

Feeling   pretty   and   presentable,   I   head

downstairs. Jesse is just then setting the new faucet into the sink, then leaning in underneath it to tighten it into place. My timer beeps, letting me know it's time to add the cheese. I take off the foil, add a thick layer of cheddar, reset the timer for another three minutes, and then turn to find Jesse leaning back against the finished sink, his eyes on me in that blatant, admiring way he has.

"You look incredible."

I duck my head at his compliment. "Thanks."

"If I'd known you'd dress up like that, I'd have brought a button-down and nicer jeans." He flips his wrench in his hand, and then holsters it in his tool belt, which he unbuckles and removes.

I laugh. "I'm not dressed up, I'm just not in pajamas anymore."

"Hey, those pajamas are—"

"The cat's pajamas?" I suggest, grinning.

"Okay, grandma. No, I was going to say they're the sexiest thing I've ever seen, but then, that wouldn't be fair to what you're wearing now."

"You like the romper, huh?"

He quirks an eyebrow. "I *like* beer and pretzels and ESPN sports highlights—I *love* that romper."

I smile happily. "Well…I'm glad you like it."

Why does this feel awkward, all of a sudden?

Jesse is just staring at me, looking me up and

down, a tiny, private grin on his face.

"What?" I ask, self-conscious under his scrutiny.

"Nothing. I just can't help staring at you." He sets his tool belt on the counter, and turns back to me. "Is it making you uncomfortable?"

I nod. "A little."

"Sorry, you're just gorgeous, and I'm not great with self-restraint."

"You're really laying it on thick tonight, Mr. O'Neill."

He shrugs. "I just calls 'em like I sees 'em." He gestures at the sink. "So, what do you think?"

I move over next to him, standing in front of the sink. "It's...it's perfect, Jesse."

He traces the side of the sink with a fingertip. "It's an actual antique, you know. Over a hundred years old, original to the farmhouse. The owners were happy to see it go to someone who would appreciate it. If I hadn't taken it they were going to see about selling it to an antiques dealer, but while it's beautiful and in perfect condition, it's not like they'd have gotten a lot for it. Better this way." He taps the countertops, which are laminate made to look like marble, a cheap, chintzy effect. "All you need in here now is to replace these countertops, paint the cabinets white, and put in glass-front doors."

"And rip out the floor and put in new tile," I

point out.

He shrugs, laughing. "Yeah, that too. Other than that, not much!"

"One step at a time," I say. "Thank you for the sink, Jesse. You have to let me at least pay you for your time."

He shakes his head. "Nope. Dinner with you is payment enough." He taps the countertop again. "I think some nice, rich, dark-stained butcher blocks would work well in here. I can pick some up fairly reasonably. You don't have, like, acres of counter to do so you're not looking at a huge expense. And honestly, stripping and painting the cabinets is something you could do yourself easily on a weekend afternoon."

"I wouldn't know how to strip them, but painting I can do."

"Well, maybe I can come over some Saturday and we can do it together."

I gaze up at him. "Why are you so willing to do all this work for me?"

He lifts one big shoulder. "It's work I enjoy doing, for one thing. I get a great sense of accomplishment and pride from seeing something improved through my efforts. For another thing, I like you, and I like being around you, so doing something I enjoy around a woman I like? It doesn't feel like work."

The oven timer dings, and I pull out the casserole.

I point at a cabinet. "The plates are in there and the forks are in the drawer behind you."

He retrieves the silverware and plates, and while I'm dishing up the food he takes a bottle of red wine from the little rack on the counter next to my fridge, opens it, and pours us each a glass, and then helps me carry everything outside to my table.

Our meal together is slow, easy, and leisurely. Comfortable. We talk about our families—his father passed away from a stroke when he was in high school, and his mom is a retired teacher living in an all-inclusive assisted living retirement community in Arizona. He has one younger brother, a career Marine Corps officer stationed in Okinawa. I tell him about growing up an only child of older parents—I was born when my father was fifty and my mom forty-five. I was an unexpected accident, something they were very clear about my whole life. We trade high school embarrassment stories, first crushes, college party stories, bad trips, bad dates, and everything in between. The wine flowed—perhaps a little too freely, but I'm enjoying myself more than any date in recent memory. At some point there's a second bottle opened, and we're sitting side by side in my lounge chairs, watching for the few stars visible in the Chicago suburbs.

The lounge chairs are close, and we're sitting facing each other, our knees brushing. Every once in awhile, one of us will gesture as we talk, and our hands will touch, or his fingers will rest, briefly, on my knee. I'm feeling good, happy, light, loose—a little buzzed, maybe. And I can't seem to keep my eyes off of his lips. I remember vividly the feel of them on mine, and I want that again. I remember the way his hands felt on my hips, and clutching my buttocks. I remember the way the hard ridge of his erection pressed against me through his jeans.

Will he kiss me? What's he waiting for?

I want what comes after kissing.

I want the rush of adrenaline; I want hands tearing at clothes, lips stuttering across bare skin, breath on breath. I want to let my desperation and hunger go free. I want to surrender to him. I want to feel small and delicate beneath him. I want to feel wanted, desired, needed.

Hours have passed since dinner—are we are on our third bottle? I can't remember.

I'm getting impatient.

Jesse gets up, excuses himself to use the bathroom, and I follow him inside. I'm a little unsteady, a little dizzy.

I use the bathroom after Jesse, and take a moment to fix my hair and plump up my cleavage.

When I come out, Jesse is drinking a glass of water, sitting on my couch in my living room, looking through my coffee table book of Ansel Adams photography. He looks up when I come out, and his eyes darken with desire.

That look in his eyes turns me to mush, makes my thighs tremble.

I sit beside him, take the glass of water from him, drink some, and put it down. I'm angled into him, knees against his thighs. He's so close, so big, so strong and handsome, and my lips tingle in anticipation.

I wait—a beat, two, three.

Is he not going to kiss me?

Fuck it.

I lean against him, wrap my hand around the back of his head and cup his cheek with the other hand and press my lips to his. He rumbles low in his chest, and his hands slide around my waist. For a moment, he just holds me like that, kissing me back—and then he lifts me onto his lap. I straddle him, feeling his erection through his jeans, his hands scraping up the front of my thighs from knees to hips and then he spans my hips with his hands and pulls me closer. I'm levered over him, bent over to kiss him, gasping against his tongue, tasting him, hands playing in his hair.

I grind against him, writhing my hips, telling him silently what I want and how much I want it.

Except, instead of taking the hint, he breaks the kiss, panting.

I frown down at him, licking the taste of him off my lips. "Wha—why did you stop?"

He rests his head against my chest, his forehead just beneath my chin. "We've had a lot of wine, Imogen."

"Yeah, so?"

"I'm no lightweight, but I'm feeling it," he says, his voice heavy and slow. "And I know you are, too."

"Maybe a little," I admit, my chest tight with foreboding. "So what, though? If we're both in the same place and we both want this, what's the problem?"

He captures my wrists in one hand, holds them against his chest, and uses his other hand to brush a tendril of my hair away from my eyes. "If we'd already slept together, I wouldn't have a problem with it. Half-drunk sex can be awesome, but—I don't want our first time together to be half-drunk."

"Why not?" I whisper, rejection stinging hard.

"Because I want you to go into it totally sober, totally in control, absolutely feeling and knowing everything." He tries to meet my eyes, but I won't let him.

"I appreciate you trying to do the honorable thing here, Jess, but I know what I want, and I'm not so drunk that I don't know what I'm doing." Goddammit, I hate how my voice quavers.

"Imogen—please don't think this is easy for me. I want you more than I can say—"

"So don't tell me—*show* me. Please," I say, my voice breaking into a whisper on the last word.

"God, I fucking want to. But you're only just out of a ten-year marriage, Imogen. You've been through a lot, and I just cannot and will not let you jump into something half-drunk. I will *not* be something you regret rushing into."

"I'm not rushing, I just—"

He cups my face in one hand. "Imogen, please understand. This is honestly the most difficult thing I've ever done, but I know it's the right thing."

My raging hormones don't agree. I rub my core against him. "Jesse, again—I appreciate what you're doing, and I really respect you taking the honorable route, here, but..." I choke on my words. "But I *need* this. You don't understand."

He snarls wordlessly when I rub against him, and all but throws me off of him onto the couch, shooting to his feet and pacing away, fists clenching and releasing. "Fuck, Imogen. I can tell *exactly* how much you need this, and I'm right there with you. But I won't start it with you when we're both like this." He digs in his pocket and tosses his keys on the coffee table. "For fuck's sake, I'm not even in any condition to drive home. It wouldn't be the way it's supposed to be, if we go there now. It won't be what I want it to be, for you and for myself."

"Dammit," I hiss. "Fine. Whatever. Go ahead and do the right thing, then, Sir Galahad."

"Imogen, I'm just—"

I shake my head, refusing to cry about this in front of him—it's a losing battle right now, and I'm clamping down hard on the tears, on the lump in my throat. "Don't. Just...go."

He scrapes his hand through his hair again, growling. He glances at me, mouth opening as if to say something, but then closes it again and he stomps angrily for the door. I want to stop him, but I don't.

I want to pin him against the door and kiss him and jump into his arms and beg him to make love to me, but I don't.

I've already embarrassed myself enough, throwing myself at him, begging, pleading, and now crying. So no, I won't go that last step. I sit on the couch, barely stifling the tears, as he tromps down the steps he built, across the lawn, and vanishes into the midnight shadows of my neighborhood, on foot.

I wait until I'm sure he's gone, and then I rise to my feet.

A wave of dizziness washes over me, and I have to sit back down and try to stand up again, more slowly and carefully this time. I go up the stairs, holding the rail, pulling myself up. The stairs waver and multiply, and then somehow I'm in my room, falling into my bed.

I feel warm wetness on my cheeks, staining the pillow even as I drift and spin.

I fucked it all up.

Threw myself at him, but got too drunk and he rejected me.

He'll never want me now.

Just like Nicholas.

I fall asleep in a cold wet spot made by my own tears.

ELEVEN

I WAKE UP WITH A POUNDING HEAD, MY MOUTH DRY AS A desert, sun blazing into my room, making me sweat like a pig. My sheets are tangled and soaked in sweat. I'm still in my romper; at some point in the night I tried to take off my bra, apparently, but only partially succeeded—the cups are pushed up over my breasts, one arm is pulled out of the strap, but it's still hooked around my back.

Images from last night blast through me, each moment vivid—right up until the point that Jesse refused to have sex with me.

I remember getting angry, feeling rejected, and—

Now I know why I feel so crappy: I'm hungover. I barely remember coming up the stairs last night. Which means I was a lot more drunk than I'd thought.

And Jesse had been right. He'd done the most honorable, moral, decent, ethical thing possible, and I'd gotten mad at him for it. I know he'd wanted me—I'd felt the evidence of it.

I'd begged him. Thrown myself at him with all the desperation of a woman long-scorned.

And he'd still had the strength and honor to do the right thing.

If I'd had sex with him last night, I don't think I'd regret it this morning, but I do think it wouldn't have been what it could be and should be—exactly what he'd said.

I fall back asleep berating myself.

A couple hours later I wake up again. I still have a raging thirst and my head is still pounding, but I feel marginally better.

God, how did I do this almost every night of the week in college, and then still wake up for morning classes? It boggles my mind, now.

Slowly, painfully, I work myself upright, and then pause to let my head stop pounding before I get out of bed and remove my clothes and put on my pajamas.

I trudge listlessly downstairs, make coffee, and drink several glasses of water while the coffee is brewing. My stomach roils, but I know I need to eat, so I scramble some eggs and nuke some frozen sausages. It's hard to get anything down at first, but after a few bites I become ravenous and devour it, washing it down with several cups of coffee. I take my last mug of coffee out onto my front porch.

As I open the front door it's then that I remember that I have a *new* front porch to enjoy my coffee—thanks to Jesse. I see that his truck is gone; I remember him walking out and leaving his keys on my coffee table, so he must have come by earlier this morning when I was sleeping. Now I feel worse than ever.

My house faces east, so I get the morning sun over the tops of the houses across the street. My neighbor is trimming her shrubs. She waves, and I wave back. The movement hurts my head.

I think about Jesse as I sit down on the top step.

Did I ruin things with him? Probably. That'd be my luck.

I need to talk to him, fix things. Try to make amends, and hope that I didn't totally mess everything up.

I need to get past the worst of the hangover though.

I go back inside and have to hunt for my phone—I find it wedged between the cushions of the couch. With another glass of water in hand, I call Audra.

"Hey," she answers, on the second ring. "Don't tell me—you need my advice again."

I groan. "Yes. No. Maybe. I don't know."

Audra laughs. "Well that covers all the possibilities." She speaks again, but she's shouting, and not at me. Her voice is muffled as if she's half covered the microphone with her hand. *"Keep your back straight, Sarah! Good! Now squat lower this time, as far as you can go. Good! Now push up—push the bar up with your whole body, not just your legs. Great! Two more."*

I moan. "Please don't shout, Audra."

She laughs again. "Aha—you got drunk last night, didn't you?"

"Uh huh," I murmur.

"And you had sloppy sex instead of earth-shaking sex, and now you're mad at yourself?"

I whimper, a sound that was meant to be a laugh but didn't quite make it all the way there. "Worse. Or better, I don't know. He came over, installed a beautiful antique farmhouse sink for me, and then I made him dinner and we ate together. It was the best date I've ever had. We talked for hours, about literally everything. And we drank, like, three bottles of wine. And I threw myself at him."

"Atta girl."

"No, not atta girl. I was drunk, but much more than I realized."

"So you feel like he took advantage of you?" she conjectures, anger starting to tinge her voice.

"No!" I protest. "He *wouldn't* have sex with me. He stopped us—stopped me. Said he wouldn't start something with me when we were both half-drunk. And I—I got mad. I was so horny, Audra, you don't even know! But I didn't realize how drunk I really was until I woke up this morning. He left mad last night because I was a bitch about it. And now I'm hungover and I'm scared I ruined things."

"First, did he drive home?"

"Nuh-uh. He left his truck here and walked home."

"Honestly, Imogen, I'm impressed. It takes a man with serious integrity and fortitude to turn down a girl who's throwing herself at him when he's as in the bag as she is. I think a lot of guys would have gone with it. It's not like you were wasted and he was sober. It would have been informed consent, right?"

"Absolutely. But it wouldn't have been what it should be, and that's exactly what he said to me." I sniffle. "And I was such a bitch about it."

"Okay, a couple things, here. One, stop beating yourself up. He'll understand. If he was willing and able to stop you both while under the influence, that means he's really into you. So he'll understand. Second, you need to sober up before you try to talk to him about it."

"I'm trying. I ate, and I've had a boatload of coffee, and a lot of water."

"You do know what the best cure for a hangover is, don't you?"

I groan. "Don't say it."

"You need to sweat it out."

"That sounds like a special circle of hell."

She laughs. "I know, but trust me, it works."

"I hate you."

"Can you drive, or are you still too fucked up?" she asks.

"I don't think I should. I'm still a little unsteady."

"Okay, then just wait for me. I'm working at the gym across town today. I'm done with this client, and I have some time before my next one, so I'll come over and kick your ass."

"I don't wanna," I whine, only partially joking.

"I know, but it'll do you good, and you'll feel better when I'm done with you."

"Fine," I grumble. "But I'm gonna hate it."

"You'll thank me later. Now get that big beautiful ass of yours into workout gear. I'll be there in fifteen."

"*Big?*" I squeal. "You think my ass is *big?*"

Audra sighs. "Imogen. This is not news to you. And it's a good thing—I guarantee you your sexy Mr. Tighty Blackies harbors a deep and eternal appreciation for the size and shape of your derrière." I hear gym noises, and then parking lot noises, and then her car door open and close and the dinging as she starts the car. "But, if you're really feeling self-conscious about it, come into the gym with me a few times a week and we can work on toning it up."

"It's not just my butt that needs toning, unfortunately," I lament.

A laugh. "No, it never is. But fortunately for you, your best friend is a master personal trainer. Commit the time and effort to me, and I'll have you in killer shape in no time."

"If by killer you mean kill me, then yes," I say, in a droll tone. "Love you," I intone in a nasally drawl.

"What would you do without me?"

"Let's not find out," I say.

Audra arrives ten minutes later. She's decked out in workout gear—hot pink Lycra capris, a thin white hoodie zipped less than halfway up, sleeves pushed up to her elbows, nothing on beneath it but a royal blue sports bra, and cross trainer shoes that look like Jackson Pollock got hold of them—an explosion of colors in drips and stripes and dots and smears. She pops her trunk and pulls out two black kettlebells, closes her trunk with her elbow, and carries the weight to the middle of my front yard. I'm in all black—full-length yoga pants, black sports bra, black tank top, and my trusty old New Balance running shoes.

For the next forty-five minutes, Audra tortures me to within an inch of my life, all with a single 25lb kettlebell—she makes me swing it, hold it and do squats, press it over my head, bend over and row it, sit and do twists with it, stand and just hold it as long as I can. She doesn't allow me any rest, either, or very little. Just enough to catch my breath, and then she's slave-driving me on to the next movement, until I'm whimpering from exhaustion and sweat is dripping in buckets from every pore.

When she finally tells me we're done, I collapse onto my back in the grass, gasping raggedly.

She sits down beside me, barely breathing hard and with a dainty sheen of sweat on her forehead. "That wasn't so bad, was it?"

I rip a handful of grass out and toss it at her. "You suck."

She just laughs and tickles my nose with a blade of grass. "You secretly love it, don't you? That feeling of exhaustion after a hard workout is addicting, isn't it?"

I laugh. "I don't know about that, Audra. I mean, yeah, I do feel better now, so it works as a hangover cure, but I'm not sure I'll ever be addicted to working out."

She just pats my thigh. "We'll get you there."

I sit up, groaning a laugh at the soreness in all my muscles. "I can't believe I got that drunk," I say, grimacing at Audra. "It was *so* not cool of me."

"Don't beat yourself up, Imogen. You were ex-cited and nervous, and it's been over ten years since you've had to worry about how to figure out a relationship with a new guy. Overindulging a little in response is perfectly normal."

"So should I just, like, call him? Or have him come over so I can apologize in person?"

"Definitely don't call him," she says, weaving blades of grass together. "Or rather, don't have that conversation over the phone. But don't apologize, either. Just make it clear you haven't changed your mind about what you want, that it wasn't the booze talking."

I frown, disagreeing with my friend—and not for the first time. "I overindulged by *a lot*, and was a super bitch when he was being the amazing gentleman he is. I'm apologizing. I owe him that much at least." I feel my cheeks heating. "But I'll definitely be making it clear that I haven't changed my mind about what I want, and that it wasn't the booze making me so horny."

Audra grins and wiggles her butt with her arms over her head, doing a seated version of an erotic dance. "Get—it—*on*, girlfriend!"

I slap her on the arm, but I'm laughing with her, because that's exactly what I plan on doing. After I make amends for my idiotic behavior.

Putting her kettlebells back in the trunk of her car, Audra leaves, after eliciting a

BFF-double-pinkie-promise from me that I'll start working out with her at least twice a week, if not three times.

With Audra gone, I head back inside and clean up from last night, and spend the afternoon on additional house chores—deep cleaning the baseboards and dusting in weird places and scrubbing the shower. When my house is as clean as it can be, I finally take a long, leisurely, scalding hot bubble bath in my clawfoot tub; the tub was one of the main selling points of this house for me, along with the backyard and the plentiful windows. When I'm clean, shaved, and trimmed, I do something I haven't done in quite a long time: I brush out and curl my hair into loose spirals, put on makeup, and zip myself into my favorite going-out dress, a little red dress with a mid-thigh hemline, a plunging neckline, a low back, and plenty of cling on my generous curves. My gold heels and some understated jewelry completes the outfit, along with a little clutch containing my wallet, phone, lip gloss, and the other essentials.

By this time it's past eight in the evening, and I opt to text Jesse instead of calling him: *Are you and your friend at Billy Bar?*

He answers a few minutes later: *Yep. You feeling okay? ;-)*

The winking face makes me think he may not be

too mad at me, which lifts my spirits a little.

Me: *I was pretty rough this morning, but my best friend is a personal trainer, so she came over and helped me sweat it out. I'm feeling much better now. I was thinking I would come out and meet the rest of your friends.*

Jesse: *Cool to have friends like that. A good workout after a big night is always a good way to get past a hangover. I did the same thing this morning myself.*

Jesse: *I'd love it if you came out. It's just me, Ryder, Franco, and James.*

Jesse: *I can't say I'm sticking to water, but I'm definitely taking it easy tonight.*

Me: *Yeah, I will be too.*

Jesse: *So I'll see you soon?*

Me: *In just a few minutes. Leaving now.*

Instead of typing a reply, he merely sends a looped gif of Carlton from *Fresh Prince of Belair* doing the Carlton Dance, which makes me snort in laughter as I get into my car.

I park in the middle of the Billy Bar lot, next to Jesse's truck—which is the fourth in a lineup of big, masculine trucks decked out with racks and lights and toolboxes and, in Franco's case, a bed cap. I assume the one truck I'm not familiar with is Ryder's. Instead of a big, rugged pickup, Ryder's is a classic 1940s Chevy box truck, heavily customized and beautifully restored. I remember Jesse saying Ryder is an electrician, so it makes sense he'd need a special truck to hold all the special equipment.

Next to their big butch man-mobiles, my little red 1998 Toyota Camry looks like a Matchbox toy.

I've driven past Billy Bar a zillion times, having been born and raised in this area, but I've never been inside—it's just not the sort of place I, or anyone I know, would typically go. When you think of a local dive, Billy Bar is the kind of place you think of. It's an old Pizza Hut building that was converted and renovated into a bar when I was in high school. It will forever be a Pizza Hut building—there's no disguising that unmistakable roof. I'm not sure what to expect inside, but my Judgy McJudgerson instincts have me expecting the worst—dank, dark, sticky, smoky, and possibly featuring a stripper pole in the back, with lots of neon everywhere.

Inside, it's well-lit, clean, smoke-free, stripper pole-free, with zero neon. Instead, the walls feature a lot of huge beer company mirrors, posters of classic motorcycles and hot rods, posters for car parts and oil and transmission fluids, and even an antique gas pump mounted on the wall. On another wall is what looks like a deconstructed transmission or something, with each piece mounted in place a few inches from the adjoining parts. The bar stretches along most of the length of one side of the building; the bar top itself is a single enormous piece of polished and stained hardwood, mounted on a long series of truck bed gates. The stools are motorcycle seats complete with old license plates and tail lights, mounted on giant springs. The owners left the windows in place, so there's actually natural light coming in, as well as plenty of warm, soft incandescent lighting; they got rid of the original can lighting and replaced it with hanging light fixtures made from old steering wheels strung with loose, dangling Edison bulbs. There are booths lining the walls, each made from the benches of old cars and trucks, complete with seat belts and buckles, and there are a dozen or so high-top tables in the middle, also crafted from car parts and other industrial materials. The whole effect is rugged and masculine and inviting and cool. In a back corner by the entrance to the kitchen there's a pair of pool tables, a handful of coin-op arcade games, and a dartboard, which is where I find Jesse and his crew.

They're crowded around Franco, who is hunched over a pinball machine; the boys are all shouting at him in what sounds like a mixture of insults and advice. As I close in, I can see why they're all so excited—Franco is within a thousand points of the high score, set by JB, with the second highest score set by JON, which I assume is James Bod and Jesse O'Neill. As I watch,

Franco passes the high score, and then taps out less than a hundred points past the high score.

"Boom, bitch!" Franco says, smacking the side of the machine, and then whirling to face James. "Beat you!" And then he dances over to face Jesse. "And you!"

James swigs from a bottle, shaking his head and rolling his eyes. "Oh ye of little faith. You know you can't top the pinball master for long."

Jesse snorts. "Okay, pinball master. The only reason my score is second highest is because Ryder's clumsy ass spilled his beer on me. You know I'd have smashed that high score otherwise. I've been beating you in pinball since third grade."

"You mean we've been going back and forth since third grade," James shoots back.

"Sure, go ahead and think that. But let's review the facts. Who still holds the high score on the Voltron machine at Electric Ed's back by our old high school? That'd be me. Who holds the high score in the bar we went to in college? Oh, that's right! That'd be *me*. I've been to both places recently, and I'm still on top, baby!"

I laugh, startling all of them. "Arguing about pinball game scores? At your ages?"

They turn away from the game and Franco chuckles. "You have no clue who you're talking to, do you? To these two yokels, pinball isn't just a game, it's a religion."

Jesse and James bump fists. "Pinball isn't just a game," Jesse reiterates, "it's the ultimate test of focus, reflexes, and manual dexterity."

When the laughter dies down, the handsome redhead in the group turns to me.

"Ryder," he says, in a deep, silky voice. "You must be Imogen."

"My fame precedes me, I see," I joke. "Nice to meet you, Ryder. Hi guys, good to see you again."

James and Franco I've both met, but Ryder I haven't, yet. He's a redhead, complete with pale skin and freckles. His hair is short on the sides and messy on top, with a full beard trimmed close, somewhere between too long for stubble and too short for a true beard. He's just as good-looking as his three friends, and just as different in build; Ryder is the shortest of the four, only a few inches taller than me, but he's impressively and scarily muscular. He has a calm, warm air to him, though, and his smile is bright and eager, and his grip as he shakes my hand is gentle.

"Your fame does indeed precede you," Ryder says, laughing. "This butthead won't shut up about you." He finishes this with a jerk of his thumb at Jesse.

Who, I believe, just might be blushing under that bushy beard.

"I talked about her *one* time, dude. Once. Hardly counts as *won't shut up about her*." Jesse narrows his eyes at Ryder. "And you're one to talk. The last girl you dated, you were all 'Elizabeth this, and Elizabeth that' for three months straight, until you realized she was batshit crazy and dumped her loony-ass."

Ryder shrugs. "Loony, yes, but her ass was also tighter than a fuckin'—" he cuts off with an embarrassed grin at me. "Uh, I mean—she was...she had a...umm..."

"Hey, you're a group of guys at your local place. No need to filter your conversation for my sake," I say with a laugh. "Besides, it's not like I'm unaware of how men talk."

Jesse just guffaws, smacking Ryder on the back. "Tight ass or not, she was a nutjob."

I drink a couple beers with the guys as we talk, and it's surprisingly fun and easy to hang out with them. They had lots of funny stories about various construction jobs and I had a few stories of my own about the crazy stuff that can happen in the medical business. After a couple of hours, James and Ryder excuse themselves to go to the bathroom, and Franco heads outside to return a phone call, leaving Jesse and me alone. The music in the bar is loud enough to drown out the conversations around us, but not so loud that we have to shout to be heard.

I trace the rim of my glass with a fingertip. "So, about last night—"

Jesse holds up a hand. "Imogen, I know you're probably—"

"Wait, wait, please—just hear me out first." I cover his hand with mine. "I wanted to apologize for how I acted. I was a lot more drunk than I thought I was, and you were just being a gentleman and doing something amazing, and I was an ornery bitch to you. So, I'm sorry. And thank you. Thank you for being you, for taking care of me and being honorable and a gentleman even when I was being…well, the way I was."

"No need to apologize, Imogen—I just don't want you to think I didn't want—"

I lean close and speak over him, keeping my voice low. "I have absolutely zero doubts about that, Jesse."

"You seemed pretty pissed. I was worried you'd still be mad."

"And I was worried I'd ruined things with my drunken idiocy. But to answer your question, the instant I woke up, my first thought was 'oh shit, I'm hungover,' and my second thought was, 'oh shit, I really messed up with Jesse.'"

"So you understand why I stopped us?" he asks, his hands engulfing mine.

"I'm glad you did what you did, Jesse. I'm grateful.

I was so horny I couldn't stand it, and I wanted you so bad, and I just wasn't thinking straight. After you left I stood up, and that's when I discovered exactly how drunk I was."

He breathes out sharply through his nostrils, jaw flexing. "Not taking you when you were offering yourself up to me like a gift-wrapped present was, very literally, the second hardest thing I've ever done in my life."

I tilt my head to one side. "Second hardest?"

He nods. "The first hardest is connected to that situation I don't like talking about. It's a major downer, and I'm a lot more interested in this conversation."

"Then forget I asked." I gaze up at him through my eyelashes, shifting my weight forward and squeezing my tits together with my arms as I lean toward him. "The only real difference between last night and tonight is that tonight I'm totally sober."

"In that case, I just have two questions for you. One, do you work in the morning?"

I shake my head. "No. Well, not early, at least. I go in at eleven."

"Good, because that leads me to my second question." His thumb rubs circles against the back of my hand, and his eyes flick between my eyes and my cleavage. "You want to get out of here?"

TWELVE

JESSE DOESN'T EVEN BOTHER SAYING GOODBYE OR MAKING excuses to his friends—the moment I whisper, "Yes," he takes me by the hand and hauls me faster than my heels will safely allow out of the bar to his truck. My initial impression was that we'd get in our separate cars and drive back to my house, since that's where we've always spent time together. But no. He's got other ideas.

I follow behind him across the parking lot, clinging to his hand, until we reach the lineup of trucks—and my Camry. I let go of his hand and dig in my clutch for my purse, but Jesse puts his hand at the small of my back and ushers me forward, between his truck and my car. Only, I'm on the wrong side of my car.

"Um, Jesse? The steering wheel is on the other side of my car," I point out.

His eyes dark and smoldering, he just smirks. "I

know. But you're not driving."

"I'm not?"

He shakes his head, digging his keys from his pocket and blipping the locks open. "Nope. I'm kidnapping you."

"Oh. I—oh." He steps around the hood, leans past me, and opens the passenger door of his truck. He's so close I can smell him, feel his heat. "Where are we going?"

He presses his lips to my ear. "My house."

"Oh. Okay," I whisper, shaking all over with excitement and need and nerves. "Why?"

"Because I live outside town, on a big chunk of land, with no neighbors."

"Okay...?" I ask, prompting for the reasoning behind this seeming non sequitur.

He nips my earlobe between his teeth, and then whispers in my ear. "That way, when I make you scream so loud the chandeliers rattle, there'll be no one around to hear."

My breath leaves me in a sudden, whimpering whoosh. "Oh god, Jesse. You know what it does to me when you talk like that?"

He presses up behind me, his mouth still against my ear. "No, Imogen. What's it do to you?"

"It makes me wet." I whisper this, and I can't quite believe it's me saying it, but the thrill racing through my blood tells me it's the right thing to say. And also, it's true. So, so true.

He growls, and his hand cups my hip. His teeth sink into my earlobe again, so I *feel* his growl as well as hear it. His body behind me, the door to my left, I'm sheltered between his truck and him, in a hot tense bubble of sexuality. I smell the leather of his seats, the distinct smell of a particular person's lived-in vehicle. Feel his chest against my back. His hips against my buttocks. His erection against my tailbone. His breath on my ear. His growl vibrating throughout me.

And his hand, powerfully cupping my hipbone. Slowly, deliberately, giving me time to stop him, his hand travels down to my thigh, to the hem of my dress. I press my hands against the edge of the seat, gripping the pebbled leather hard. I stop breathing as his hand slides between my thighs and slowly floats upward, under my dress.

"Dirty talk makes you wet?" he murmurs. "Here?"

I shift my feet farther apart and twist my head so my lips graze his cheek, just above his beard line. "It does when it's you talking that way to me."

"How wet?" he asks, his fingers tracing a V around the edges of my underwear over my core.

"I don't know," I say, swallowing doubt and embracing need, "you'd have to find out for yourself."

He groans, whether from need or from relief, I don't know. It's his only response, though, other than to tease a light touch of his fingertip over the lace covering my core. I huff a breath out, head hanging. His touch has the front of my dress riding up, baring most of my thighs, and his hand covers my core. It's so erotic, watching his hand steal slowly upward from my core to the waistband of my thong, and then watching his fingers slip under the elastic. More erotic yet to watch his hand fill the red lace as his palm covers me, and then his fingertip is grazing over my opening, and I can't breathe in but my lungs are empty, and my blood is singing A whine escapes me as he drags his finger up the seam of my core yet again, still not delving in. Just teasing me, learning the shape of me.

I want to beg him to plunge his finger inside me, to touch me, to make me scream like he promised. Instead, I inhale a moan, and wait. He doesn't disappoint. This time, when his finger grazes downward, it slips between the lips ever so slightly, and I bite my lip. Upward, and a little deeper, and now I'm biting my lip so hard it hurts.

"Jesse..." I whisper, my face still turned to his, my lips brushing his cheek.

He tilts my chin so our mouths meet, and as his tongue finds mine; he delves into me, slipping a digit into my pulsing wet heat. I moan loudly through the kiss at the delicious intrusion. I whimper and gasp as he draws his finger out, only just barely brushing me where I'm most sensitive.

I smell my own essence, and open my eyes to see him pop his finger into his mouth with a groan.

"So wet, and sweet as sugar."

"Oh god, Jesse." I'm having trouble formulating thoughts beyond animal, primal instinct. "I want—I need…"

"What, Imogen?" he asks, his voice a low rumble against my back. "What do you want—what do you need?"

"Everything." It's the only possible answer.

"Then let's get going," he answers, and slides a hand under my thighs and an arm around my waist and lifts me up into his truck, gently depositing me on the seat. He reaches across to buckle me in, taking extra effort to make sure the seat belt strap rests snugly between my breasts. I laugh at this, because I'm fully aware he did it more for his own visual enjoyment than for my safety.

"What?" he says, his tone protesting his innocence.

"I am familiar with the notion of strapboob, Jesse."

He laughs with me as he climbs behind the

steering wheel. "I just wanted to make sure you were properly buckled in."

He navigates his way out of the parking lot and heads out of town. The inside of his truck is silent except for the slight buffeting of wind from the windows being cracked a few inches. I see his gaze occasionally shift over to me, slide up and down my body, and then flick back to the road.

So, feeling daring and full of my own sensuality, I decide to play a little game of chicken. I gather the hem of my dress in my fingers while he's watching the road, lifting up slightly and surreptitiously tugging the dress up higher, baring more of my thighs The next time he glances back at me, his eyes linger longer, until he has to visibly force himself to return his attention to the road.

When he checks his blind spot over his left shoulder to change lanes, I quickly reach up and tug the already low neckline of my dress down, and the cups of my bra with it, so all of my breasts except my nipples and areolae are bared.

And, again, his gaze steals over to me, and lingers, sweeps up and down and back up, until he yet has to force himself to look back at the road.

I allow a brief, secret smile at the effect my game is having.

I wait until he glances out his window to watch

a particularly fancy sports car go past, and I tug the hemline of my dress higher yet, several inches this time; it's high enough now that if I spread my thighs open a bit—like so—he'll be able to see hints of the lace of my thong.

He looks me up and down once more, and now a grin steals across his face as he wises up to what's happening. "Saucy little minx, aren't you?"

I blink innocently at him. "What do you mean?" I ask, in a breathy Jessica Rabbit voice.

He just shakes his head and laughs. "Nothing—nothing at all."

And so I continue my game.

He makes a left turn, and while he's focusing on the turn, I tug the neckline lower yet, a fine-tuning adjustment so that the upper half-circle of my areolae are visible. When his gaze returns to me, my hands are on my lap, idly fidgeting. Fortunately, for both of us, there's another stoplight, and Jesse takes this moment to let his gaze rest on my breasts for a long, long moment.

"Goddamn, Imogen—you're *killing* me."

I just grin at him. "Am I? How?"

He shifts in his seat, and then, with a glance at me, he pivots his hips upward, shoves his hand down his pants, and adjusts himself. I've never considered that particular movement to be sexy when a guy does it, but somehow, Jesse makes it sexy, arousing. Enticing.

I want to plunge my hand into his pants, feel him fill my hand, feel him swell against my palm and fill my grip. I watch every moment of his adjustment, picturing the long thick ridge from the underwear selfie, and the erection I've felt pressed against me.

"Having problems?" I ask, smirking at him.

"Yeah, I am," he growls. "I'm about to bust through this damn zipper."

"How far are we from your house?" I ask.

"Another ten minutes," he murmurs. "Which is ten minutes too long."

"Drive faster?" I suggest.

He shakes his head. "Nah, this road is regularly patrolled by Staties. There's one in particular who likes to sit parked in this little stand of trees where nobody can see him from either direction, but he can pull out in a hurry to pop speeders. I learned that the hard way," he chuckles. "Got the points on my license to prove it, too. So no, I'll go the speed limit and just hope either the zipper holds or you quit playing with fire."

"Playing with fire?" I ask. "How do you mean?"

He glances at me, his gaze hot and rife with promise. "You keep playing your little striptease game, my restraint is gonna snap and I'm going stop this truck

and rip that goddamn gorgeous dress off your goddamn gorgeous body and get the taste of you I've
been craving since the moment I laid eyes on you."

"Why don't you?" I ask, daring him with a lifted
chin and a lick of my tongue over my lips.

"Because I want you in my bed for that, so I can
take the hours and hours I'll need to explore every
inch of that luscious body."

"Oh." I glance at him, watching him shift in his
seat, squirming in a vain attempt to relieve the pressure in his jeans. "There's another option you may
not have considered."

He decelerates to a stoplight, and then looks at
me. "What option would that be?"

"This one," I say, reaching across the console.

He keeps both hands on the steering wheel, and
I see his jaw flexing, tensing as I find the button of
his jeans and pop it open, and then find the tab of
his zipper and tug it down, slowly, inch by inch, until
his jeans are sagging open and his erection is bulging
against the gray cotton of his underwear to fill the
opening.

"There," I say, resting my hand on his thigh.
"That should help relieve the pressure some, right?"
I'm intentionally teasing him, now.

"Fuck," he moans. "I don't know if that's better
or worse."

"How would it be worse?" I ask.

We're zipping down a two-lane highway now, trees on the right, open fields on our left, the moon high and half-full overhead. It's beautiful out here, peaceful, serene, quiet. I can't quite appreciate it, though—I'm far too laser-focused on Jesse.

"There's less pressure now, so I'm not in danger of popping the zipper, but you've only gotten me partway to where I selfishly want you to take me."

A tactful way of putting it.

I chew on my lower lip, trying to decide how far I want to take this. How daring am I?

I feel the thrill of a shiver run through me, and I know I'm not about to dial it back at this stage in the game. My hand is still resting on his solid thigh; I trace it upward, fingers dragging over the rough denim, across the cold teeth of the zipper, to the soft cotton and the firm-yet-soft bulge beneath. Alternating between watching my hands and his face, I hook two fingers under the elastic and tug it away and downward. The broad pink of him emerges, and I suck in a breath at the thickness of it. Holy mother of wow— seeing it in person, in the flesh is…my heart races, my hands tremble, and my breath shortens.

"Imogen," Jesse groans, "dammit, woman."

"What? Is this not helping?" I know damn well it's not. He wants my hands around him as much if not more than I want it, just like I want his fingers inside me as much if not more than he wants them there.

"Define helping."

"I could help all the way if you want." I glance at him, watching for his reaction.

He tilts his head back, closes his eyes briefly, and lets out a long, tortured growl. "Fuuuuuuck. You know how crazy it makes me when you suggest stuff like that?"

"How crazy?"

"Crazy enough that I'm tempted to tell to you to do your worst. Or your best, depending how you look at it."

Desire to see more him, touch more of him races through me, controls me, and I take his words as either a dare or permission. I do what I wanted to do moments ago—I delve my hand into his underwear and take hold of him.

My breath fails, and my heart stutters—he's *huge*. Hot and hard in my hand, spreading my fingers apart. Soft, smooth. Ripples, and veins, and the smooth roundness of the tip under my thumb, moisture leaking. He groans and his hips shift forward, and I reach over the console with my other hand to tug the underwear away so I can see better. I let him go and just look at him—a massive thick shaft of pink flesh, the head bobbing against his belly with his breathing and the bump and sway of the truck.

He makes a turn off the highway onto a narrow gravel road that winds down a hill and through a copse of trees, up another hill, and then angles across a wide field of tall grass waving in the breeze. In the distance, a house sits on a hill surrounded by rolling green hills, a ring of trees in the distance.

"That's my place up ahead," Jesse murmurs.

I have him in my hand again, hot and throbbing. I stroke, once, slowly, downward, and he growls in his chest, hips flexing, and then his hand wrenches mine away

"Not yet. You keep touching me like that, I won't last half a second. I want you too bad."

I almost whimper at the loss of him in my hand—it's almost as maddening as feeling his finger inside me for a single delving moment. More—I want more. So much more.

Everything.

He's hauling ass now that he's on his own property; we jolt down a hill and over a rut, and then he's skidding to a stop in the circular dirt driveway in front of his home. It's a beautiful white two-story Victorian farmhouse, with a wraparound stretching around the entire home, twin dormers on the roof; the shutters are painted a deep scarlet, and the front door is red as well. An acre or so of grass around the home itself is mown, fertilized, and watered, but the rest beyond it is wild and untamed.

Dust swirls in the moonlight and in the twin beams of the headlights, and then he's shutting the engine off and opening his door. He roughly refastens his jeans and hops out, circles to my side before I'm even unbuckled. My door flies open, and he hauls me out, carries me in his arms up the stairs to his porch, and sets me down to fit his key into the lock. I take the time, while he's unlocking the door, to fix my dress. He fumbles a moment or two, and then with an impatient shove, the door swings open and we step in.

The interior is obscured in shadows and slices of moonlight at first, and then he flicks a few switches just inside the front door, illuminating the home, revealing a beautiful open-plan main floor with acres of polished hardwood, gleaming stone countertops, stainless steel appliances, open face cabinets, a deep leather couch, seascape and landscape artwork on the walls. I move around the main level, which includes the living room, dining room, kitchen, a small walk-in pantry, and a half bathroom. There's a lovely rocking chair in the living room, handmade from the looks of it, and a matching side table. The dining room table and matching chairs all have a similar look as the rocking chair and side table, making me think all three pieces were made by the same person or company.

Jesse sees me looking at the rocking chair. "All the wooden furniture in here was made by Franco. He's a master finishing carpenter, and he handcrafts furniture on the side. The chair, the side table, and the dining room set were his housewarming gift to me when I finished renovating this place."

I glance around. "You renovated this yourself?"

Jesse snorts. "No—I, a professional builder, hired someone else." He laughs. "Of course I did. Took me, like, two years to do the whole thing, but I wasn't in a hurry. Obviously the guys helped. We'd finish work on Friday evening, come out here, and work on a bit here and there. This is where I spent pretty much every weekend for two years."

"It's really beautiful," I say.

He digs his phone out of his pocket and scrolls through his photographs until he finds a set. "Scroll to the right. The first few are from when I first bought it."

Standing in his gorgeous kitchen, I swipe through the photographs, and I'm truly amazed. I knew Jesse was skilled, but what he's done here is artistry. The before photographs show a house that was probably seconds from being condemned. The roof was falling in, the front porch was sagging, and the siding was missing in places. More photos showed the inside, which was in even worse shape. Walls were missing chunks, the ceilings were bulging and sagging with water damage, there was old sheet-covered furniture and garbage and animal nests and inches of dust.

"I ripped the entire roof off, and tore out every wall that wasn't load bearing. The real saving grace here is that the original hardwood floors had all been covered at some point by this god-awful shag carpeting, so they'd been really well preserved pretty much everywhere. The floors and the exterior walls are all that's original; everything else has been totally rebuilt. All the wiring, all the plumbing, lighting, everything we did from scratch."

"A real labor of love, huh?" I ask, handing him his phone back.

"Yeah, sure was." He waves a hand at the kitchen. "So, want a tour?"

I gaze up at him. "Yeah, sure." I lick my lips and go for the truth. "As long as the tour ends in your bedroom."

His smile is predatory. "Who says we need a bed for what I have in mind?"

"What—what do you have in mind?"

He just smirks. "You'll find out soon enough."

God, I hope so. Now that we've backed away from the heat of the moment, my nerves are jangling on high alert. Need hasn't abated, and neither has my desire for him, but knowing what's happening, where this is going—the anticipation is making me vibrate with anxiety and doubt and self-consciousness, on top of the need and desire.

When my hormones are in control, I have no thoughts beyond getting what I want and fulfilling my desires, but now that we're out of the moment, my brain is starting up again and questions are floating up from deep in the pool of my uncertainty and self-doubt.

What if, when I'm finally naked, I don't look as good as he thinks I will? What if my butt is too big? What if the wrinkles and dimples on my ass turn him off? What if the fact that my belly isn't taut and firm and toned—like, say, Audra's—is a turnoff? What if I'm not as wild and adventurous in bed as he wants me to be? What if he wants things I'm not comfortable with? What if sex with him is bad? What if it's incredible and I fall for him even harder than I can already feel myself falling?

He's an avowed hound dog, a lifelong bachelor with no intention or desire to jump into anything deep or committed, and I'm not sure I'm capable of a casual, physical relationship. In a lot of ways, that's exactly what I want—no-strings sex, fun and free and physically fulfilling, but without all the messy emotions that come along with being involved with someone. That sounds easy and simple and fun, and after my god-awful messy failure of a marriage and the ugly divorce being able to just have good sex and not put my heart at risk sounds kind of nice.

But I know myself. I know how my emotions work, and they operate on a hair trigger.

Jesse is eyeing me. "Where'd you go just now?"

I shake my head, clueless as to how to communicate any of this to him, let alone whether it'd be smart to do so.

What happens, happens—okay, Audra, I'll try things your way.

"Hey, there's no pressure, here, okay?" Jesse says, perhaps correctly assessing me.

He tosses his keys onto the counter beside the stove, digs his wallet and phone out of his pocket and tosses them down along with his keys, then leans back against the counter and unties his boots, toes them off and kicks them across the room to land willy-nilly by the back door. His socks join them, and then he turns back to me.

"We could skip the tour for now," he says, moving closer.

"We could," I agree, placing my palms flat on his chest.

"I'm a lot more interested in a tour of you." He lets his gaze roam my body yet again, desire crackling in his eyes—it's that look that gets me, every time. That look which says he *wants* me, that he can't get enough of even just seeing me, fully clothed or otherwise.

"You've gotten a pretty good tour already," I say, tracing the outline of his pec over his T-shirt.

"Nah, I'm gonna need the full, detailed, comprehensive tour." He spans my waist with both hands. "An in-depth tour."

"I think that could be arranged," I say, my voice low.

Yet again, his eyes rake over me, head to toe, several times. "Have I mentioned yet how goddamn incredible you look this evening?"

I shake my head. "That hasn't come up, no."

He growls. "God, I'm an idiot. It's all I've been thinking about tonight."

"What have you been thinking?"

He gestures at me, sweeping his hand up and down. "You, in that dress—you're the most beautiful woman I've ever seen."

I laugh, a barking outburst. "Let's not be ridiculous, Jesse. But thanks for the vote of confidence."

His hands tighten, and he yanks me roughly up against him. "You think I'm joking?" he growls, unamused.

Any hilarity I may have felt vanishes abruptly at

the hardness of his body against mine, at the heat and ferocity in his voice. "I—I haven't felt that way in a long time, so it's a little hard for me to believe."

"You don't have to believe it yourself," he murmurs. "You just have to know that *I* believe it."

"I think you maybe, possibly, are laying it on a little thick," I admit. "You don't have to, you know. I'm a sure thing, at least for tonight."

Jesse's growl is actually a little scary. "You've already accused me of that once, Imogen, and I don't fuckin' appreciate it." His fingers dig into my hips and he holds me hard against his big body, so I have to tilt my head back to meet his fiery brown gaze. "You need to understand something about me, babe. I don't lay anything on thick. I don't flatter, or charm, or play games. I'm giving you the raw, unvarnished truth as I see it and feel it. So if I'm standing here telling you I think you, in that sexy-as-fuck little red dress and gold heels, are the most beautiful woman I've ever laid eyes or hands on, you best believe that down to your goddamn atoms. Because I mean that shit with everything I've got."

"I believe you," I whisper. And I do. You can't fake intensity like that.

"Do you?" he rumbles. "I'm not so sure. I think maybe you need some convincing."

I'm trying to formulate a sassy, flirty response

still when he slides one palm up my back to cup the back of my head, and then his lips slant across mine. My breath catches as he kisses me—at first it's a hot whirlwind of lips and teeth, his fingers clutching my nape and clawing into the flesh above my hip. And then he slows it, softening his grip on me, softening his mouth on mine and dipping his tongue against mine. I claw my fingers into fists in his shirt and lift up on my toes, a whimper in my throat.

I'm the first to go for flesh—I need more of him, of his skin, his heat, and his muscle. My fingers release his shirt and find the hem, and slip underneath to scour the hard plane of his stomach. Pushing upward, lifting the shirt, my thumbs following the centerline of his chest, up his sternum and between his pecs. He crosses his arms and peels the pesky T-shirt off and tosses it aside, and I moan in delight at the firm warmth of his chest under my hands. I explore his torso as we kiss, palming his pecs and roaming down his sides, up his back to curl my hands over his shoulders. With each touch, each exploration of his muscled body, I press closer, delving deeper into the kiss, devouring his lips and tongue and breathing his breath.

He rumbles in his chest as I roam his body. His hands leave my nape and hip, and begin their own exploration. He tugs the straps of my dress aside and shoves them down the sides of my arms, baring my shoulders, and then his hands skate down the outsides of my biceps, then jump to my waist. For a moment, his hands span my waist, and then they edge around to the small of my back; my breath catches in my throat and I moan into his mouth as he cups my ass in his hands. A firm grip, then, before he squeezes, kneads, smoothing in circles, teasing and toying with the heft and the bounce.

He breaks the kiss, his palms possessively gripping my buttocks. "Have I mentioned yet how much I love this?" He squeezes as he says this, making sure I know exactly what he's talking about. "It's perfect."

I murmur a laugh. "Funny, because when I called Audra to come over this morning, she told me to get my big beautiful ass into some workout gear, and I got upset that she called my butt big. And she said she was pretty certain you—how did she put it? She said you probably, and I quote, 'harbor a deep and eternal appreciation for the size and shape of my derrière.'"

Jesse's response is to gather the fabric of my dress in his fingers, walking the hemline upward until my dress is hiked up over my hips, leaving my ass bare. And, did I mention the underwear I'm wearing is a thong? It's nothing but a tiny triangle of red lace over my core, a strap around my hips, and a red string. When my ass is bared, he palms it again, with a long, deep groan of unmistakable appreciation.

"Your friend is more right than she knows," he says. "Your ass is perfect."

"I guess I'm just self-conscious. I used to be in great shape, but I've slacked off over the past few years."

Jesse sighs. "Imogen. Stop. Just stop. You're absolutely perfect." He caresses my butt again. "I can't get enough."

I kiss his chest, and then his pec, and then his shoulder, my hands carving circles around his broad back and shoulders. "I think you've just gotten started, Jesse," I say. "I know I'm self-conscious, and I know it's annoying. It'll take time for me to work past it. Time, and probably a lot of compliments I'll have trouble believing."

He grinds his erection against me. "Does this feel like a compliment to you?"

"I don't know," I murmur, grinning as I kiss his neck under his beard line. "There're too many layers of clothing between me and you to be sure."

"An easily rectified situation," he says.

I unfasten his button and lower the zipper again, and his erection bulges free. This time, I push his jeans down over his butt. He steps out of them, kicks them aside, and I cup the hard roundness of his butt, over the tight gray cotton of his boxer briefs. I linger there, enjoying the feel of it, the hardness of it. And then I bring my hands between us and cup his erection.

"Feeling the compliment now?" Jesse asks. "Getting to spend time with you, getting to look at you, getting to put my hands on your incredible body...you do that to me. You make me so hard it hurts."

"I think I'm starting to feel the compliment," I say, caressing his length over his underwear. "But I think I may need to feel more of it to be absolutely sure."

He laughs, capturing both of my hands in one of his. "Not so fast," he says. "I have something else in mind, first."

"Something...*else*?" I ask, my voice cracking a little.

He doesn't answer. At least, not with words. Still pinioning my hands together, he reaches around behind me and unzips my dress. Keeping hold of my hands, he nudges the dress straps down, letting the dress sag a little lower. Instead of letting me go so the dress falls off, he transfers his grip on one wrist to his other hand, slides his fingertips up my arm, captures the other strap and drags it down. I'm breathless and helpless to do anything except comply as he guides my arm out of the loop of the strap, and then repeats this on the other side. The dress is tight enough that it won't fall off on its own, requiring a little…help, to come off. Again, Jesse deviates from my expectations by leaving the dress on. It's sagging, drooping, but catching around the bell of my hips. He still has a firm grip on both of my hands, refusing to let them go, retaining utter control over me.

He raises my hands over my head, transfers both into one of his and, with a brief, intense locking of eyes, presses his lips to my sternum, just above the valley of my cleavage. And then downward, to the slope of one breast. Slowly, with delicate gentility, his beard silky and scratchy at once against my skin, he kisses me, and then moves to the other breast. Down, kissing closer and closer to the edge of bra and the neckline. Back upward, then, up to my sternum, to the base of my throat. I gasp, and tilt my head back, and he accepts my offering, kissing up my throat to the underside of my chin, and then around to underneath my earlobe, behind my ear, then the shell of it, his breath hot on my flesh. I shiver, and a ghost of a whimper escapes me as he brings his lips to my cheekbone, the corner of my lips. My mouth opens, and I eagerly meet his kiss.

He starts the kiss slowly, this time, gradually building the intensity of it, feeding my hunger for his tongue on mine and his breath and his lips until I'm ravenous and greedy, and then, as our kiss crescendos in a clash of mouths and moans, he uses his free hand—up until now clinging to the small of my back to press me against him into the kiss—to grasp a handful of my dress and tug.

The scarlet fabric pools on the floor around my feet, and my heart slams in my chest—I haven't stood in nothing but undergarments in front of any man for so long—and especially not one like Jesse. It's a thrill, and utterly terrifying. I know he finds me attractive—I don't doubt that. It's my own fears and insecurities at play, and I argue them, combat them, try to hold on to the desire and the need and the wild abandon, cling to the ever-fleeting confidence to stand as I am and let Jesse look without flinching from his gaze.

And indeed, he releases me and steps back three paces.

It requires an effort of will—my nerves crashing and fear slamming in my blood and in my gut, doubts preying on me—to stand tall, shoulders back, head up, as he gazes at me.

"Fuck, you're beautiful," he murmurs. "Is that what you were wearing when you flashed me as I was backing out the other day?

I nod. "Yes."

He rakes his hand through his hair. "Perfect."

I offer a hesitant, shy smile. "Better be careful, Jesse. You keep saying that, I might just start believing it." I indicate his body with a sweep of my finger. "You're pretty damn perfect yourself, you know."

He steps toward me in a predatory swagger, mouth curling up in a hot grin. "Good. Then I'll say it every time I look at you until you do. Because you are. You're perfect." His hands slide over the small of my back, trace the underside of my bra strap, and follow the circle of my thong's waistband. "But you'd be even more perfect if we took these off."

Oh god, oh god. I swallow hard, fighting desperately for the confidence to let him strip me naked, right here, in the brightly lit kitchen, with open windows all around.

The last several times I was naked with a man, the lights were off, the blinds were closed, and the entire process lasted less than five minutes from start to finish, leaving me vulnerable and frustrated and alone as he rolled over and went to sleep. Last several times? Try every time for several years. I don't remember the last time I stood confident in my nudity for a man.

He senses something. "You okay?"

I nod, but have to blink and swallow and work past the lump of fear and doubt. "Just...nervous."

He pulls me against him, his palms on my back. "Don't lie to me, Imogen."

"Fine. I'm terrified." I meet his gaze, my eyes stinging. "I want this—I want you. I want *everything*—that hasn't changed in the slightest. I want it all more than ever. But…"

"What do you need?" he asks.

"Can we go to your room? And maybe…turn the lights off?"

He frowns. "Imogen…Jesus. That bastard really did a number on you, didn't he?" He shakes his head. "I'm not letting you hide. I'm not letting you give doubt and fear the win."

"Easier said than done. When things are hot and heavy and I don't have time to think, I'm fine," I tell him, allowing brutal honesty to emerge. "And I have moments where I feel bold and beautiful and even sexy. But then other times, I just…I doubt myself. I don't doubt that you're attracted to me, or even that you think I'm perfect, somehow. It's not you I doubt, it's me. It's hard to know who I am, now. After everything that's happened, I'm not the woman I was. I'm someone else, and I don't know who that is. I want to be someone bold and strong, I want to be confident and I want to take what I want. But it's hard. I'm trying, but it's so hard. And you're so effortlessly cool and handsome and confident and strong, and you say such incredible things, and the way you touch me is magical. And I just…it's all so mixed up."

He cups my face and tilts it up. "Can you do something for me?"

"What?"

"Show me the photo you sent me."

My purse is on the counter beside his phone, keys, and wallet—I don't even remember bringing it in or putting it down, but there it is. I get my phone and bring up the photo. On either side of it in the photo feed are some of the other photos I took that I didn't delete and didn't send.

I hand him the phone. "You can swipe both ways. There are a couple others I didn't send you. They're unedited and not super great, but—"

He touches my lips with a finger to shut me up, and I'm thankful, because I'm nervous letting him see those, and I would have kept babbling. He swipes through the photos, taking time to carefully scrutinize each one. He shows me the screen: it's one of the ones I didn't send, but nearly did. I'm on my back, left arm curled under and around my breasts to squeeze them together and prop them up, with the phone held up and out to the side to capture almost all of my body—my legs are crossed at the thighs and my hips are twisted away to shield my core from the camera. The only reason I didn't send that one was because the angle of my turned-aside thigh reveals an unflattering amount of stretch marks and cellulite.

"Why the hell didn't you send me this?" he demands. It's almost comical how legitimately offended he sounds.

I gesture at the offending area on the photograph. "Because of this."

He snorts in derision, shaking his head. "That's bullshit."

I frown. "I can't change how I feel about myself just by wanting to, Jesse."

He backs away from me. "Stand there, just like that."

"What are you doing?" I demand, reaching for my phone.

He holds it up, pointing at me with the other hand. "Stand there like you were. Please?"

Reluctantly, I comply, crossing one arm under my breasts, the other reaching up to toy with a lock of my hair. One foot is crossed over the other, my sparkly gold heels still on, and I'm leaning a hip against the edge of the counter. He snaps a few photos, and then glances at me again.

"Now, turn around. Please."

I panic. "No, no. Jesse—come on."

He just grins. "I'm proving a point. If you don't like the photos, you delete them."

I sigh shakily and then, with a nervous duck of my head, I turn around. "Take your picture and be done."

He laughs. "Oh no, not so fast. Stand upright,

and look at me over your shoulder."

In order to do so, I have to shift my weight to one side, popping my hip out. But what do I do with my hands?

Jesse has the answer. "Put your middle fingers along the creases of the underside of your butt, like you're trying to lift it up. You're framing it, sort of."

I snort. "You've done this before, sleazeball."

He chortles. "No, I haven't actually. Swear to god." He winks at me. "I just have a great subject in this case, so it makes it easy."

I do what he says, and as he snaps a photo, I find myself adjusting the pose a little, flexing my buttocks and actually lifting them a little, tossing my hair just so, and actually smiling at him as he snaps another few photos.

He sidles up behind me, brings the phone around in front of me, and, swiping back to the beginning of the series, and shows them to me. "See? Look how sexy you are in these."

I swipe through, and damn if I don't actually look pretty damn good. The red lingerie compliments my tan skin and brown hair, and my body actually looks…

Sexy.

I smile at him. "You're just a good photographer," I say, still not quite willing to give it up, for some stupid reason.

He just shakes his head. "You couldn't take a bad picture if you tried."

I laugh. "You haven't seen me first thing in the morning."

His grin is fierce. "Not yet, I haven't. But I plan to."

Heat boils through me. "What if I'm ugly and have bad breath?"

"You're never ugly, and I have mouthwash." He sets the phone on the counter, and now he's towering behind me, his arms imprisoning me between them. "I want to take a few more pictures of you, if you'll let me."

I sigh. "I get the point, Jesse." I tap the phone screen. "I actually do look pretty good in those."

His hands skate down the sides of my hips, and then upward, grazing my belly and coming to a halt just beneath my breasts. "Trust me," he murmurs.

I want his hands to go upward, but instead, I whisper my acquiescence. "Okay." I straighten my spine and summon my courage. "How do you want me, Mr. Photographer?"

He chuckles, a sound that manages to convey amusement and arousal at the same time. "How do I want you?" He puts his lips to my ear, whispering, "I want you on your hands and knees in my bed. I want you above me, those big beautiful tits bouncing in my face. I want your thighs wrapped around my face. I want you bent over this counter, screaming my name."

I whimper, leaning back against him. "I like the sound of all of that."

He slides his palms up over the cups hiding my breasts. "I've been dreaming of these night and day."

"Well, there they are," I murmur, in a fit of wild originality.

He touches his lips to my nape, and his fingers dance and traipse around to my back. With a flick of his fingers, he unhooks my bra, and then his hand slides smoothly up the bare skin where the strap used to be up to my shoulders, brushing the straps away. I clutch the cups in place for a moment, and then let my arms fall to my sides before reaching up and behind me to grasp at him, at his hair, his beard.

My bra topples to the counter with a soft thud. Jesse's hands spread across my stomach and then, once more, carve upward. I catch my breath, and my lip between my teeth, as his big strong hands finally, at long last, alight beneath my breasts.

Hesitantly, reverently, he cups their weight, lifting them, caressing them. He moans against the back of my neck, and I feel his erection against my buttocks, throbbing hard and thick behind his underwear. I have my hands bunched in his hair, my head tilted back to rest on his shoulder. He spends several long moments just playing with my breasts, cupping and kneading, thumbing my nipples until I'm gasping and flinching.

And then, without warning, he lets them go. I open my eyes to see him with my phone in hand, swiping from the lock screen to activate my camera. Standing behind me, he holds the camera away facing us, and snaps a photo of us like this. He taps the thumbnail and we see the photograph: he's huge behind me, his chest broad and his tattooed arms vanishing behind the camera angle, his hair a wild mane of black, his eyes merry and hot and aroused. I look sensual, erotic—my hair is loose and still curly, my eyes smoky, lips red, skin tan, and my breasts are firm and round, my nipples thick and tall from his attention.

It is possibly the hottest photo I've ever seen— and it's of *me*. Of *us*.

I'm about to comment on this when he tosses the phone onto the counter. "I can't wait any longer," he growls.

There's no time to wonder what he means—he slides to a crouch behind me, fingers hooking into the waistband of my thong. His lips touch the small of my back, and then the upper bell of my left hip, and I'm breathless from his kiss, from the touch of his lips to my flesh. His lips kiss downward to the waistband of my thong, and as he kisses along it, he tugs it lower and lower, following its descent with his lips, from one side of my buttocks to the other. I grip the counter and endure his kisses, gasping now and then. I can't even gasp when, finally, he tugs them past the swell of my ass so they tumble to the floor at my feet. And, just like that, I'm naked.

But he's not done.

His mouth continues to lave kisses over my thighs and buttocks, while his hands curl around my legs and inch upward, his fingers dancing along the insides of my thighs. Up and up and up his hands dare, and my lungs contract until I'm dizzy and have to suck in air. My breath is shot right back out of me the next instant, though, when his fingers dance up to the juncture of my thighs, and pause.

"Jesse?"

He murmurs in response, a wordless answer to my inarticulate question. My core trembles, soaked and slippery with desire, as his touch inches nearer. I clutch the counter with a white-fingered grip, barely breathing. His teeth sink into my left buttock, nipping sharply, eliciting a shriek from me—the shriek morphs into a drawn-out moan as he traces my seam with a fingertip. There's not the gradual intrusion as in the parking lot; this time, he sweeps his finger up my opening once, and then presses two fingers to the hypersensitive nub of nerves at the apex of my core. It hardens at his touch, begging for attention; two slow circles of his fingers, and I'm gasping. Three, four, five—faster and faster, and I'm shaking, knees quaking, hips helplessly flexing. Two fingers, and he has me undulating on the edge of orgasm faster than I've ever gotten there in my life, even on my own. His other hand cups my breasts, one and then the other and then both, playing with them and caressing. As I start to move into his touch, he starts to play with my nipples, flicking them, pinching, twisting, thumbing, until I'm a writhing, seething mess of dripping arousal, moaning and whimpering and utterly desperate for the edge to come so I can topple eagerly over it.

But when I'm moments from reaching the cusp of climax, he stops, grabs me by the hips, and spins me around. It's an abrupt, rough maneuver that leaves me gasping and dizzy, my breasts jiggling from the movement.

"Jesse, I—please, don't stop now. I was so close!" My voice cracks into a whisper at the end.

He just smirks up at me. "You think I'd leave you like this?"

"I don't—I don't know."

He palms my ass and pulls me closer, shifting to his knees on the floor, gazing up at me. I knot my hand in his hair as he leans closer to me, as I realize his intent. Oh god, please, please, please—it's been so long since I've gotten that, and I want it so badly, I want to feel his tongue and his beard and his—

Thoughts fly out of my head as he kisses my core—a true kiss. And another kiss, and another, each one hotter, each one more passionate, and then the kisses turn into his tongue slathering against my seam and slipping between my lips and finding my hardened center. I cry out, a sobbing moan of pure ecstasy as he laves tonguing kisses over every inch of my core. I writhe against his mouth, sagging back against the counter, groaning gasps and crying and sobbing as he worships me with his mouth.

He growls in that feral, utterly masculine way of his as he works me to climax. When I reach the edge, I can't help but scream. I've never felt anything like this in my life, never known this intensity, this wondrous, pure, fiery perfection. He licks and laps and kisses until I'm weak in the knees and openly crying from equal parts relief and ecstasy and wonder.

And then, when I can handle no more, I have to push his face away. "Stop…" I whimper. "I can't—no more."

He kneels before me, gazing up at me between the pendulous globes of my breasts, my essence beaded in his beard. "You're a goddess, Imogen."

And then he rises gracefully to his feet, hooks

his hands under my thighs and lifts me into the air. Instinctively, I wrap my legs around him, and his hands cup my ass to support my weight.

I cling to him as he walks with me to the stairs near the front door, and I can't help but kiss his forehead and his cheeks and his neck as he carries me effortlessly up the stairs.

His bedroom is at the top of the stairs, but I see nothing of it, only the retreating view of the stairs as he carries me into his room and to his bed. He stands at the foot his bed, holding me up, my legs tangled around his waist, gazing into my eyes for a long moment.

And then he bends over, laying me on the soft, downy comforter. I'm surrounded by softness and warmth, and he's above me, a beautiful, powerful, attentive, incredible man who just gave me the most stunning, breathtaking orgasm of my life.

"I need more of you, Imogen," he says.

I'm spread naked beneath him, every part of me bare to him, offered up to him. He's tasted me, felt me come. He's touched every inch of my body.

Yet he still wants more?

I reach for him, and this time, he lets me.

THIRTEEN

IS HANDS HANG AT HIS SIDES, LOOSELY CLENCHED, and his breathing is slow and even, as if he hadn't just carried me up a flight of stairs. When I sit up and reach for him, his lips curl into a grin. His erection tents the front of his underwear. I lick my lips in anticipation of seeing all of him, which for some reason makes him snort a laugh.

"What?" I ask, my fingers hooked in the waistband. "Are you laughing at me?"

"No, never. I just didn't realize it was possible until just now that someone could be adorable and erotic at the same time."

"Adorable?"

He nods. "The way you licked your lips? It was just...adorable. And erotic."

"I'll take adorable and erotic."

"I'll take *you*," he growls.

"Didn't you just do that?" I tease.

He shakes his head. "That was just…a preview."

If that was a preview, I can't wait to find out what the full program will do to me.

I'm stalling.

Sitting on the edge of his bed, my fingers hooked in his underwear, I let out a slow breath and glance up at him. He just smiles at me and briefly toys with my breasts, as if he just can't help himself.

My heart is crashing in my chest as I draw the elastic away from his body and peel the cotton undergarment downward. He steps out of them and toes them aside.

Ohhhh god. Holy hell.

Talk about perfection. Standing straight upright against his belly, he's a thick shaft of veiny, throbbing arousal. The round head gleams wetly, begging for my touch. I reach a hesitant hand out, and then grasp him. One hand isn't nearly enough—it takes both of my hands to fully encompass his entire length. With one small hand wrapped around his thick erection, I stroke him slowly, watching the path of my hand up to the head, watch my palm wrap over the bulbous, pre-cum-leaking tip, and then slide back down.

I glance up at Jesse: he's got his arms crossed over his chest, and his jaw is tensing, flexing, and his breathing is coming fast and ragged. "You okay?" I ask.

He nods, tightly. "Better than okay. I wish I could

feel your hand around me like that forever, without having to come. But as it is, I'm riding the edge here, and I need you." He pulls away from me, out of my grip, and then prowls forward. I crawl backward on the bed as he crawls forward onto it, predatory and male and primal. Every inch of him is beautiful, the way his muscles shift powerfully as he crawls toward me, the wild mane of his jet-black hair, the soft, shaggy beard, the tattoos. My breath catches at this vision: Jesse, crawling for me, hunger in his eyes, his arousal bobbing and swaying as he moves, his muscles shifting in the moonlight coming in from the windows.

I reach the head of the bed, leaning against headboard and pillows, and he's above me, reaching for me. His hand curls around the back of my neck and he lifts me up to him, taking a dizzying kiss from me. Again, as with every time I've ever kissed Jesse, I'm soon lost in it. In him. In the sweep of his tongue and the slant of his lips and the warm huff of his breath. He's just as lost in the kiss, I want to think, lowering himself over me, burying his mouth against mine, moaning into my breath. Curling me closer, his hands exploring my body without purpose except to feel me, to touch me, to indulge in the pleasure of my feminine flesh.

The drugging potency of his kiss dizzies me, leaves me gasping. "Jesse..." I whisper.

He brushes a thumb over my cheekbone. "Imogen?"

"Kiss me again. And...please, don't stop."

He levers an arm beside my head, supporting his weight on it as he opens a drawer in his bedside table. Withdrawing a box of condoms, he rips the top open with a glance at me. "Brand-new box because I've never brought anyone here. I bought these today, hoping and fantasizing about bringing you here someday. I didn't think it'd actually happen today, though."

He rips a square free and tosses the box and the rest of the strip aside, and moves back to his knees. Hands shaking with need and with anticipation, I take the wrapper from him and tear it open to reveal the ring inside. I remove it, fit the latex to the thick, round head of him, and roll it down, hand over hand, enjoying the way he groans incoherently at my touch.

Instead of moving over me, he reaches for me, extending his hand. I take it, and he draws me upright to a sitting position. He sinks back to sit on his heels, and pulls me to him.

"What are you doing?" I ask, unsure of his intent.

His only response is to guide me up onto my knees and then to sit on my heels in a mirror of his own position, so we're both on our knees, sitting on our heels facing each other. He draws me closer yet, palming a breast as I lean into him, his other hand going for my ass. My own hands begin their own exploration, sliding over his massive shoulders and down the serpentine S of his spine to his firm buttocks. His lips find mine, and now I can delve into this, now I can trust him to know what he's doing with me. When he kisses me, the world fades and my doubts vanish and my fears are erased and everything is right and perfect, because he's kissing me.

The deeper our kiss goes, the wilder my pulse hammers, the hotter and wetter my core becomes. The more I need him.

I lift up on my knees, smashing my breasts against his chest, clutching his face in both hands. His palms cup my ass, lifting me higher, and now I understand.

"Yes," I breathe.

He lifts me up, pulls me close. My pulse is a coruscating crescendo in my veins, and my heart—the physical one—is squeezing madly, while my metaphysical heart is blossoming open like a flower stretching upward for the sunrise. I reach between us, clutch the latex-sheathed magnificence of his erection and guide him to me.

I have to break the kiss to whimper as the head nudges my opening.

"*Jesse...*" I sob.

His voice is as ragged as mine when he answers. "God...*Imogen.*"

He grips a buttock in each hand, holding me up, and I clutch him, drawing out the moment.

It's up to me, I realize.

He's waiting for me.

I press my forehead to his and breathe in slowly, take his upper lip between my teeth, and claim a fierce, wilding, ungentle kiss. He moans, a sound I feel in the crush of my breasts against his chest—he needs me, that's what the moan says: don't draw it out any longer.

I sink down onto him, sobbing as he fills me. His roar laces through my sob, and he releases my ass to let me slap down onto his thighs. He fills me and stretches me and I can't take anymore, but I'm still stretching around him, and I'm filled by the burning aching swell of accepting his enormity inside me. He's fully impaled in me now, and I'm sitting on his thighs. My breasts are pressed against his face, and he takes the opportunity to bathe my nipples with kisses, and then he moves to the undersides, in the tender flesh where they meet my chest, the delicate inner skin, and then finally he takes my nipple into his mouth and suckles until I moan, and have to move.

I rise up, whimpering as he slicks out of me, until just the fat thick head remains inside me, and then I crush downward, a loud shriek leaving me as he spears into me. His voice joins mine, a guttural cry as he drives in, our hips meeting once more. He cups my breasts and lifts them to his mouth, worshipping them one and then the other in alternating rhythm.

I lift up again, and this time, I know there won't be any stopping. I clutch his shoulders for support as I rise, drawing him out, and then take another kiss from his mouth as we merge and crash together, our voices united in mutual ecstasy. Jesse clutches at me as I rise up again immediately, needing the fullness of him, needing the slide of his throbbing arousal through me. His hands hold me hard against his chest, holding him as he thrusts deep into me, my buttocks smashed flat against his thighs, my breasts in his face, his breath on my throat, his hair tickling and pungently male.

He falls backward without warning, taking me with him, and now I'm on top of him, straddling him, and his hands roam my back and my hips and my ass and then slide up to cup my breasts and flick my nipples, before palming my face and bringing my mouth to his.

"Ride me, Imogen," he breathes, our lips brushing, his words felt as much as heard.

I have no choice but to obey—it's what I need, more than my next breath, more than anything, I need to ride him to our mutual completion. There is nothing but sensation. Only him, only his scent, the powerful bulge of his muscles, the hard plane of his chest beneath me, his hips angular under mine, his arousal throbbing and hot and thick inside me, his hands exploring me, tangling in my hair and carving down my spine to cradle my ass, encouraging me to move.

Move; *move*.

I need it. I need the slide and grind—I claw my hands into his chest, leaning against him for balance, for support, my hair draping in brown curtains around our faces, blocking out all the world and even his room and the walls and the silver wash of the moonlight. I don't want this to end, I don't want to stop, I don't even want to come yet, I just want to feel this forever, for as long as I can. I've never been so full, never felt so filled, never felt so stretched. My core aches and tingles from the thickness of him spreading me so far open, and I'll know I'll be so sore it'll be hard to walk later, but it's perfect right now and I don't want to stop.

He thrusts, and I whimper; he drives deep, and now I can tilt my hips and sink against him and he goes even deeper and the sense of fullness and completion is so overwhelming another gasping sob is ripped from me. I sag forward, pulling away from him, moaning at the emptiness throughout me at the loss of him, and then I fall back, slamming my ass against him, *hard*. He groans in shock, and the next time I pull forward and begin my downward slide, he thrusts to meet me—his hips crash against me with a resounding slap, and his erection is all I feel, moving in me and through me, deep and deep and deeper. The next thrust, I lift up, balancing upright, stretching him away from his body and sitting down on him, impaling him deeper than ever.

His hands circle my hips and now he lifts, guiding me upward, and controlling the downward force, so I take him harder than ever, faster yet. I feel a crescendo rising in me, feel the swell in my core, the heat building and the pressure intensifying. My softness and his steel clash and merge in an ever-faster rhythm, slaps and moans filling the air, his grunts and my shrieks woven around each other.

I can hold it back no longer—I've been pushing the climax away, not wanting this to end, but he is relentless.

He senses me approaching the edge, perhaps feeling it in the way I clench around him, perhaps hearing it in the way my breath catches and the whimpers turn to screams. His hands cup my breasts and he relinquishes control over my rhythm, letting me take myself to the edge and past. He pinches my nipples, and I cry out—he flicks them, licks them, and I lose myself to the crushing force of my climax. I press my hands to his belly, just above the joining of our bodies, and now I can't stop the approach of the climax even if I wanted to. I embrace it, now.

"Come for me, Imogen," Jesse growls, and his words may as well be a command, one that I have no choice but to obey.

I writhe on top of him, grinding him through me, hips gyrating in wild, helpless circles, and my breasts shake and tremble and bounce and sway, and his hands are on my hips, encouraging me to go faster, faster—which I do. Faster, faster. My hands stab into my hair, yanking it back, and then as the climax becomes inevitable, a tsunami of smashing, inundating, scream-eliciting ecstasy.

"Jesse!" I cry, not just crying out loud, but actually sobbing, a scream of his name as I reach the cusp of climax.

"Let me feel you come, Imogen," he snarls, driving relentlessly into me. "Let me feel you come around me."

My right hand steals automatically to my core, two fingers pressing and circling, and I fling myself into oblivion.

"God that's fucking hot," he growls.

My eyes snap open and I realize he's watching me, devouring my every move—my left hand is clutched to my left breast, cupping and squeezing, while my right drives me to the furthest, highest peaks of orgasm; he has my left hip in a crushing, bruising grip I can't get enough of while his right kneads my right breast, flicking my nipple with his thumb, adding to the fury of my orgasm.

I'm screaming and screaming and screaming as I come—not wordless screams, though, but his name, over and over and over.

When the orgasm is wrung out of me, I'm left limp, and he's still hard inside me.

"God, Jesse," I whimper. "Oh my god."

His grin is predatory. "My turn," he rumbles.

"Your turn?" I breathe, incredulous. "You haven't come yet?"

"Did you feel me come? Did you hear me come?"

"No," I say, my voice faint.

"Because I didn't. I was waiting for you. I needed to feel you come first." He lifts me up, pushes me backward, off of him. "And now it's my turn."

"Oh—oh god," I whisper. "Please, Jesse, I need it." I reach for him, aching at the loss of him. "Give it to me."

I'm on my back now, and I've never wanted anything so badly as I want to feel him on top of me. He crawls over me, and I widen my thighs for him, welcoming him. Begging for him. His eyes rake over me, spread out beneath him, breasts drooping heavily to either side, belly heaving, breathless, from the still-quaking aftershocks of my orgasm, my core wet with soaking need, waiting for him.

"You are…*so* fucking beautiful, Imogen."

Now why the *hell* does that make me cry? Actual tears drip from my eyes, at his words, unbidden and unwelcome and unstoppable.

His thumbs wipe them away, and his expression is…I would say tender, if it wasn't for the ravenous, primal, seductive hunger in his eyes. I grasp him as he approaches me, taking his thick, latex-sheathed erection in my fist and guiding him to me. He lets me, shifting toward me, shuffling on his knees.

He doesn't just flop over me in the usual missionary position—oh no, Jesse O'Neill does nothing so pedestrian as that. He remains on his knees, and he takes my ankles in his hands and tucks my feet into his armpits, stretching my legs apart, thighs in a wide V, knees pushed backward—opening me wider than I've ever been, so I can take him deeper than I've ever been filled. I cry out, a strangled, sob-laden, shock-laced sound of abandon.

Jesse starts slowly, as if we've just begun. As if I haven't already come harder than I've ever come in my life. His hands cradle my inner thighs, gripping the tender silk of my flesh just to either side of our joining. And he drives, slowly, deliberately, into me.

Pulls out. Slides in. With each thrust, he adjusts his angle so every time he fills me it feels slightly different, a new sensation, a subtle difference in the way his arousal strikes into me. It's like he's searching for something with his thrusts, as if they're questing, seeking the perfect angle.

What is he looking for? I don't know.

I can't ask, I'm too breathless, too lost in sensation. Too lost in him.

And then, with a shattering detonation, he finds it. He finds the perfect angle. He knows when he finds it, too, because I scream without warning, my hips crashing helplessly against him. He thrusts now at that precise angle, faster and faster, each thrust dragging another scream out of me, forcing my hips to move, to match him, each thrust accompanied by a guttural grunt from him and a breathless scream from me.

"Jesse—" I gasp, "holy *shit*, Jesse, what are you doing to me?"

He has no words for me in reply, and I want none, need none—as long as he doesn't stop.

He increases his pace with each thrust, never varying his angle, and I'm shaking with the force of his lovemaking—if you can call it that. It's more carnal than that, I realize. It's far more primal and animal than lovemaking. The raw carnality of this is undeniable, exhilarating, freeing.

He's fucking me, and I can't get enough.

I abandon myself to the furious eroticism of this, with Jesse, taking each pounding thrust and begging for more with my screams and my driving hips and my clawing hands.

How long can he last? I feel like we've been moving together for so long, for hours. Longer than I've ever had sex, certainly. And he seems no closer to his own release than when he started. I'm losing it, losing the battle to keep from coming yet again. I can't deny myself the climax, can't deny him his mastery over my body. He knows exactly what he's doing.

"One more, Imogen," he snarls. "Give me one more."

"God—Jesse, I—oh god," I breathe. "I need yours."

"I'll give it to you—as soon as you give me one more." His strong, work-roughened hands cup my inner thighs, pressing my legs farther apart, until he's gripping me at the creases where thighs meet core, and his thumbs spread my stretched, tender hood further open, and then the wide pad of his thumb finds my hypersensitive center and circles, as if I needed further stimulation to reach the edge. "Now, Imogen—come for me, *right now*."

He barks the command, and I obey, yet again.

I thrash under him, writhe in his hands and grind against his thrusting erection. I take him deep, and ache with the fullness of him, and scream with the wrenching, spasmodic fury of my third orgasm.

He drives into me through wave after wave of climax, and I'm sobbing yet again.

And once more, I realize he's not done with me yet.

He pulls out of me entirely, and kneels over me. "Hands and knees, Imogen."

"Wh-what?" I squeak.

"Remember what I said, earlier? I want you on your hands and knees in my bed."

I need him. I need his orgasm. I need his release. I *need* it.

So, despite being shaky and weak and breathless from three earth-shaking orgasms, I roll to my belly and push up on my hands and knees. I've never in my life felt so self-conscious as I do in this moment, my big flabby ass in the air and spread out in front of him. My chest tightens, and my throat closes, and I'm close to losing the thread of arousal, so terrified am I that seeing me like this will turn him off.

Nicholas never wanted me like this.

As if the thought of my ex had been an audible thing, Jesse snarls. "Quit that shit, Imogen."

"Wha—? What?" I breathe.

"I can fucking feel you shutting down right now."

"I don't feel sexy like this," I admit, the words barely audible.

He actually laughs—he has the gall to laugh. "Imogen, Jesus. How the hell do you not know how goddamned perfect you are?"

I can only shake my head, trying not to cry. I twist to look at him over my shoulder. He meets my eyes, and there is nothing in his expression but pure, unfiltered need. God, he's gorgeous: Kneeling behind me, erection thick and upright and enormous and perfect, wet from me, his muscles shifting and powerful, his tanned skin slick and beaded with sweat from making me come so hard, his hair as untamed as the man himself, a jet-black mess of thick locks around his eyes and jaw. He's staring at me, his eyes devouring me. I cannot deny the arousal in his gaze, and he's looking at *me,* like this, in a position I find…not demeaning, not humiliating…I'm just self-conscious and unsure like this. But the look on his face as he kneels behind me is undeniable.

As is the reverence in his hands as he reaches out to palm my buttocks. "So fuckin' beautiful," he murmurs, his eyes sliding to mine. "How do you not understand that you're perfect? You're exquisite, Imogen."

I swallow, and breathe. "Just, like this, I feel like—"

He caresses the generous curve of my ass. "You think *this* is too big? Is that what you're so self-conscious about?"

I nod, not trusting my voice.

He presses his hips forward, rubbing his arousal against the left cheek. "What does this feel like, to you?" he says, taking himself in hand, rubbing himself against the other side now. "Does this feel like I'm turned off?"

I shake my head. "No."

"What's it feel like, Imogen?" He drags the head against my seam. "Don't you feel how turned on I am?"

"Yes," I breathe. "I feel it."

"I'm so hard it hurts," he snarls. "I've never been so fucking turned on my life."

"Don't lie to me, Jesse," I whisper.

He drags himself downward between the cheeks of my ass, a thick hard ridge between them, and then, using his fingers to find my entrance, notches himself inside me. "Does this feel like a lie?"

God, he feels bigger and harder than ever. "No…" I breathe, on a whimper.

He slides in, slowly. "You feel how hard I am?" he demands, his hands palming my ass.

"I feel it."

"I'm not gonna last ten seconds like this, Imogen," he growls. "So get ready."

"Jesse, god…" I gasp, feeling him push into me. "I'm ready."

"Are you?" he murmurs. "I'm not sure you are."

"I feel you, Jesse. You're so big, so hard."

He pulls back, and drives in, so, so, so slowly. As if savoring every millimeter of slick sliding wetness of me. "Because of *you*. Because seeing you like this, on your knees for me, seeing this ass of yours—yes, this big, gorgeous, juicy *perfect* ass—" he caresses the round weight of me as he speaks, a tender, reverent, worshipful touch, "—all spread out just for me, getting to take you like this, feeling you like this…it's fucking heaven, Imogen."

"Jesse…" I gasp, his words hitting me as hard as his slow, inexorable thrusts. "Keep talking. Tell me everything. I need to hear it from you."

He leans over me, reaching under to cup my breasts, pushing into me, his hips squashing hard against my ass. "You need to hear me say it? I told you before how much I love this," he says, one hand caressing my butt as the other kneads my breast. "How much I love your ass."

"I don't think I believed you," I admit.

"Do you believe me now?" he demands, leaning

backward again, upright on his knees behind me, both hands on my buttocks now, pulling their heft apart so he can drive deeper with his slow thrusts.

"I'm starting to," I say.

"What else do you need to hear to believe? Your ass is perfect, Imogen." He has my ass in a palmed grip, braced for each thrust. "I can't get enough of it."

"Take all of it, then," I say. "Show me how much you like it."

He speeds up, as if he can't help it. Each thrust finds his hips slapping against my butt, and each thrust drives him into me so I whimper, and gasp, and shriek at the beautiful penetration of him. And then, on his next thrust, he pats his hands against my buttocks.

"How about that?" he says, "you like that?"

I nod, turning to watch him over my shoulder. And, in this position—no longer on my hands and knees, but only on my knees, my entire torso flattened against the mattress to lift my ass high into the air, I can see the beauty in my curves. I see the sensual eroticism in the uplifted spread of my ass, in the curve of my spine, in the power in my legs. And now, as he taps my buttocks in time with each thrust, I begin to feel the burn of arousal scorching away the doubts, a conflagration of need searing away my self-consciousness.

He smacks my ass harder. "You like that,

Imogen?" he demands.

I nod. "Yeah," I breathe. "Do it again."

He drives into me, his hips smacking hard even as his hand slaps even harder. The sting is beautiful, adding to the crashing heat of my building climax.

"You like it when I spank you?" he growls.

"Yes, Jesse."

"Say it."

"I like it when you spank my ass," I breathe, almost breaking into giggles hearing myself say that. But it's too dirty and too arousing to be funny—especially as I realize he's actively holding back.

His jaw is clenched, and his thrusts are more measured, and he's gasping raggedly, growling with each thrust. I need his orgasm. God, I need it. I've had three—almost four now—and I want to feel him lose control.

"Jesse, please," I whisper, brazenly begging. *"Please."*

"Please what, Imogen?"

"Come," I breathe. "Give it to me. Spank me, fuck me—let me feel you come."

"I don't want it to end," he says, even as he thrusts harder. "I don't want to stop."

"I don't either." I push back into his thrusts, now, and my orgasm is not being brought on by his touch or my own, nor by his mastery over my body, but by raw arousal, by the raging, driving, coruscating need for him brought on by our joining. "But I need you. I need to feel you come. Please, Jesse."

He's growling helplessly, and his thrusts speed up to a wild, manic, furious onslaught. He stops spanking me and just claws his hands into the trembling, bouncing flesh of my ass as he thrusts; his growls turn to grunts, and then his grunts turn to a roar, and he's gone, utterly animal now, all control lost. I watch him over my shoulder and give myself to the moment, my own climax—my fourth—tearing through me like a wildfire, my screams meeting his bellowing snarl of orgasm.

Each of his thrusts is accompanied by a greedy caress of my buttocks, and this, the way he palms and kneads and caresses my ass as he gives me his orgasm, does more to erase my self-consciousness than anything he could say. He could conceivably fool me and lie to me with his words, but he can't fake that, not as obviously gone as he is into the depths of climax. His possessive appreciation for me in that moment of abandon cannot be faked.

"Ohhhh…" he breathes, his moment of release turning him breathless, his roars and grunts gentled to a ragged, helpless groan. "Ohhhh fuck, *Imogen*…"

I'm with him, then, squeezing and clenching around him, crying out, taking each slow hard grinding thrust with a backward drive, wanting it deeper, needing him harder.

We come in unison.

I feel him release even as my climax crescendos inside me, turning me into a writhing, thrashing, lust-crazed beast.

His orgasm is endless, it feels like, thrust after thrust of grunting, groaning, cursing release, his hands slapping, cupping, gripping, kneading, and ca-ressing my ass through it all.

Finally, after a beautiful eternity, I collapse for-ward and he goes with me, all of his weight on me for a moment, leaving me unable to breathe and feeling exhilarated.

And then he rolls over, and I—out of some kind of instinct I didn't know I possessed—roll with him, needing to be close, needing his strength and heat and hardness and comfort after what we just experienced together.

I hear his heart under my ear, a slamming, frenet-ic, racing beat. Even in the intimacy of cradling me in his arms, he finds a way to keep a hand on the outer curve of my ass, which makes me smile a secret, pri-vate smile of delight.

I drowse.

But I feel him, still—Jesse, his breathing ragged still, his heart hammering, his hands clutching me.

He's not relaxing—he's tense.

I lift up on an elbow and look at him. His expression is usually open and readable, his emotions on his sleeve. For once, I can't read him.

"Jesse?" I say.

He glances at me. "Hi," he murmurs.

"Thank you," I say, smiling at him.

He frowns, wrinkling his brow. "What? Why are you thanking me?"

I laugh. "Because that was—that was the most—" I shake my head, unable to encapsulate how I feel in words. "You made me feel—"

"How you should always feel," he cuts in. "How it should always be."

"But that's not how it's always been, and I don't think I've ever felt how you made me feel, so...thank you." I rest my hand on his chest, lean up on an elbow against him—his eyes roam my body, his hand still clutches the curve of my hip, but he's tensed and restless, and his eyes won't meet mine.

"You shouldn't be thanking *me*—I should be thanking *you*," he says.

"For what?"

"For the gift of yourself," he says. "For...just for...*you*."

I blink, unsure how to respond to that, and he won't look at me.

He shifts under me, restless.

"Are you okay?" I ask.

He nods. "I just need to get this off and clean up," he says.

I roll away, and he gets up. I watch him go, enjoying the sight of his beautiful nude body as he goes into the bathroom. I kick my feet under the blankets—the bed had been neatly made, and the vigor of our sex sent all the blankets and sheets askew. Now that the heat of the moment has faded, the air is drying my sweat and cooling me off.

When Jesse returns, he stands a few feet away from the bed, staring at me. As if trying to come to terms with the sight of me in his bed. I didn't bother covering with the sheet, only tugging up enough to warm my legs. His eyes skate over me, as if he can't help devouring me with his eyes, but his expression is not one of arousal now, but of...

Discomfort.

Tension.

There's an awkwardness in the room that I don't know how to identify, how to rectify, what to do with.

I want him to climb back into the bed with me, and I want him to touch me, and to kiss me. I want to feel his body against mine. I want to drowse with him in the silence and the afterglow. I want to cling to him.

I want to slide into arousal with him, and take

him a dozen different ways before dawn.

He blinks at me. "I—" but he doesn't finish.

And realization hits me. The usual clichés apply—apply—like a freight train, like a ton of bricks, with all the force of a hurricane. They all apply.

He doesn't want me in his bed, now that it's over.

He's never brought anyone here.

Which means he doesn't do…this. The afterward scene. I bet when he's done, he leaves. Maybe a drink or a smoke between, some chitchat, another go, and then he leaves. That's why he'd never bring anyone here—he can't make his escape. If we'd done this at my house, he'd have made an excuse for leaving. He has to work early. Maybe fake an emergency phone call from James—but no, it's one thirty in the morning, and James is out of town, and Jesse guaranteed no emergencies.

So what now?

I realize my mistake—I assumed intimacy where there is none.

This was just sex.

For him, and for me.

Incredible, stunning, breathtaking, earth-shaking, life-changing, expectation-shattering sex.

But still just…sex.

And now it's over.

The cuddles afterward, resting my head on his

chest, listening to his heartbeat, his arm around me, cradling me…that's not what this is, and not what he wants. He never promised that, or anything like it.

I choke back whatever stupid thoughts and emotions are boiling inside me—I deny them, shove them down, shut them down, and fake a breezy, unaffected casual confidence I in no way feel.

"So, I should go."

Jesse doesn't react. Fists clenched at his sides, jaw ticking, chest rising and falling—if I didn't know better I'd think he was warring with his own thoughts and feelings.

I kick my feet free of the blankets and leave the bed. I don't feel sexy or sensual or powerful anymore, but somehow, neither do I feel self-conscious in my nakedness. I wait for a response, but, uncharacteristically, I get nothing from him.

I'm baffled, now. I stare at him, trying to figure this moment out. He's not the single-word, grunty, macho, no-reply kind of guy. I've known those, and dislike it intensely. You know what's sexy? A guy who can communicate. That's what I like about Jesse, what has me falling for him—

Oh.

Oh shit.

Oh no.

I breathe through my panic. I'm not falling for

him. I'm not. I can't be.

I make for the bedroom door, naked, panicking inside, still faking a confident casualness that's less and less believable by the second. I need to get away from him before I lose the ability to fake it anymore. I'm a terrible actress—I don't fake orgasms, and I don't fake emotions. This feels illicit, yucky, trying to make him feel like I'm unaffected when everything inside is a mess.

I want to cling to him—I want to beg for more of him. Give me more orgasms. Let him taste me. Take me until I'm ragged with exhaustion.

But I can't have that, it seems.

That's not what this is.

He got what he wanted, and so did I.

I don't let myself run, as I head for the stairs. I force myself to not hurry, to act like everything is hunky-dory fantastic fabulous, like I'm ready to go, like I got what I wanted and I'm as done as he is.

I feel him following me, feel his eyes on me, and feel the weight of unspoken words between us.

I ignore it.

I dress in the kitchen, facing away from him— step into my thong, tug it into place; hook my bra in front and spin it around, shrug into the straps, tuck the cups into place, tighten the straps a hint; step into the dress, zip it, and find my purse.

Where are my heels? I had them on—how long? I don't remember. Did I have them on during sex? Maybe. I think I had them on for part of it, and then kicked them off at some point. I don't know where they are and I don't care. I just need to get out of here.

"Imogen," Jesse says, sounding wildly uncharacteristically hesitant. "I'm not—I don't want you to think—"

"I have to go," I say, going for breezy and fine. "Can you drop me off? If not, I can call a cab."

"I'll take you," he murmurs. "Cab would take an hour to get out here."

I wonder what we could do with that hour? I think it, but I don't say it. We're past that, I think.

Why does that hurt? The loss of the witty, clever, lascivious banter hurts.

He finds his jeans on the kitchen floor and shoves his legs into them one after the other, tugs them up, tucks his junk into them and carefully zips them up. His shirt is by the front door, but he ignores it, finding instead a faded black pullover Blackhawks hoodie hanging from a hook by the front door. He tugs it on and nudges open the front door. He's out onto the porch before he stops abruptly.

He snorts in frustration. "Keys. Need keys."

It should be amusing to see Jesse this obviously flustered, but it's not—it hurts. It's confusing. And I don't want to ask what's wrong because I don't want to know the answer. I wait on the porch while he snags his keys, phone, and wallet, and then we both climb his truck.

The drive back to Billy Bar is long and quiet.

He's deep in thought. He has his window open, his left wrist draped over the wheel, right elbow on the console between us, fist clenched, his thumb repeatedly and obsessively switching from finger to finger, cracking the knuckles.

I try to speak a dozen times, but can't figure what to say that won't open a can of worms I know I can't handle.

I just need to go home and be alone. Maybe ice my vagina, because *holy shit*, am I going to be sore I'll savor the soreness, and I'll hoard the memory of sex with Jesse.

Back in the parking lot of Billy Bar, he pulls to a stop next to my little POS Camry, slamming the shifter into park. I don't get out right away, hoping he'll say something. Hoping, deep down, that he'll say or do something to salvage this situation.

He doesn't, and I can't hold back a sigh.

I shove open the door and unbuckle. "Thanks for the ride," I say. And then, in one last attempt, I smirk at him. "And for driving me back to my car."

His smile is slow and unsure. "Imogen, listen—"

I hold up my hand. "Jesse, don't. I'll ask you no questions, you tell me no lies."

"It's just that—"

"Thank you, Jesse. You made me feel beautiful and wanted in a way that—in a way I'm not sure I've ever felt, ever in my life. So thank you for that." I smile, but it's sad, regretful, and I can't hide that. "I'm going to go now, Jesse. Goodbye."

"Imogen, wait."

I don't. I close the truck door, unlock my Camry—the old-fashioned way, with my key in the lock—get in, start the motor. Thank god it starts—with a sick, rattling squeal, but it starts.

I pull away, seeing Jesse jumping from his truck and jogging after me—I hear him telling me to wait.

But I don't.

I don't want to know his reasons. I know he has them, and I'm sure they're good reasons.

He was clear at the start that he doesn't do heartbreak. He keeps things clean. I went into this knowing exactly what it was—no-strings, no-expectations sex. And as sex goes, it was goddamn spectacular. Fireworks. Ten out of ten.

Hell, twenty out of ten.

But that's all it was, and I don't need to hear what he has to say. Excuses, reasons, logic, justifications—I just need to clarify my own emotions, get myself clear of the assumptions I was fostering. The hope I was nurturing.

I make the fatal mistake of looking in the rear-view mirror—and I see Jesse, hands in his hair, looking distraught.

I take the extra precaution of shutting off my phone as I drive home, just in case he tries to call.

I don't cry, but I want to.

FOURTEEN

I HIDE FROM JESSE AND AUDRA FOR THREE DAYS. THEY both blow up my phone, but after six calls from each, I shut it off and leave it off. I ask for, and receive without question, three days off from Dr. Waverley. I buy a plane ticket to Florida, rent a convertible at the airport, and I visit my parents. They're overjoyed at my unexpected visit, as I haven't gotten down to see them more than once or a twice a year for the past several years, even though I talk to them regularly.

We don't have the kind of relationship where I would ever, ever, ever talk about what's currently bothering me—they certainly sense it, as I'm out of sorts and mopey most of the time. Instead, they go out of their way to make sure we have lots of fun, keeping the conversation light and happy. We drink wine on their back porch and go see movies at the luxury theater nearby, and go to a comedy show and binge on a season of a period drama on their Netflix account and, honestly, it's a much-needed getaway from everything.

I finally turn on my phone in the waiting area at my gate while waiting to board my flight home: I have nineteen texts, mostly from Audra, and several from Jesse. I don't read the ones from Jesse, because I'm chickenshit. The preview line for the thread reads: *—always been bad at that, and I'm sorry. Call me if you want.*

I don't dare read the rest.

Audra's texts are angry. Mostly along the lines of how dare I ignore her, we're fighting, I promised her details, she knows I'm having a breakdown and if I don't call her we're over, we're totally having a BFF breakup.

I shut my phone off for the flight back home; leave it off for the drive home. It's late evening by the time I get back to my neighborhood, and as I prepare to turn onto my street, I have a panic attack. What if I go there and he's there. He could totally be there, if he's not there already. If I see him, I'll spill everything.

And I don't dare do that.

We had casual sex. That's it. No big deal. People do it all the time. He's a pro at it. I'm not, but I can figure it out. Audra will teach me how. Maybe I'll go to a club with her and pick up some younger guy and we'll have casual sex and I'll become a casual sex junkie like Audra and Jesse.

The thought is so patently ridiculous that I actually laugh at myself—as I drive right past my house.

There's only one place to go, and it takes me less than ten minutes to get there.

Audra's place is a sixth-floor condo, and I have a key. I'm not thinking as I let myself into her building and ride the elevator up—I'm acting on instinct, avoiding thinking or examining my emotions until I know it's safe, and it won't be safe until I'm in Audra's condo, wrapped up in her giant king-size microfleece throw blanket, eating Thai delivery and drinking a vat of wine.

I let myself into her condo, and it's not until I've let the door close behind me that I realize I've made a serious mistake.

Audra is bent over the arm of her couch, miniskirt up over her butt, a guy at least ten years younger than her drilling her for all he's worth. Audra is biting down on a throw pillow to muffle her shrieks, and he's muffling his grunts by biting her shoulder.

They don't even notice me at first.

Actually, they don't notice me at all, and I'm too stunned to move.

He finishes with one last hard slam, grunting, biting her, and pulls out.

She gasps, spitting out the pillow, straightens—and

shrieks in surprise when she sees me. "Imogen! Holy shit! What—what are you—?"

The guy is blanking totally. His jeans are around his ankles, his shirt hanging off the back of the couch—he's still hard, the condom full, and he's dazed, staring at me, and then at Audra, and then back to me again.

My mouth is open, and I'm struggling to look away.

Audra recovers first. "Price—go clean up," she snaps, shoving her skirt down.

He blinks at me, and then her. "Uh. Yeah."

He tugs his jeans and underwear up most of the way—awkwardly, clumsily, and vanishes into the bathroom.

I blink at Audra. "I—I'm sorry. I didn't—I wasn't thinking. I'll leave."

Audra snorts. "Don't be stupid. Just give me ten seconds to get rid of this guy."

"Audra, for real, I'm leaving. I'm sorry I interrupted."

Audra grabs my arm to prevent me from leaving. "Imogen, please, it's totally fine." She grins at me. "He got his O, I got mine, and we're good. One and done, babe, you know that."

I'd normally give her friendly grief about that, but under the circumstances, I dare not.

A moment later the guy, Price, emerges from the bathroom, and beelines for Audra, snagging his shirt on the way and digging his phone from his pocket. "So, can I get your number?" he asks. "So we can meet up later?"

Audra pats his cheek, her tone cold and condescending. "We talked about this before I brought you up, Price."

"But I thought—"

"That I'd change my mind once I got a taste of the D?" she interrupts, her tone amused; he clearly did think exactly that. "Nope. You can go, now, buddy."

"Audra," I hiss. "At least be nice."

She rolls her eyes at me, but offers him a nice smile and a less bitchy tone of voice. "I really did enjoy myself, Price. Or rather, you. But I'm not really in a place for anything more than that, okay?" She rolls the excuse out with practiced smoothness. "It's just where I'm at. It's nothing personal."

He nods. "I gotcha." He offers her a grin that's probably meant to be sexy and charming, but just seems goofy, at least to me. "If you change your mind—"

"You'll be the first person I call," Audra says, ushering him to the door and out of it. "Bye, Price. Thanks!"

He waves and grins and tries to get another word

in even as she closes the door in his face, turns the lock and attaches the chain *and* the deadbolt, and then whirls on me.

"What the hell happened, Imogen Catherine Irving?" Audra demands. "You vanished on me! No calls, no texts, no details, nothing. You ignore me for *three* days, and when I hunt you down at your new job your boss says you took time off to go visit your folks? Spill it, bitch!"

I head for the couch, but think better of it considering what I just saw. "You couldn't even get to the bedroom with him?"

Audra laughs. "Oh, we made it to the bedroom. And the bathroom. And the kitchen. He was getting ready to leave and I decided I wanted one more. He's young and virile enough that he had one more in him."

I cringe. "Oh."

She looks at me like I'm stupid. "You think I'd go to all the trouble of bringing a dude to my condo for one measly fuck? Forget the one and done motto. If that's all I'm after, I'll jump him in the car. No, they don't get to come up here unless I'm sure they can go the distance."

I make a face. "Audra."

She just laughs. "What? I met him at the gym a week ago. I let him take me to his place after a workout for a nooner, and we got it on like *Donkey Kong*. He had the goods and the stamina, so I let him take me on a date, *and* I brought him home. He's lucky. Most guys don't even get a date out of me."

I laugh. "God, you're crazy."

"Hey, I have very high standards. My condo is a sacred space, and I only allow the best sex up here."

I sigh. "I wish I could be more like you right now."

"You wear your heart on your sleeve, honey." She frowns, and then turns her attention to me. "Oh. Ohhhhh. Something *happened*."

"You think I'd vanish to Florida for no reason?"

Audra eyes me. "Do I need to order Thai and open a bottle of wine?"

Too overwhelmed to care anymore, I slump onto her couch—on the opposite end from where the action took place. "Yes. Order everything on the menu, and a case of wine."

"Oh boy."

While we're waiting for the food to come, Audra takes a quick shower and emerges in her bathrobe, hair wet around her shoulders, makeup gone—without makeup and her hair loose and damp instead of in a tight updo, she looks both older and younger than usual. Softer, less polished, less perfect, but more beautiful in a personal, informal sort of way. I realize the face she puts on for just about everyone—even me, most of the time—is a careful mask meant to hide a facet of herself I think few ever see.

The food comes and I pay for it and set it out while Audra pours wine, and we curl up side by side on her couch, devouring food and wine before we get into the conversation; it's our way, for as long as I can remember—food and wine, and then talk.

"It was either really bad, or really good," Audra guesses, after we're both full.

"Really good," I answer.

"Too good?"

I nod. "Way too good."

"So take me through you running away to Florida, and not answering your best friend of almost thirty years."

"Stop making me feel old. I'm having a hard enough time as it is."

"Fine. Not even twenty-five years, then."

I grimace. "That's not much better."

Audra whacks me on the arm. "Quit being a crybaby. Age happens, get over it. You know what's nice about hitting forty? I can get away with not giving a shit in a way I couldn't in my twenties or thirties."

"My age is not the issue."

"Then what is the issue?"

"The sex was mind-blowing," I say. "Best sex of my life."

Audra raises her eyebrow. "And…?"

"And when it was over it was just…over. I rolled into him, you know? Out of instinct or something. And he actually did hold me like that for a minute, but then he clearly was trying to figure out how to get me out of his bed and out of his house without pissing me off."

Audra winces. "Ouch."

"I tried to go into it without expectations, Audra. I really did. I knew going in that he didn't—as he put it in so many words—'do heartbreak,'" I use air quotes around his phrase. "He made it clear that he doesn't do relationships, or long-term, or any of that. I *knew it*. And I'm not even looking for it myself. I'm not even two months divorced yet. I went into it with him *knowing* it wasn't anything but casual sex."

"And you still latched on?" she conjectures.

I nod. "I haven't really processed it yet. I ran."

"He kicked you out?"

I shake my head. "No. I acted like I didn't care. Like I had to go. He drove me to my car at Billy Bar, and I left. He tried to explain, but I just—I didn't want to hear his excuses."

Audra is quiet for a while. "So, let me get this straight. You and Jesse have mind-blowing, best-ever sex, you go to cuddle, he freezes, and you bolt."

I shrug. "More or less. He wouldn't say anything.

He always has something to say, Audra, *always*. But he just looked at me like—like he didn't know what to do with me now that we'd had sex. Like, this chick is in my bed and I can't figure out how to get her out of it. He said he never brings anyone to his house—or rather, that he never had, until me. So his usual method of escape was out of the question. Like, usually he just leaves, you know? So I made it easy on him—I acted like it was all totally fine, and told him I had to go."

"How many times did you go?"

I shrug. "Only once, but it was…a *lot*."

Audra is silent again. "What did he actually *say* to you?"

"I didn't really give him much of a chance to say anything, actually. He tried to make excuses, you know—" I turn my voice as deep and growly and gruff as possible, mimicking him, "Imogen, listen, it's just that I, you know…" I trail off and resume in my normal voice. "That kind of thing."

Audra pours us each another glass of wine, and takes time thinking in silence, drinking her wine and staring hard at me over the rim.

After a long time, she sets her wine on the coffee table and takes my hand in hers. "Imogen, honey, I think you fucked up."

I'm taken aback. "What?" That's not what I was expecting her to say.

"I don't want you to be like me—you're you, and I'm me. You know what I went through, why I'm like I am about guys and sex. You don't have to be that way. You went through a shitty situation, and I get that. He was never good enough for you, and I was never shy about saying that. And listen, I'm your best friend, right? So I won't be shy about saying I fucking *told* you so. I've never said it, but I'll say it now."

I rear back, stung. "Are you serious?"

She just lifts her eyebrow. "Oh, I'm not done, babe, so hold your offense until the end." She stabs my chest. "I *told you* Nicholas was a douchebag, and that I didn't trust him. When you slept with him the first time, you said it wasn't amazing, and I told you to dump his ass then. I told you he'd hurt you. I told you you deserved better. You insisted you knew what you were doing, and I let it go. I stood up for you at your wedding even though you knew I disagreed with you marrying him. I told you I had a car waiting so you could run at the last second, and I wasn't kidding. I had a cab and a getaway driver ready and waiting. I even had an overnight bag packed for you. But you married him anyway."

Tears sting my eyes. "Audra, come on—"

"No, you need to listen." She takes my wine from me and sets it down, and I know she's serious as a heart attack if she doesn't want us drinking during this. "Nicholas was only doing exactly what was in his nature. He never loved you, and you never loved him. You wanted stability, you wanted to be nurtured, and you wanted to nurture." She's sympathetic now, but keeps going. "You wanted kids. You wanted a family."

I'm so hurt and angry I can't speak. "Audra, I didn't come over here for this."

"Too damn bad. You're here now and this is what you're getting." She pauses, breathes in slowly and lets it out even more slowly. "He was never going to be able to give you what you wanted. Not in any way. He dulled your spark, Imogen." She sounds emotional, more so than I've ever heard her. "You gave him everything you had, literally and metaphorically. And now it's over, it's finally over, and you're still desperate for the one thing you've always wanted."

"Goddammit, Audra," I hiss. *"Don't."*

"You were an accident. Your parents love the hell out of you, and they did their best, but they were retired by the time you were in high school. You're lonely. You were lonely in college, you were lonely when you met Nicholas, and you're lonelier than ever now." She smiles sadly at me. "And trust me, I get it. But with Nicholas, you had to know, deep down, that he was a slimy piece of shit and that he'd only end up hurting you. You settled for a douche-canoe, and you paid the price. Or, rather, you got what you paid for.

You can't play the victim, here. You suspected he was cheating on you and you stayed with him. Even after you had proof, you took another *year* to divorce him. You were willfully blind and stupid. Yeah, it hurts, but it's over. He doesn't deserve another second of your time or thought, and certainly not you feeling some ridiculous sense of being heartbroken."

"I got what I deserved, you're saying."

"You didn't deserve it, no. He was a piece of shit. He stamped out your fire. You used to be a fire-cracker. You used to be down for anything. You used to be wild and fun and take no shit. I realize it was a response to how you grew up, but it was fun. He dulled you. And now you're just starting to get that back. This guy, Jesse, he's made you more alive than you've been in twelve years, Imogen! You feel that, you see it, and you're scared of it. He makes you feel things you're realizing Nicholas *should* have made you feel but never ever fucking did, and you're angry at yourself for wasting twelve years of your life on that bastard."

I can't see. Can't breathe.

She's not done. "Guess what, Imogen? You don't get that time back. Just like I don't get back this time I'm spending on guys half my age who are never anything but toys and distractions. I recognize that. But you know what you can do? You can change what happens. You don't have to react based on how Nicholas made you feel. You don't have to be the victim."

"I'm not playing the fucking victim!" I shout.

"Yes, honey. You are." She squeezes my hand. "You made a shitty choice, Imogen. Now you have to move on."

"What does any of this have to do with Jesse?"

"You fucked up, that's what."

"How?"

"He's bent over backward to do things for you. Tens of thousands of dollars of work, for free or dirt cheap. He's charmed you, wooed you, and made you feel sexy again when Nicholas made you feel like shit. You've had fun with him. You *like* him. He challenges you. You've been on a dry spell for a year and a half— we both know that. Which means you were, on top of everything else, horny as hell. Desperate for sex. Desperate for actual P-in-V sex, with a man. And he made it easy. He presented a no-strings scenario without making you feel cheap, and you went for it.

"I encouraged it because, if nothing else, you'd get sex and hopefully stop being such a whiny, reclusive stick-in-the-mud. But the problem is, not only have you not had sex in a year and a half, you also haven't had any kind of validation or intimacy or male attention in a year and a half. And, unlike me, you can't fool yourself into thinking good sex is a decent stand-in for any of that. So you were desperate for just basic *attention*, period. And Jesse gave it to you. Sounds like he gave it to you *good*, too, girlfriend, because even crazy nympho Lee never left you saying the sex was mind-blowing, best of your life. And it's not like Lee was your first by any stretch of the imagination."

She's dropped so much on me at this point that I don't even know where to start, but she still isn't done.

"And yeah, maybe your guy Jesse is a player or a hookup artist or whatever, but from what you told me, it sounds like he was trying to figure out how to *keep* you in his bed, not get rid of you. You panicked, because you're scared of falling in love. And you're scared of being hurt even worse than Nicholas hurt you, because you can see yourself feeling things for Jesse you never did for Nicholas. So you ditched him. You bolted. He may have driven you home, but you didn't give him a chance to say boo, much less process how *he* may have been feeling about you. Because it sounds to me like he has feelings for you, Imogen, and maybe he's as confused and mixed up and scared as you are, but he's a dude, and when dudes are faced with emotions they don't understand or can't handle, they shut down. But instead of seeing that, you reacted out of your own bullshit, shut him out, and ran."

"Fuck," I whisper.

"Yeah. And something tells me that Jesse could be the best thing that ever happened to you."

"He already is," I say.

"He brought you to his *home*. It's a big deal for me, so I'm guessing it is for him."

"So that guy, Price—"

"This isn't about me."

"Audra."

"Fine. I really liked him. But he's too young, too broke, and too emotionally needy. I'd end up momming him as much as I fucked him, and I'm not here for that. So he had to go. But he really was sweet and cute and great in bed, and if I was fifteen years younger and a lot less jaded and fucked up, I'd have let him stay…for who knows how long."

"Audra—"

"We can talk about me another time, okay? Forget Price. My point is, taking someone home when that's way outside how you do something—that's a big deal. He wouldn't do that lightly. He wouldn't have done that if he was expecting to make a getaway after a quick fuck. You only bring someone into your own home if you're willing to deal with the next day awkwardness."

"How do you deal with next day awkwardness?" I ask, honestly curious.

"If I bring a guy home and I'm ready for him

to go? Usually I suggest we go out to breakfast separately. Or I blow him and then make excuses about work."

"Why blow him first?"

She shrugs, grinning. "Because a guy will do pretty much anything you want after you've sucked him off. It softens the blow of asking him to leave. Also, I just like giving head."

I shake my head. "You do? Like, you actually enjoy it?"

She wrinkles her nose and grins at me. "Well, yeah." She frowns at me. "I mean, do I enjoy it like I enjoy getting eaten out? No, but it's a different kind of enjoyment. Just being honest about it, I like the power of it. I like the manipulation of it. I get off knowing just my hands and mouth can make a guy desperate and willing to do whatever I want. And, under the right circumstances, I like making a guy feel good. But that's a different kind of BJ."

"It is?" I've given them, of course, but only as foreplay, and usually in a quid-pro-quo sort of scenario, so I've never thought about giving oral in the way Audra's talking about it.

She laughs. "I mean, of course. " She sighs and waves a hand. "You're distracting me from the topic. Get me talking about giving head and I lose my train of thought."

I roll my eyes at her, laughing. "Audra, you're too much."

"So say all the men," she quips, and I don't think she's joking. "My point is, I don't think you gave Jesse a fair shot."

"He sent me texts and left voicemails, but I've been avoiding them—and him."

"You came straight here from the airport, I'm guessing?"

I nod. "Yeah."

She shakes her head, sighing. "This time, I'm not gonna tell you what I think you should do. This one is all on you. What I will end my rant with is this it doesn't have to be love, as in True Love, capital T, capital L, with hearts and bubbles and glitter and a mushy happily-ever-after ending. It can be something real for both of you without being that. You can have your cake and eat it too, in this case, Imogen—there *is* something between casual no-strings sex and diamond rings and wedding vows."

I sigh. "Maybe you're right."

"You know I'm right." She holds out her hand flat, palm up. "Your phone."

I hesitate, but then hand her my phone—she knows my passcode, of course, and uses it to open up my thread with Jesse. We read his messages together—there are seven.

Jesse: *Can we talk? Even on the phone?*

Jesse: *Imogen? I don't like how we left things, and I want to say a few things.*

Jesse: *I don't like trusting important things to text messages. There's too much chance of things getting misunderstood. Call me. Or tell me you're home and I'll come over.*

Jesse: *Screw it. It's been two days and you're not answering your phone. So if you don't answer this message, I'm coming over, and I'll wait until you're home to say what I have to say.*

Jesse: *You're not home. I waited twelve hours and you never showed up. And since you know how I am, you know I didn't spend those twelve hours idle. So...your welcome.*

Jesse: **you're*, because when your mother is a retired English teacher, you're required to have proper grammar even via text.*

Jesse: *Still not saying everything, but I'll say at least this much, in case you ever read these. Or maybe you're reading them and ignoring me, I'm not sure. Whatever. Here it is. I told you I had something like a serious relationship once, and that's true. There's a lot more to the story, and it's a very, very hard thing for me to talk about. But it's made me approach relationships hesitantly, to say the least. I tend to clam up when I'm overwhelmed or feeling emotions I'm not comfortable with, and all I'll say is that I definitely felt things with you that made me clam up, because of that long and hard to talk about story. I've always been bad about that, and I'm sorry. Call me if you want.*

The voicemails are just him saying "Call me" in a gruff, terse tone.

I click the phone back to sleep and look at Audra. "I fucked up."

"Yeah, babe, you did."

"What do I do?"

"I mean, if it was me, I'd show up where he worked, tell him I was sorry, and then blow him. And maybe bring food with me, because men think with their stomachs as much as their dicks." Audra shrugs. "But that's just me."

I consider.

And actually, she may be on to something.

She sees the speculative look in my eye. "Imogen, I was joking."

I frown at her. "No, you weren't."

"Okay, no, I wasn't. But that's not the kind of thing you do."

"No, but you also told me this is a chance in my life to become someone I've never been. Reinvent myself. And god knows after the way Jesse treated me the other night, I probably owe him a little something."

Audra leans closer to me and, on cue, we both

grab our wine. "Is it finally time for details?" she asks, wiggling her eyebrows suggestively.

And so, I give her details. Every last little one.

When I'm done, Audra sinks against the couch, dramatically fanning her face. "Whooooo boy! And he has three friends, you say? Each sexier than the last?"

I shrug. "I mean, I personally think Jesse is the sexiest, but something tells me you'd find Franco pretty damn jaw-dropping."

She quirks an eyebrow. "Franco? Is that first name or last?"

I laugh, frowning. "Actually, I don't know. It's the only name I've heard for him."

She eyes me speculatively. "I have an idea, if you're serious about doing what I said."

"And what's your idea?" I ask, wary.

She just grins lasciviously. "Let's just say it'll let you make your move, Jesse's girl, and give me a chance to check out this allegedly jaw-dropping Mr. Franco."

I cackle when I hear her plan. "You know what? Let's do it," I say.

FIFTEEN

"THIS WAS STUPID," I HISS TO AUDRA, AS WE approach the Waverley job site. "I'm not doing this."

Audra grabs my arm and keeps me walking. "It's very stupid, which is why you're doing it. You never do anything dumb and reckless. And this is calculated recklessness." She speaks casually, not whispering. "It's to a purpose."

"Remind me what that purpose is, again?"

"Apologize for running from him, not giving him a chance to say anything, and then avoiding him, and not answering his calls or messages. And to then communicate that you're still into him. And, as a side bonus, you try something new, even if it's a little scary at first. Because trust me, it is. But it's exhilarating and fun and a hell of a rush. And he'll *love* it. Which means, if he's half the lover you say he is, he'll repay you a million times over, because to him, giving you multiple orgasms during sex is what he's *supposed* to do, and to him, you don't owe him anything because he doesn't keep score. Or if he does, it's one for him for every three for you. Either way, you win."

"What if someone sees?"

"It'll be his buddies, and they won't care."

"I'll care if they see me doing that. I know them. I've drunk beer with them."

"Then don't get caught." She grins, tosses her hair, sucks in a deep breath, and tugs her top down a little bit. "Showtime. Do I look okay?"

"Audra, you look as incredible as ever. What about me?"

She glances at me. "Bitch, please. He'll get hard at first sight." She shoots me a look. "Promise me you're not kidding about Franco being hot."

I laugh. "You won't believe me until you see him."

"Because I need something jaw-dropping in my life. I've had a streak of guys that have been, at best, decently hot." She grins salaciously. "And my jaw needs a little workout, anyway."

I don't say anything because I'm pretty sure if anyone can give Audra a run for her money, it'd be Franco.

The house is…incredible. Done in the French Manor style, it's three stories, royal blue with slate gray roof tiles, surrounded by two acres of pristine grass—the area directly around the house itself is dirt still, because the landscaping hasn't been done yet, according to Jesse. The house looks mostly done, which jives with Jesse's reports that it's down to finishing details. The front door is standing open, and I hear a radio blaring something unintelligible; more of Jesse's screamy, thrashy, headache-inducing heavy metal. Overlapped around the music are the voices of the guys, each distinct, with a few others thrown in. I see a plumber's van, someone that appears to specialize in renewable energy, and outside the house a crew of three young men are laying bricks in the circular driveway—which features a marble fountain that isn't flowing with water yet.

Audra and I are each carrying giant bags full of carryout burgers and fries from a local pub and grill, and each of us has a twelve-pack of beer.

The bricklayers stop and whistle at us. "Hey-yo, you got some of that for us?" one of them asks, grinning at us.

Audra, always up for a little nonsense, hands her bag off to me, and cracks open the box of beer cans while sashaying sexily toward the three young men—who look to be barely out of high school, and probably hired to do the unskilled labor the more skilled crew doesn't want to waste their time on.

"Sure, boys." She puts a little extra pop to her hips as sidles over to them, offering them the beer. "Go ahead," she says, breathily, leaning over a bit more than necessary.

They each take one, laughing and chattering. And then Audra sashays back to me, still putting on a show for them, just because. And she doesn't look back as we enter the home itself, even though we both know all three are staring at us—Audra especially.

"You're shameless," I whisper-laugh.

She just smirks and shrugs as we enter the house. "It's harmless fun. It'll be a memorable part of the day for some young kids doing hard work on a hot day for probably shitty pay."

"Actually," a voice says, surprising us both into startled gasps. "They get paid double what most would pay for that job."

I whirl, and see Franco at the window beside the open front door—he'd been in the process of painting the trim around the window. He'd seen the whole thing.

"Hi, Franco." I try for familiar and friendly, hoping Jesse hasn't said too much.

The wary hardness in his gaze tells me Jesse has definitely said something to his friends. "Imogen." His gaze goes to Audra, looking her over. "Who's your friend?"

Normally, this is where Audra takes over. Her patented seduction routine goes into overdrive, and she has the guy eating out of her hand, if not somewhere else, within seconds. Only, she's mute. Staring at Franco, jaw open. I swear she has a dot of drool at the corner of her mouth.

I glance at Franco again, and understand: it's a hot day and the other truck out front of the house is an HVAC technician, so the A/C in the house isn't hooked up yet—meaning it's hot in here, since it's easily over ninety outside today. Which means Franco is shirtless, in the Sexy Contractor look—dirty, ripped, paint-spattered, faded jeans, heavy work boots, and a tool belt slung low around his hard, narrow hips. And Franco is, as I've said...jaw dropping. A man with the dedication to his body that Franco shows...well, that's like catnip to a fitness addict like Audra.

Franco frowns at me. "You both lose your voice?"

I start. "Oh. Sorry. This is my best friend, Audra." I elbow her. "Audra, this is Franco. That friend of Jesse's I was telling you about?"

"Abs!" Audra bursts out, apropos of nothing. She blinks, shakes her head, drags her wrist across the corner of her mouth, glancing at me worriedly, and then back at Franco. "Um. I mean. Audra. My name is—my name is Audra."

A slow, amused smile spreads over Franco's face.

"Tits. I mean, Franco. My name is Franco."

Audra, in a rare fit of extended dumbfounded speechlessness, glances down at her chest. Which, admittedly, she has put on rather obvious display: a "sports bra" that's more lingerie than sports bra, and tight white form-fitting workout shorts that barely cover her ass. I'm pretty sure her sports bra has push-up technology, and god knows Audra's monster tits don't need any help in that department.

"Oh." Audra shifts her glance up to Franco, her gaze slowly traveling the length of his body. "You're jaw-dropping. I mean, Franco. You're Franco."

He just smolders at her even harder. "Yep. That's me."

I hand Audra the bag she'd given to me. "Well, umm…I need to talk to Jesse."

Franco's gaze, when he shoots a look at me, tells me he's not thrilled with me. "Upstairs. Master bathroom."

"Franco, I—"

He shakes his head. "Save it for him, Imogen."

"Thanks." I gesture at Audra. "I'll just leave you two to your awkwardness competition."

She's just staring at him, very much like a cartoon character. I snap my fingers in front of her eyes. "What?" She jerks her eyes to me. "What's up?"

I laugh. "I'm going to go find Jesse. You've got

this, yes?"

Audra nods, slowly, not taking her eyes off Franco. "Yes. I'm good. Oh, I'm *so* good."

I carry my bag of food and case of beer in search of the stairs; on my way, I pass an entry to the kitchen, where I see James and Ryder engaged in conversation—judging by the quick way they clam up, they were talking about me. I pause, and James just jerks his thumb in the direction of the stairs. Yeah, I've not made any friends.

I wander upstairs, following the music. As Franco said, I find Jesse in the master bathroom, on his knees caulking around the base of a huge clawfoot tub big enough for three people.

He doesn't hear me.

I glance at my reflection in the mirror, and tease my hair a little, and plump my cleavage. I'm dressed casually, in my most flattering pair of skinny jeans and a cream shirt with a daring V-neck, just translucent enough to give hints of my black bra underneath. I suck in a deep breath, and say a word of thanks that he's in here, alone, and that I don't have to try and lure him anywhere. This way, I can just...

Lock the door.

He hears that, turns, and sees me. His brows lower, and he takes in the sight and smell of the food, the case of beer, and then my outfit. "Hi, Imogen."

I don't smile; I can't, not yet. "Hi."

"You're alive. I was wondering."

Apologize, and then make my move; I take a deep breath, preparing myself. My nerves jangle, adrenaline races. I'm nervous, but excited.

"Did you just lock the door?" he asks, looking past me at the door.

I nod. "Yeah."

"Why?" He's suspicious. Wary. Confused, maybe.

I set the food and beer on the counter nearby, and then turn back to him. As I approach, he stands up, setting the caulking gun on the floor.

"I just…I—" I owe him the truth. "I panicked. I ran off, and I didn't give you a chance to—I don't know…say anything."

He frowns harder. "I was trying to figure out what to say. And then you just shut down and I was—" He shrugs, as inarticulate as I am.

"I thought you were trying to figure out how to get rid of me," I admit. "And I was scared. Because I was feeling things, but I assumed you didn't and couldn't possibly feel the same. So I just—yeah, I shut down."

"I wasn't trying to get rid of you, Imogen," he murmurs. "The opposite, if anything."

I step closer to him. "I came to say I'm sorry."

He nods. "I get it. After what you've been

through, and with how I said I usually am about relationships—"

I touch his mouth. "I came to say I'm sorry," I say again. "And to bring you something to show you that I'm still interested in…whatever this is, or…or whatever it could be."

He eyes the items on the counter. "Burgers and beer certainly helps."

I sink to my knees in front of him. "That's just because it's lunchtime and I thought you might like lunch. That's not what I brought."

He quirks an eyebrow. "Oh no?"

I shake my head. "Nope."

His eyes roam over me. "What'd you bring, then?"

God, I can't believe I'm about to do this. I'm tempted to go double-check that I locked the door, but I don't. I shift closer to him, sitting on my heels in front of him, and reach up to unbuckle his tool belt. I set it carefully on the floor nearby; it's a lot heavier than it looks. He's breathing very slowly, very carefully, his eyes following my every move as if not quite willing to believe I'm about to do what he thinks (hopes?) I'm about to do.

I unbuckle his thick black leather belt, and then undo the button of his jeans, and then lower the zipper.

"Imogen, you don't have to—" he breaks off as I tug his jeans down, and he grabs my wrists before I can go further. "Imogen, wait. You don't have to prove anything, or whatever it is you're doing. I should have communicated better, not let you think—"

"What if I *want* to prove something?" I ask. "Maybe this is my way of saying I'm sorry for hurting you."

"I thought you'd gotten what you wanted," he admits. "You acted like you didn't give a shit, like you were just done and ready to go."

"That was all bullshit. I was a mess." I tug at my wrists, trying to free them. "I wanted…more."

"So did I," he breathes, still not quite letting go of me yet.

I gaze up at him. "This whole thing, everything about us, Jesse…it's new. It's different. And I like it. But it's scary." I wiggle my wrists, and he lets go. "I'm not proving anything to *you*, right now—I'm proving something to myself."

He breathes shakily. "When you got in your car and drove off, and then didn't answer me, I thought you were done with me, with this whole thing."

I pull his jeans down so they're around his ankles, and then push his plain white T-shirt up. It's sweat-soaked and smells like him, and the scent drives me wild, for some reason. I lick my lips and feel a tremor of eagerness run through me. I *want* this. And more than anything, I want to show him how much I want *him*. He tears the shirt off and tosses it aside, and slides his underwear down. He's hard, bobbing with his shallow breaths.

God, he's even more beautiful now than he was that night.

I glance up at him as I reach for him. "Jesse?"

He grunts an affirmative, as if he's forgotten how to speak. "Uh—yeah?" He blows out a harsh breath, and tries again. "What, Imogen?"

"Don't—don't stop me."

"No promises." He grins, and I return it.

I stroke him, slowly, savoring every exquisite inch of him sliding through my hands. This time, I take all the time in the world to just touch him, exploring his length and thickness with my hands. When he's clenching his jaw and breathing hard, I lean forward. Lick my lips.

The windows are open, and a bird chirps. The music still grinds from the Bluetooth speaker sitting on the counter. I can hear voices filtering up from the lower level, both through the floor and the window. It's broad daylight, and I'm in my boss's unfinished house, and I'm about to…

I keep my eyes on him as I lower my mouth over him. He grunts as I take him into my mouth, and then he groans as I sink him as deep as I can take him. I stroke him with both hands as I slide my lips back up his length, fluttering my tongue against the slick, veiny side. Down, licking, stroking. He hisses, and then buries his hands in my hair, tangling tight but not attempting to guide what I'm doing.

"Jesus, Imogen."

I gaze up at him, and he's...well, he looks like he's in heaven, in an agony of ecstasy. As if what I'm doing feels nearly too good to bear. So I keep doing it. Licking, suckling, tonguing him, stroking. Long, slow, deep, and then short and shallow, using my tongue as much as possible, swirling it around the head, tasting the pearls of essence leaking out of him.

"You have to stop," he growls.

"Mmm-mmm." I hum the negative.

He reaches for me, and I snag his wrists, guiding his hands back to my hair, not slowing the rhythm of my bobbing. When he knots his fingers into my hair with a curse through grated teeth, I smile around him, meeting his eyes with mine.

"Oh fuck, Imogen. What are you doing to me?"

I let him free of my mouth just long enough to murmur, "Exactly what I want to, Jesse." I take another slow, deep mouthful of him, and then back away again. "Now shut up and enjoy it."

"You want this?"

"Mmmm-hmmm," I murmur the affirmative, breathily. Because god, do I want it. He was in such tight control last time, until the very last second. This time, I want him to be in my control. Not about manipulation, but about knowing he wants to give that over to me, so that I can do this for him. It's exhilarating, and scary. I almost wish I hadn't locked the door, just to make it a little scarier.

I like the way he's responding, the helpless tilt of his hips, the breathless groans as I slide my mouth around him, the growls in his chest as I stroke him and tongue the tip.

"Imogen, I'm—" he huffs, hips flexing involuntarily. "I—god, I'm gonna come…"

"Mmmm-hmmm?"

"Fuck—right now."

He isn't lying, either. I'm not ready for it—he surprises me even as he warns me. The sudden rush of it, the snarl of his voice, the musky taste and the flood of salty tang in my mouth, and his thickness sliding through my lips, and the wild cry as he releases, a strangled, helpless, almost mewling sigh as he releases and releases.

When he's finally finished, I take a few more moments to savor him, the taste of him, the feel of him in my mouth, softening now, and then he's pulling away and sinking to his knees with me.

I wipe at my lips with my wrist, grinning at him. "Hi," I murmur. "So, do you believe that I still want more with you, now?"

He laughs. "God, Imogen. You're ridiculous. I hope you understand I didn't need you to do *that* to know you want more."

"It was partially just because I've never done anything like that and wanted to surprise you. And myself."

"Well...I'm surprised," he says, righting his jeans. He eyes the food on the counter. "So. Burgers and beer?"

I smirk at him, licking my lips. "I think just had lunch, actually."

He laughs. "Gotta wash it down, then."

We sit on the marble floor and—after we both wash our hands—we dig into the food I brought, washing it all down with beer. And, like with Audra, once we both eat, Jesse sits back and eyes me, clearly about to say something heavy.

"The story isn't entirely mine to tell, so I'll only tell my side of it." He cracks another beer. "I was with a girl for five years. We were...pretty serious." He's clearly struggling with what and how much to say. "I told you James is my brother-in-law, right?"

I nod. "Yeah..." I frown. "But I've never heard anything about his wife, who would be your sister, right? He also doesn't wear a ring."

Jesse nods, head hanging. "Um. So I was super into this girl. Love and all that, right? And James was married to my sister, so my best friend was married to my older sister, which was weird at first, but if anyone could have been good enough for her, it was James. And things for them were great, you know? He was head over heels for her. Had been our whole lives, honestly. Just…gaga for her."

I smile. "That sounds sweet."

He nods, not smiling. "Well, um. Renée, my sister—she—ah…she passed away. She died." He blinks hard, and my heart squeezes, because this is still very obviously painful to talk about. "And James, he—he lost it. It just…my best buddy since third grade, man, he just…" Jesse shakes his head. "It was bad."

"God, Jesse, I'm so, so sorry."

He just nods. "Yeah, well…um. I saw what it did to James when his wife died, you know? And I'd been thinking of proposing, you know? She'd been hinting, and I'd been planning. Had a ring picked. But then Renée died and James went haywire, and…I guess I panicked. I broke up with her instead. Like, why would I put myself at risk for that same kind of heartbreak? You never know what'll happen in life, who'll die and leave you broken. Why bother? It was fear, grief, all that. It was stupid—I was stupid. She was amazing, and I—" He glances at me apologetically. "Sorry, I guess this isn't what you probably want to hear after…"

I take his hand. "Jesse, no, it's fine. I mean, it's not fine, but I understand. This is your story, and I want to hear it."

He sighs. "By the time I realized I'd fucked up, she was long gone. Left Chicago, met another guy, moved on. I talked to her a long while later, and she said she was still messed up over the way I broke it off, but that she'd made peace and forgiven me. And I just…after that, I couldn't bring myself to even go near that kind of thing again. I'd hurt one girl already, *and* myself, and—it's taken James so long to heal, and he's still not totally okay, if he ever will be, and so… yeah, I keep things…shallow, I guess."

I hang my head. "And I don't know what I want, to be honest," I say. "I mean, I just got out of a marriage that really messed me up, so I'm not really looking to jump back into that, but…" I exhale sharply, tasting him on my breath. "It wasn't good, my relationship with Nicholas. It was never good. And this thing with you and me…it's already—I want to say better, but that implies Nicholas was something even decent, and he really wasn't. I put everything I could into him, into us, trying to make it work, trying to convince myself it was working, but I was never anything but lonely." I look at him, locking eyes with him. "And with you...I'm not lonely. I'm feeling things I didn't know were possible. And then you go and show me how sex can really be, and that just scares the shit out of me, because...god, I was missing out on *that* this whole time? Where were you, twelve years ago? But am I looking to jump into something huge, with rings and declarations of love and all that? I don't—I don't think so. But Jesse, I *do* want more than just no-strings sex."

He pulls me onto his lap. "Imogen—it was *never* no-strings with us." He sighs. "That's what I was trying to figure out how to say, but I couldn't because I was dealing with leftovers from automatically avoiding anything real. But it can't be anything *except* real with you. It already *is* more. So much more."

"Really?" I hate how the sniffle escapes me, as I say that.

He taps my nose. "Really really." He does this in a Shrek voice that's so bad it's good.

I laugh. "Don't make fun of me. I can't help being a little emotional."

He just smiles at me. "I'm not making fun." He quirks an eyebrow at me. "Remember what I said about you being adorably erotic? You're also erotically adorable."

I feel something growing under me, and I boggle

at him. "Already?"

He grins, a hot, eager smirk. "Baby, you have no idea." He stands up, lifting me to my feet. "How about you sit on that counter and talk to me while I work? I've only got a few more things left to do in here, and then what say you and me head to your place? You haven't been by yet, have you?"

"No," I admit. "I was avoiding you, so I went to Audra's."

He juts his chin at the counter. "Sit. Talk to me about ways I can get you to apologize like that again."

I laugh as I hop up on the counter. "Hey, if you're that…generous…every time we have sex, I'll feel like I need to *apologize* just to make the number of orgasms between us equal. So you'd end up getting apologized to a *lot*."

He smolders at me as he finishes caulking around the tub. "I was in a hurry that night. I was fucking desperate to have you, so I kind of rushed it a little. Usually I'd make sure you had at least four or five orgasms *before* we started having sex."

"Oh," I squeak, breathless, and then find my own heat bubbling up into my gaze. "If that's the case, you'll be getting a whole lot of me stopping by with lunch."

He grins. "I could live with that arrangement."

Two hours and a lot of innuendos later, we're at

my house. Audra and Franco disappeared, apparently, and she was my ride, but we're in Jesse's truck. Which is, honestly, becoming one of my favorite places.

We're at my door, and he's hesitating. "I, um. Got bored waiting for you," he says, by way of explanation. "So…yeah."

I unlock the door and push in; there's nothing different in the foyer or living room, which means it's in the kitchen.

I stop in the doorway, gaping. He replaced all my counters with butcher blocks stained a deep, rich, dark brown, and painted my cabinets white, took off the doors and replaced them with glass, and ripped up the shitty old laminate and replaced it with sleek gray slate.

I feel my eyes sting. "Jesse."

He scuffs a toe against the floor. "The guys helped."

"Why, when I was so rude to you?"

"Both of us messed that up, and I wanted to do this. I wanted to—I had to…" He sighs. "I like doing things for you. I like making you happy. It's obvious no one has ever really taken care of you before, and I feel good doing things for you."

"Thank you," I whisper. "It's perfect. It's amazing, it's…"

I look at it all again, over his shoulder. My kitchen

is unrecognizable from what it looked like before I met him.

"You love it?" he asks, searching me with his eyes.

"So much." I grin at him, jumping up and wrapping my legs around his waist. "Take me upstairs so I can say thank you."

He growls eagerly. "You could thank me right here, up against this counter."

I slide down off of him, grinning harder. "Okay," I whisper.

I peel off my shirt, kick off my jeans, make quick work of bra and underwear, and before he can even blink three times, I'm naked. I turn away from him, sliding my hands across the smooth, cool surface of the counter. Lean over it, wiggling my butt at him.

He's just staring at me.

I writhe, undulating my ass at him. "Jesse?"

He shakes his head, as if to clear it of hypnotism. "Sorry, I just—you're so fucking sexy, sometimes I just…" he trails off. "I don't know how to say it."

"Don't tell me, then," I murmur, reaching between my legs. "Show me."

He growls again, reaching for me. "God, I love the way you think." He frowns. "I don't have any protection with me. I don't carry it in my wallet like I used to."

I smirk at him. "Purse." I point at my purse on

the counter. "I bought some, just in case."

"Did I mention that I love the way you think?" he says, digging them out of my purse.

In seconds, he's behind me, reaching for me. I bend over the counter, and he fills me, his hands carving over me, showing me how beautiful he finds me with his touch, with his lips stuttering over me as he moves, as we move together. And with his words; he gasps, as we find completion together: "So perfect, Imogen—you're—god, you're so perfect."

"You're perfect too, Jess," I say, clinging to him, afterward.

"Nah, we're just perfect together." He doesn't try to move away, this time, as we lay on the new slate floor of my kitchen, bathing in the afterglow. He glances at me. "Is your shower big enough for two?"

I laugh. "Ha! You're funny. No, it's not even big enough for one."

He rumbles in displeasure. "I have to fix that." He stands up, picking me up with him, and carries me upstairs. "We'll make it work."

We make it work.

Later, my phone beeps, a notification from Audra. It's a picture of her, from the cleavage up, hair a mess...with Franco beside her, eyes closed.

Jesse is beside me, and he sees the photo. "Audra better be careful. Franco is...a lot like me. Except worse, in some ways. He's not real great with emotions or commitment."

I laugh. "I'd say the same about Franco—he oughta be careful. The term man-eater was invented for Audra."

Jesse rumbles a laugh. "This could get messy."

Indeed it could. I pull Jesse close to me, so his head covers my breasts, and we take a selfie together—it's obvious what we were just doing, but nothing is visible. I send it, with a caption—

Me: *Jesse says you better know what you're doing with Franco.*

Audra: *Dude, I'm scared.*

Me: *!! What? Tell me!*

Audra: *He makes me FEEL THINGS. It's icky and I don't like it.*

Me: *You've known him what, a few hours?*

Audra: *I'm telling you, he scares the shit out of me. But he's so good I can't stop myself.*

Me: *Audra, seriously. Chill. It's been a couple hours. It's just insta-lust.*

She sends another selfie, this one of her face—she's biting her lower lip, eyes wide, glancing to the side at Franco laying next to her—and yeah, his body is truly stunning, if you're into that sort of thing. Her expression in the photo is funny, but it also communicates, somehow that she's not entirely kidding about being scared. Her caption comes a second later—

Audra: **YOU DONT UNDERSTAND!!! HE'S GOT A MAGICAL DICK AND I'M FEELING THINGS!!!**

Audra: *Uh-oh. He's waking up. Time for round...3? 4? I've lost count. Tell me I'm a cold-hearted man-eating bitch with no soul. Tell ME!*

Me: *You're a cold-hearted man-eating bitch with no soul? Only, you're not. So...you're on own with this one. Except if you need me of course. I've got All Thai'd Up on speed dial, and three bottles of Josh in the rack.*

Audra: *if this goes south—or anywhere except nowhere, you'd better make it four bottles. Or maybe even six. Because we're either going to be incredible together, or we'll destroy each other. There will be no in between.*

I sigh, putting the phone aside.

Oh, Audra, I hope you know what you're doing.

I laugh at that, because does anyone know what they're doing? I sure as hell don't.

A while later, after a pizza delivery, Jesse glances at me. "So...we're together?" he asks, oh so casually.

I nod. "No expectations, but…"

He shakes his head, finishing his bite. "I wouldn't mind some expectations."

I stare hard at him. "What kind of expectations?"

He shrugs. "I guess we figure that out as we go. This is new for both of us."

Figure it out as we go. That's not how I usually do things. I like to know where things lie, where we're going. Nicholas and I set things out from the start. We knew what it was and where it was going from the outset.

But…Jesse isn't Nicholas. And I don't need to know. I can be okay taking things one step at a time.

Figure things out as we go.

I just grin at him. "Will you still help me update my house?"

He smolders at me. "I'll have to charge you."

"I don't have a lot of money," I breathe, holding back a smile.

"Then we'll have to figure out an…alternative… payment program." He reaches for me. "It'd involve a lot you, naked, underneath me, screaming my name."

"Where do I sign?"

He just laughs, but then neither of us are laughing…

Because underneath the banter and the sexual tension, I can tell…

This is…something.

As in…Something. With a capital S.

What, I don't know yet.

But I'm willing to find out.

Hell…I'm *eager* to find out.

Want more of Audra and Franco's story, and the world of Dad Bod Contracting?

Book two: *Drilled*

Coming soon!

Jasinda Wilder

Visit me at my website: **www.jasindawilder.com**
Email me: **jasindawilder@gmail.com**

If you enjoyed this book, you can help others enjoy
it as well by recommending it to friends and family,
or by mentioning it in reading and discussion groups
and online forums. You can also review it on the
site from which you purchased it. But, whether
you recommend it to anyone else or not, thank you
so much for taking the time to read my book! Your
support means the world to me!

My other titles:

The Preacher's Son:
Unbound
Unleashed
Unbroken

Biker Billionaire:
Wild Ride

Big Girls Do It:

Better (#1), Wetter (#2), Wilder (#3), On Top (#4)
Married (#5)
On Christmas (#5.5)
Pregnant (#6)
Boxed Set

Rock Stars Do It:

Harder
Dirty
Forever
Boxed Set

From the world of *Big Girls* and *Rock Stars*:

Big Love Abroad

Delilah's Diary:

A Sexy Journey
La Vita Sexy
A Sexy Surrender

The Falling Series:

Falling Into You
Falling Into Us
Falling Under
Falling Away
Falling for Colton

The Ever Trilogy:
Forever & Always
After Forever
Saving Forever

The world of *Alpha:*
Alpha
Beta
Omega
Harris: Alpha One Security Book 1
Thresh: Alpha One Security Book 2
Duke: Alpha One Security Book 3
Puck: Alpha One Security Book 4

The world of Stripped:
Stripped
Trashed

The world of *Wounded:*
Wounded
Captured

The Houri Legends:
Jack and Djinn
Djinn and Tonic

The Black Room
(With Jade London):
Door One
Door Two
Door Three
Door Four
Door Five
Door Six
Door Seven
Door Eight
Deleted Door

Standalone titles:
Yours

Non-Fiction titles:
You Can Do It
You Can Do It: Strength
You Can Do It: Fasting

Jack Wilder Titles:
The Missionary

To be informed of new releases and special offers, sign up for Jasinda's email newsletter.

Made in the USA
Middletown, DE
19 July 2018